"The police detective who t[akes up the case has the] cooperation of Peter Dulut[h ...] assistance. That is where he [... it is Peter's wife] who discovers the key to this [... and a very] neat job she makes of it. Hats o[ff ... to] Patrick Quentin."
—Isaac Anderson
The New York Times Book Review
September 16, 1945

"It's no surprise that Hugh Wheeler, co-author of the Patrick Quentin mysteries, went on to write *A Little Night Music* and *Sweeney Todd* (winning Tony awards for each), and the film (among others) *Something for Everyone,* for his novels are supremely theatrical, intricately plotted, full of colorful detail and eccentric characters."
—Hal Prince

Mysteries by
PATRICK QUENTIN
Featuring Peter Duluth

PUZZLE FOR FOOLS
PUZZLE FOR PLAYERS*
PUZZLE FOR PUPPETS*
PUZZLE FOR WANTONS*
PUZZLE FOR FIENDS
PUZZLE FOR PILGRIMS
RUN TO DEATH**
BLACK WIDOW**
and
MY SON, THE MURDERER** (*with Jack Duluth*)

*available in a Library of Crime Classics® edition
**forthcoming

Series Consultant: Douglas G. Greene

PATRICK QUENTIN

PUZZLE FOR WANTONS

A Peter Duluth Mystery

INTERNATIONAL POLYGONICS, LTD.
NEW YORK CITY

PUZZLE FOR WANTONS

Copyright © 1945 by Patrick Quentin (psuedonym for Hugh C. Wheeler). Renewed 1972 by Hugh C. Wheeler. Reprinted with the permission of the estate of Hugh C. Wheeler and Curtis Brown Ltd.

Library of Congress Card Catalog No. 90-80764
ISBN 1-55882-063-9

Printed and manufactured in the United States of America.
First IPL printing June 1990.
10 9 8 7 6 5 4 3 2 1

Part One

DOROTHY

One

"MY THIRD HUSBAND was no gentleman. I shall be glad to get rid of him." Dorothy Flanders, big and gorgeous and blonde as champagne, slid a sixth shrimp canapé between bougainvillaea lips. "The night before I left for Reno, he chased me all over the apartment with a steak knife."

For the last fifteen minutes the luscious Mrs. Flanders had been giving us an uncensored and uncalled-for account of her sex life. My wife was watching her, fascinated. So was I. I had never seen anyone so beautiful who ate so much.

"Yes, Lieutenant Duluth." Dorothy Flanders' swooning blue eyes contemplated space as if it was something delightful to eat. "In a way it was lucky he lost that leg at Saipan. Otherwise he'd have caught up with me. With the steak knife, I mean."

I gulped. Iris, whose dark loveliness was rather subordinated by so much massive blondeness, asked politely, "Just why did your third husband chase you with a steak knife, Mrs. Flanders?"

"Oh, you know how men are, dear." Mrs. Flanders shrugged shoulders bare and blatant enough to have wrecked the entire Barbary Coast. "I've always had trouble with men. Sometimes I wonder why I keep on marrying."

After fifteen minutes of her I was wondering how she'd managed to keep one lap ahead of a steak knife all these years.

Our yellow patio chairs splashed color onto the evening grayness of the interminable terrace. We were the first of Lorraine Pleygel's house guests to have dressed for dinner, and the façade of our hostess' impossible mansion, which was practically all plate glass, was having its own private sunset. Beneath us, beyond the lush gardens, the Nevada shore of Lake Tahoe gleamed emerald, like something from Tiffany's that Lorraine had become bored with and thrown away. The sleek noses of her speedboats were just visible at the dock.

Less than forty-eight hours before, I had left my ship and eight months of fighting in the Pacific behind me in the mists of San Francisco. This was only the second of my fifteen-day shore leave. Civilian life hadn't quite come into focus yet. I had forgotten that women like Dorothy Flanders were allowed to exist and that people could still be as idly and ideally rich as Lorraine.

But even the Pleygel fortune, which had kept Lorraine solvent through the wildest escapades, couldn't keep this landscape under control. There was too much sky. The barren peaks of the Sierras, indifferent to chic, scowled blackly across the lake. The rough scent of sage drifted in from the foothills, snuffing out the jasmine.

Nevada had been Nevada long before Lorraine Pleygel had swooped down to woo it with her millions. Like a cowboy wooed by an heiress, it hadn't bothered to change its denim shirt for her or to clean its nails.

"Yes," said Dorothy Flanders suddenly, managing to look voluptuous even as she shoveled ripe olives into a cupped hand. "He said he'd kill me if he ever set eyes on me again. Men are so depressingly jealous. But then women are jealous, too." She gave me a look of immense candle power as if she had delivered herself of a rare profundity. "I'm frightfully hungry. Where's Lorraine?"

Iris said, "She drove to Reno with Chuck Dawson to pick up some other guests from the train."

"She's always dashing off just before meals. What guests?"

"She didn't say. Just people from Frisco."

"They'll probably be ghastly women." Dorothy sighed and stirred inside what there was of her evening gown. "Lorraine has a genius for filling this house with the ghastliest women. I should have stayed on in Reno, had my· divorce in peace, and not let her kidnap me. But you know how Lorraine is."

I knew exactly how our hostess was. With her pop eyes, her mad hair, and her intense charm, Lorraine Pleygel was not merely the most warmhearted and feather-pated multimillionairess in existence. She was also an irresistible force.

In the old days when we had first known Lorraine, I had made a living producing plays on Broadway while my wife was winning respectable critical acclaim as an actress. The War came. I joined the Navy and was transferred to the Pacific Fleet. Iris condescended to a Hollywood offer and came West to be near me. It had seemed the most sensible arrangement at the time. But during the eight months of my latest absence at sea, some studio magnate in a burst of hysterical inspiration had decided that my wife was something for which a war-torn world was hungering. When my ship finally docked for repairs at San Francisco and our long awaited chance for two quiet weeks together came, I found to my dismay that Iris had been ballyhooed into the most reluctant movie star in history.

Our first day had been a hell of autograph hounds and cameras and telephone pleas for benefits and canteens. Iris had only one piece of war work on her mind—me. But we were beaten before we started.

After the sixth fan-magazine female had collected material

from us for an article to be entitled, "Look to Your Laurels, Brunette-Bombshells," Iris collapsed.

"It's not my fault, darling. I swear it isn't," she had moaned. "It just crept up on me after Mr. Finkelstein saw me in a sweater. What a thing to come home to. You married a woman and what are you stuck with? A brunette-bombshell."

We were clinging forlornly to each other in the hotel suite, with the receiver off the hook, when Lorraine burst in, both hands outstretched, caroling, "Darlings, I hear you're being mobbed. You poor lamb-pies. Something has got to be done."

She lured us with talk of the Nevada moon, the peace of the mountains, the glories of Lake Tahoe, and a private suite of our own.

"If you want to be alone, pets, you can be alone. If you want fun, there'll be gay people there. It's a simply divine idea. The car's outside."

At that particular moment Lorraine seemed sent direct from heaven. Before we really knew what had hit us, we had been shanghaied to this insane Shangri-La which a Wild Western whim had made her build some forty miles from Reno.

We hadn't been left alone, of course. We might have known that Lorraine was incapable of leaving anyone alone for a second. Fortunately the other house guests were so obsessed with their own problems that none of them gave a hoot whether Iris was a brunette-bombshell or not.

Lorraine gathered "gay" people with the indiscriminate abandon of a squirrel gathering nuts. Dorothy Flanders was another victim of our hostess' passion for having people live at her expense. The week before, in one of her periodic commando raids, Lorraine had descended upon Reno, scoured all the hotels, and returned triumphant with the toothsome Dorothy and the two other divorcee-to-be house guests, Janet Laguno and Fleur Wyckoff. She hadn't seen any of the girls for ten years, but they had all been at school together in San Francisco. Lorraine had thought it was a divine idea to have them sit out their various divorces under her wing.

And when Lorraine thought anything was a divine idea, you might as well think it, too, because you'd find yourself doing it.

"Of course," said Dorothy Flanders, "I'm devoted to Lorraine and delighted to see her again after all these years. She was a hideous child at school, I remember—all teeth and neck." She was reduced to eating the olive out of her Martini now. I half expected her to chew up the toothpick, too. "But I must admit I would never have dreamed of coming here if I'd known Janet and Fleur were staying with her."

She paused significantly.

Iris was tapping rather formidably on her chair arm. "Don't you like the Countess Laguno and Mrs. Wyckoff, Mrs. Flanders?"

"Oh, yes, I like them. After all, we move in the same set in San Francisco. But——" Dorothy rustled her weight over onto her sheathed left hip, looking like something out of *Esquire* that you pin up in an army camp. "It's just rather embarrassing, dear. That's all."

I was struggling with the implications of that cryptic utterance when clicking female footsteps sounded behind me. I turned to see the two women in question coming toward us down the flagged terrace.

Janet Laguno—or the Countess Laguno or whatever she currently called herself—walked several paces in front of little Mrs. Wyckoff. That was her way. She was an angry woman with the wrong figure and a face that looked as if it had defeated the most expensive beauty parlors. She had made a small fortune with an exclusive woman's dress shop, but she was her own worst advertisement. Clothes hung on her as if they hated her.

She flopped into a chair and grumbled a greeting.

Dorothy, without turning her head, said, "Hello, Janet. That's a sweet dress."

"Phoo. I know I look a mess." Janet Laguno plucked up a cigarette and scowled at it. "I despise this so-called gown. It makes me feel like a life belt. And my hair's repulsive. It's all Stefano's fault. I saw my lawyer this morning and I've been brooding about Stefano all afternoon. Thinking about my husband ages me sixty years. I feel ill."

"Nonsense, dear," drawled Dorothy. "Stefano's terribly attractive even if you are going to divorce him."

"Attractive! He's a black rat. Bogus, too. Count! Why I call myself a Countess I can't imagine. If Stefano was ever anything in Italy, he was a swineherd." Janet Laguno stared at the tall crystal cocktail shaker. "Martinis! I loathe every part of them, but I might as well drink." She poured herself a cocktail and flourished the glass. "To the happiest day of my life, the day I caught my husband trying to hock my pigeon blood rubies. To Count Stefano Laguno—a sneak thief and a B-feature one to boot."

My experience of Reno women was slight, but I was getting on to the idea that husband-reviling was the only fashionable topic of conversation. That was one of the reasons why I liked and was curious about little Fleur Wyckoff. She was so completely atypical.

She had sat down unobtrusively in a chair next to Iris. Fleur was pretty—just terribly, terribly pretty, like her name—with tawny hair, a spring-flower face and small still hands. She must have been almost thirty to be contemporary with the other divorcees-to-be, but she looked no more than nineteen. Since I had met her, she had never mentioned the husband she was about to dispose of; she had never mentioned much of anything. There was a kind of quiet dread in her eyes as if she was thinking about the same thing all the time and being frightened of it.

Janet brandished the shaker. "Hi, Fleur, you're a maladjusted female, too. You might as well drink."

"Oh, no, thank you. David always makes Martinis a special way for me with practically no gin and——" Fleur Wyckoff broke off, a flush burning across the girlish skin of her cheeks. With a flutter of her hands, she stammered, "Oh, yes, I suppose I will have one, please."

"I pour liquor into myself," muttered Janet. "I hang clothes on my back. I stuff food in my stomach. And where does it get me? You, Dorothy! You eat enough in five minutes to keep a good-sized horse alive for a decade. And you still keep the right curves. How do you do it? Pay protection to Satan?"

A butler—miraculously, Lorraine still had one—came out with another unnecessary shaker of cocktails. Janet Laguno tugged at some refractory part of her dress and asked, "When are you expecting Miss Pleygel back, Bowles?"

"I really couldn't say, Madam. But I don't think she'll be long. I heard her tell Mr. French and Miss Burnett that dinner was to be at eight."

Walter French was Lorraine's older half-brother. Mimi Burnett was his little horror of a fiancée he had picked up somewhere in Las Vegas.

As the butler moved pontifically away, Janet said, "Thank heavens we've been spared the lovebirds this afternoon. How in the world did Lorraine manage to have such a dreary brother—half elk, half slug. Ugh!"

"He's only a half-brother, dear." Dorothy Flanders yawned. She looked like a beautiful python settling down to a snooze after a nice snack of antelope. "He's not so bad. He certainly doesn't deserve to be stuck with Mimi Burnett."

"Nobody deserves to be stuck with Mimi," said Janet. "I

know those little elfin things. Stars in their eyes, ants in their pants."

Fleur Wyckoff leaned forward rather fiercely. "Janet, why are you two always so beastly about every one? Mr. French has been very kind to me. And I think Mimi's sweet."

"Sweet!" Janet laughed. "Fleur dear, you could grow up with Lizzie Borden and still say she was sweet to her parents."

Dorothy nodded and gave me an automatically seductive smile. "That Mimi Burnett's a bad character, Lieutenant. A very bad character."

I was strongly tempted to say, "You should know," but I managed to control myself. After several months on the high seas, you're apt to build up a sentimental and dewy-eyed picture of the little women left behind. I wasn't used to seeing real little women—in the raw.

Iris was watching me anxiously. I knew she was worried sick that Lorraine's house party was going to be as much of a fiasco as San Francisco. She leaned toward me and squeezed my hand. I could smell her perfume, the only perfume I've ever liked.

"Can you bear it, Peter?" she breathed.

I grinned encouragingly. As a matter of fact, I was rather fascinated by these preposterous women. They had a soothing effect. They were so completely removed from the world of Zeros and submarines in which I had been living.

"If it gets too grim," whispered my wife, "I'll buy a red wig and bands for my teeth and we'll go back to Frisco."

As she spoke, I saw Walter French and Mimi Burnett strolling up through the darkening garden. Lorraine's half-brother and his fiancée always made an entrance. Mimi saw to that. Tonight they walked with their arms amorously entwined around each other's waists. Mimi dangled a solitary white rose in her free hand. I was pretty sure she was thinking that we were thinking how fragile she looked—like Mélisande, maybe, or something wispy out of Sir James Barrie.

Walter French had been unfortunate enough to have been born to Lorraine's mother by an earlier husband, before she struck it rich with old man Pleygel. He had also been unfortunate enough recently to have lost his slender all in some Hollywood promotion scheme. But life, he seemed to feel, had compensated him for everything by giving him Mimi. Mimi, who was a pain in the neck to everyone else, was the very air he breathed. He had thrown himself body and soul into playing Romeo to her Juliet—a plump Romeo with owlish spectacles and at least forty-five years under his tightening belt.

They reached the porch, still lovingly interlocked. Mimi stretched out the white rose.

"Lover and I have been reading W. B. Yeats out loud in the summerhouse, and Lover picked me this rose, didn't you, Lover?"

Walter French seemed to thrive on her nauseous habit of calling him "Lover." He beamed adoringly and said, "Why, sure, Mimi."

Mimi drifted from one woman to the other, kissing them with butterfly kisses. She reached me and extended the rose.

"Smell, Lieutenant Duluth."

I smelt. She pirouetted away, clutching the rose intensely against her thin breast and half singing, "Oh, you nice people."

She was dressed in some floating pink thing which was meant to look childish and appealing and probably a tiny bit tubercular. It didn't. She wasn't quite young enough. And, although her oval face had a certain dark prettiness, its whimsey wasn't plausible. The trouble, I think, was her eyes. There was something knowing about them—knowing and sly.

She had perched lightly on the edge of Dorothy's chaise longue, flapping the rose around. Dorothy stared at her with steely contempt and drawled, "For Pete's sake, take that revolting rose away or I'll eat it. Isn't Lorraine ever coming?"

"Haven't she and Chuck come back yet?"

"No. They're foraging for more guests."

"Oh, I do hope they're men." Mimi laid a light hand on Dorothy's arm and her eyes glinted. "For you, dear." She tossed back the page bob curls and gazed starrily at her fiancé. "I don't need men because I have my lover, don't I, Lover?"

Janet Laguno made a hawking noise in her throat. Lover beamed again.

"Why, sure, Mimi."

Janet Laguno lit a match with a spurt and snapped, "Lover, why don't you marry the girl? Then you can get yourself a nice clean divorce like us—and relax. I've never read a line of W. B. Yeats, but I should imagine he comes under the general category of extreme mental cruelty."

Lover looked shocked. Mimi swung on Janet, the pink skirt swirling around her thin legs. For a split second her face was positively vicious. Then she laughed her high, tinkling laugh and stooped to kiss Janet's forehead.

"Cute one," she said, "you say such amusing things."

Somebody might well have scratched out somebody else's eyes if Iris hadn't said at that moment, "Listen! Isn't that Lorraine's car?"

It was. The throb of its engine, coming up the long drive, suddenly made the countryside more important than the people. I was conscious again of the dark, brooding Sierras, the tang of the sage, and the vast blackening dome of the sky above us. I hadn't realized just how much tension had been engendered on the terrace. We all sat in silence, listening to Lorraine's automobile coming closer and closer. For some queer reason it sounded ominous. It linked up in my mind with the drone of an approaching enemy plane. It was as if the car were bringing to each of us our individual doom.

The car stopped at the far side of the great house. Even then, none of us spoke. Soon there were sounds in the livingroom, footsteps and the high chattering of Lorraine's voice. The plate glass things, which were some modernistic variations of French windows, burst open, and Lorraine Pleygel was upon us, the huge swaggering figure of Chuck Dawson behind her.

Lorraine was wearing a scarlet man's shirt, denims that might have been four generations old, high leather boots. A ten-gallon hat flapped on a cord behind her wild, cropped curls. She probably wanted to look like a cowhand, but she didn't. She looked exactly what she was—one of the richest and most publicized women in the country. She swooped toward us.

"Darlings, how are you? Drunk, I hope. What a ride. So beautiful. I suppose you're starving. Chuck has been moaning about food all the way home." Her gesticulating, thin-wristed hands seemed to caress us all individually. "Sugar-pusses. Babies." She spun round, grabbing Chuck's huge arm. "Chuck, lamb-pie, find yourself a drink and stop squawking about meat and potatoes. Just for an instant, while I dress. Be an angel."

Chuck grinned and swallowed a cocktail at one gulp. Husky and handsome, with yellow hair, teeth that dazzled, and muscular bulges in all the right places, Chuck Dawson was an Eastern stenographer's dream of what a cowboy should be. Draft exempt as a rancher, he was quite a character in Reno, and had recently opened up a glittering new gambling club. No one knew where he or his money came from or exactly who he was. But Lorraine, who shed fiancés as rapidly as she picked up guests, had been engaged to him for over six months—an all-time record for her.

Our hostess had patted Mimi's hand, kissed Iris, and was now squatting on the edge of my chair.

"Peter, darling, I was talking to a naval captain or something in the Del Monte. And, my dear, he knew you and told me all sorts of wonderful things about you in that battle—where was it now? I forget. But, my dear, you're a hero, saving people's lives and winning medals and things. Why on earth haven't you told us?"

I started feeling horribly embarrassed. This was neither the time nor the place to explain how you get scared under fire and do crazy things just because you are scared. I said, "Just wait, Lorraine, until Iris' publicity department get on to it. You'll be able to read all about me in next month's *Screen Lovers*."

Iris grimaced and said, "Peter, darling, don't say that—even in jest."

"But it's wonderful, my dear, simply wonderful." Lorraine drifted off. "Sometimes I think I don't really think enough about the War."

Dorothy Flanders was watching her from behind long, lazy lashes. "This is a very cosy entrance, Lorraine, but what about those other guests. Did they manage to escape?"

Lorraine laughed. "Oh, no, sweet. I left them in the hall struggling with suitcases and things. It's ghastly. I don't seem to have half enough servants any more."

Mimi Burnett, who was clinging girlishly to her plump Lover, said, "Are they women, dear, or men?"

"They're men, baby." Lorraine stroked little Fleur Wyckoff, grinned at Janet, and ended up holding Dorothy's hand. "My dears, it's the most wonderful idea. First, Mr. Throckmorton's coming in a few days." She beamed around at us as if we should receive that news with joyful clapping of hands. But since no one had the faintest idea who Mr. Throckmorton was, it didn't go down so well. "Yes, darlings, Mr. Throckmorton's my favorite friend and so divinely clever and—but that's not what I mean. What I mean is the whole thing came to me last night. Nevada's so ravishing. The mountains. The moon. Little quarrels and things seem so petty. Anger, misunderstanding, all that just simply vanishes in Nevada. Everyone knows that. Everyone says the same thing."

It always took some time to catch on to what Lorraine was trying to say. Her strange pop eyes which gave her face its piquancy—a sort of crazy cross between Bette Davis and a pretty Boston Bull—stared earnestly around the little group. "Of course, dears, I don't want to meddle. I haven't seen you sweet things for years and years and I don't know who feels what. But I do think everyone ought to be happy and I called them last night on the phone and when I explained they seemed delighted to come. Angels, it's such a divine idea and, don't you see, that's where Mr. Throckmorton comes in. Mr. Throckmorton's a lawyer and so clever and he can do all the right things about stopping proceedings and everything. And apart from anything else, think what expense it will save."

I had a horrible hunch that I knew what Lorraine was leading up to. She turned suddenly as three male figures appeared through the French windows and stepped out to join her on the terrace. Lorraine laughed that toppling, infectious laugh of hers that could have made a torture chamber seem gay.

"Darlings, I think most of you know these sweet men. Let me present: Bill Flanders, the Count Laguno, and Dr. David Wyckoff."

My horrible hunch had been right. I didn't realize, however, just how hideously sour Lorraine's latest divine idea was until I saw the reaction of the women sitting around me.

Fleur Wyckoff shuddered as if some dreadful thing inside her was tearing her apart. She half rose, and her lips stammered the word, "David."

Janet Laguno flounced up in a cloud of ugly dress and half screamed, "Stefano."

Dorothy Flanders uncurled from the chaise longue, a sinuous wary snake ready to attack or be attacked. In a strange, husky voice she breathed, "Bill."

Iris and I exchanged a look of blank dismay. Of all Lorraine's giddy escapades, this attempt to reconcile three wives with their discarded husbands was surely the most disastrous.

Lorraine moved forward with the three men. As they became more distinct in the half light, I saw that one of them had only one leg and walked with a crutch. Dorothy Flanders was standing now, silhouetted against the evening landscape, as magnificent as a Renaissance Venus.

The three men paused in front of her in an almost straight line and all three were staring at her as if she were the only thing in the world to see.

Count Stefano Laguno was the first to speak. His flat, lizard eyes slid to his wife. He bowed sleekly from the hips.

"Janet, my dear, Destiny or Miss Pleygel has decided that we meet again."

He extended his hand for hers. Janet ignored it, her sallow face wry with astounded fury. I expected her to storm away, but shock or an instinctive respect for the drama of the occasion kept her rooted to the spot.

Dr. David Wyckoff had turned to his little wife. One of his hands went out in a gesture, but blundered into nothing as he saw the icy stillness on Fleur's face. He didn't say anything and shuffled away, his gaze shifting back to Dorothy.

I noticed that his shoulders sagged as if some almost unendurable burden had been set upon them.

It was the man with the crutch whose personality dominated that criss-cross jangle of emotions. Bill Flanders was not tall, but he was broad and chunky with a military carriage which made his civilian clothes seem like a masquerade. His eyes never leaving his wife's face, he hobbled forward on his crutch. The flapping stump of trouser where his leg should have been looked poignantly helpless.

He limped so close to Dorothy that she must have felt his breath on her peach-smooth cheek. His eyes were blazing with an intensity that was completely unaffected by the fact that the rest of us were standing around him.

"Well, baby," he said, "I guess you're glad to see me."

It wasn't what he said. It wasn't exactly the harsh, crude menace in his voice. It was the expression on his face that made that so naked a moment.

It was the expression of a man who hated so much that he was almost in love with his hatred.

Lorraine waved a Martini.

"Darlings, let's all drink to three happy reunions. I know everything's going to be lovely. The moon, the desert, the lake, Mr. Throckmorton——"

Her voice, echoing in a silence, petered away. I think even she was beginning to have a dim notion that things were not as divine as they might have been.

Iris had moved close to me. I felt her fingers slip into mine.

"Peter," she breathed, "did you see Bill Flanders' face?"

I nodded.

She gave a little shiver. "If he gets his hands on a steak knife here, there'll be no stopping him this time—Mr. Throckmorton or no Mr. Throckmorton."

And that was exactly what I had been thinking.

Two

DINNER WAS EVEN WORSE than I had expected. The room itself was partly to blame. On chartreuse walls, dyspeptic Marie Laurencin women and nude Matisse bodies, looking as if they had been parboiled in brine, loomed from pickled frames. Indian masks, which might have been homey in a Guatemalan medicine man's hut, but which were most discomforting at meal times, snarled at us from corner brackets. The glass-brick table around which we were spaced was heaped with Mexican pottery. They supposedly represented fruit, but to me they suggested something abandoned after a post-mortem by an untidy pathologist. In her time Lorraine had been a patron of almost everything anyone can be a patron of. While she was building the house, interior decorators had been her passion. She had thought it a simply divine idea to have a different one create each room.

The one who created the dining room must have had stomach ulcers.

And in this indigestible setting, nothing was functioning normally except Dorothy Flanders' appetite. There was a splendor about the way she ate. Gorgeous, monumental, apparently impervious to the uneasiness for which her presence seemed largely responsible, she shoveled her way through rich course after rich course.

Hardly anyone else ate. Lorraine never ate, anyway. For years her incandescence seemed to have been fueled by an occasional nibble of lettuce or a gulp of buttermilk. Having changed from her cowboy outfit into something weird, puce, and fabulously smart, she sat at the head of the table, chattering into a void. Either she was being a perfect hostess or she was as oblivious as Dorothy to the fact that her dinner party was one of the worst in history.

Iris and I, as a sample of happy married life, tried to be socially adequate, but our thin trickle of pseudo-airy banter gave out with the soup. Lover French looked plump and discreet, while Chuck Dawson wolfed down his food as if the Lowestoft china was a tin plate and the *squab béarnais* a mess of beans. Mimi was no help either. She had found a large pink hibiscus and spent most of dinner brooding into its depths as if waiting for a pixie to flutter out of it and kiss her lightly on the forehead.

The divorcing couples might never have heard of Emily Post. Dr. David Wyckoff and his pretty little wife sat side by side as ominously rigid as an early daguerreotype. Janet Laguno, at the right of her discarded count, was mauling a tired bit of squab. Her hair was untidy and her yellow evening gown bulged in the most unlikely places. Suddenly she snapped, "Lorraine, you shouldn't have used such good silver tonight. Stefano will almost certainly steal it."

The Count, with Continental composure, merely glanced up and smiled. Lorraine, startled out of a rambling girlhood reminiscence, exclaimed, "Janet, sweet, what nonsense. I'm sure the Count doesn't steal things."

"He'd have stolen the teeth out of my head if I'd stayed with him another week." Janet shot her impervious husband an evil glance. "If you had to drag these grisly men back into our lives, you might at least have spared me from sitting next to Stefano at meals. I was brought up to keep animals out of the dining room."

That bright little bit of dialogue didn't add to the general festivity. In the thick silence that came after it, I found myself wondering why on earth the three rejected husbands had accepted Lorraine's lunatic invitation. According to her, they had been delighted at a prospect of reconciliation with their wives, but it must have been obvious to all three of them, unless they were out of their minds, that any sort of reconciliation was out of the question. And yet, at the first opportunity, they had been willing to leave their various employments in San Francisco and come rushing after their wives.

Why? The more I thought about that "why," the less I liked it.

It was Bill Flanders who had me really worried. His crutch propped against the back of his chair, he sat in the place of honor on our hostess' right, but I was pretty sure he had not heard a single word of Lorraine's babbled monologue. He was sitting unnaturally straight before an untouched plate, his eyes bright and hectic in his square, pugilistic face. It was painfully clear that every part of him was obsessed with the thought of his wife. If only he had spoken to Dorothy or even looked at her, it would have relieved the tension. But he didn't. He just sat stiffly, grinning like a mummy.

I had seen shell-shocked sailors on my own ship after an aerial bombing. They had sat like that, still as mice, with that same fixed grin on their faces. And then, without the slightest warning, they had gone berserk.

Anxiety for what might happen at the table kept the palms of my hands damp.

Lorraine was floundering in some saga about the difficulty of getting gardeners in wartime when Bill Flanders suddenly swung himself around to her.

"If you need a gardener, why not hire me? I'm nothing fancy, but I used to fool around with plants on my father's farm when I was a kid."

His voice was light, but there was a dangerous overtone.

Lorraine's birdy hand fluttered to her perfectly matched pearl necklace. "But, Mr. Flanders, surely——"

"I used to be a boxer. Maybe you don't none of you know

that. A pretty successful boxer. When I married, I had a fighting chance for welterweight champ of the country. I was in the chips." The words were spilling out now in a crescendo of uncontrolled violence. If you'd never seen someone on the verge of a nervous breakdown, you'd have said he was drunk. "Then Pearl Harbor came. You don't make much dough as a buck private in the Marines. Ask the Lieutenant here. Fifty-some bucks a month—and your leg blown off." He laughed. "I wouldn't make much of a boxer any more with a leg blown off, would I? I gotta do something."

"You really mean——"

"Yeah. I had over thirty thousand bucks in the bank when they shipped me overseas. I fixed everything swell for my wife, fixed it so's she could get at the dough with her checks. Household expenses, she said." His face was working convulsively now. It was horrible to see a grown man stripped as naked as that. "When they discharged me, they couldn't keep me at the marine hospital I was so keen to get back to my wife. I wouldn't even stay till they got me my artificial leg, taught me how to walk with it. And when I got back to my wife, guess what there was in that bank account? Fifteen dollars and seventy-five cents."

One of the worst things about it all was that Dorothy Flanders went on eating. Lovely and unruffled as a pagan goddess, she sat there, making no attempt to check that impassioned flow of words.

"Fifteen dollars and seventy-five cents." Bill Flanders turned to his wife then. There were tears trickling out of the corners of his eyes. "In a couple of years she'd thrown away every red cent I ever put by. And that was just chicken feed to her. God knows how much more she chiseled out of all the men in Frisco she let make her." His hands, clenched into fists, were trembling. "That's the woman I married, that woman sitting over there, stuffing food into herself, the two-timing hot-pants—if I had any guts, d'you know what I'd do? I'd— I'd——"

He stopped abruptly, burying his face in his big hands. Sobs, harsh and gruff as a dog's bark, wrenched his whole body. Until then I had been worried but amused by Lorraine's motley guests. Now I hated them, hated them for being so safe and smug, hated them for sitting there seeing what the War, which had never touched them, had done to Bill Flanders.

They were all staring at Dorothy as if this were some sort of theatrical spectacle in which the next move was hers. She did look up. She let her fork drop by her crêpes suzettes. She passed a languid hand over her blonde upswept hair.

She drawled, "After that pretty little speech, I suppose one of us should leave the table. I'm afraid it will have to be my husband. I have every intention of finishing my dessert."

I could gladly have killed her myself then. But Bill Flanders was beyond hearing anything. Fumbling for his crutch, he pushed himself up. With clumsy stabs of the crutch, he stumbled toward the door.

Lorraine had half risen, her funny face crumpled with misery. She had the warmest heart in the world. She couldn't bear to see anyone suffer.

"The poor boy," she breathed. "The poor, poor boy."

She started after him, but I called at her, "No, Lorraine. Leave him alone."

I knew he couldn't have borne having anyone fuss over him. Lorraine apparently realized it, too. She went back to her chair. The door slammed after Bill Flanders.

What was laughingly called dinner went on without him.

Nobody talked. It must have been as much of a relief to the others as it was to me when Lorraine got up and suggested moving to the trophy room for coffee and liqueurs.

In her earlier days Lorraine had spent a year in Darkest Africa and Darkest South America indulging a violent though temporary passion for big-game hunting. The trophy room was a monument to that tomboyish year—a huge, cavernous place decorated with the heads and necks of almost every known species of game and the grimmest mementoes of the Amazonian arts of love and war.

The trophy room, I felt, wasn't exactly a suitable room for coffee and liqueurs. But then no room in Lorraine's house was suitable for anything.

In a jittery band, we all trooped into the trophy room to find that Bill Flanders was already there, sitting in a corner under a great hunk of elephant. Although the ex-marine looked white and drawn, the passion seemed to have gone out of him. He did not even glance at his wife as she strolled by and started guzzling kümmel less than three feet away.

No one referred to the episode at the table. The evening was so far out of control that there was nothing anyone could have said, anyway.

To get away from it all, Iris and I moved off to one of the glass-topped trophy cases. It happened to be filled with blowpipes and poisoned darts which presumably had been projected at Lorraine by indignant but incompetent Amazonian marksmen.

Sitting next to the cabinet on a high thronelike chair was the most terrifying object in the trophy room. Several years ago Lorraine had been persuaded by a "ravishingly clever" female to sit for a life-size portrait doll. Lorraine had thought it a divine idea, but the finished product had been a little too much even for her. For some reason, however, she preserved it in the trophy room, where it perched in a long lime-green evening gown, staring at the world with a simpering idiot smile. Iris and I gazed at it lugubriously, wondering how we were going to get through the evening.

Lorraine must have been wondering, too. After a few sour minutes in which her divorcing couples sat around clattering coffee cups, she jumped up in a swirl of puce, smiling the devastating smile which always signaled the birth of another divine idea.

"Babies," she said, "it's so dismal here. Let's all get in cars and drive down to Chuck's place in Reno and gamble. There's nothing like roulette. Really there isn't."

Lorraine's remedy for all sticky situations was to dash off and have fun. Whether or not her theory was valid, I had never seen an idea accepted with such enthusiasm. Everyone scuttled from the trophy room to get coats and wraps. Iris and I were in the fore. We almost ran upstairs to our unnerving zebra-striped bedroom suite—the product, no doubt, of an interior decorator who had got too drunk too often at El Morocco. I closed the door on the emotional maelstrom of the house.

Iris, looking lovelier than even Mr. Hurrell's glamour photographs of her, tossed back her hair the way she does when she's worried.

"Peter darling, tell me. Is the leave being a frightful flop? These ghastly people. You don't want to go to Reno, do you?"

I knew my wife had a wanton passion for slot machines. I kissed her, which was something I could have done indefinitely.

"We'd better go, honey. Lorraine's got herself into such a messy situation. Someone ought to stick by her. Besides, I'm getting used to having a movie star for a wife. I'll enjoy showing you off."

Iris stared at me. "You really mean that, Peter?"

"Sure." I wasn't going to have her eating her heart out feeling she'd double-crossed me because Mr. Somethingstein of Magnificent Pictures had turned her into a national product like corn flakes. "Get your wrap, beautiful."

Iris pulled her cape from the closet, slung it over her shoulders, and came back to me.

"Peter, why did those husbands accept Lorraine's mad invitation?"

"I was trying to figure that out, too."

"That poor Bill Flanders. Darling—you don't really think he'd try to kill Dorothy, do you?"

"I wouldn't blame him," I said. "A little killing would do Dorothy the world of good."

"Maybe he will," mused Iris. "Maybe I'll get mixed up in a murder and get thrown out of Hollywood on a moral turpitude clause. Wouldn't that be wonderful?"

Somehow that didn't sound quite as funny as it should have. My wife crossed to the dressing table, unlocked a drawer, and produced a plump and obscene blue pottery piggy bank. She tucked it under her arm.

"Okay, darling," she said. "Let's go to Reno and show ourselves off."

The function of the horrible pig was to save Iris from herself and the slot machines. Some atavistic New England instinct in her was against gambling, and she salvaged her conscience by saving her winnings to buy War Bonds. She was very prim about it. She had even bought me a similar nightmare pig, but I was too proud to be seen with it, and it was locked away in a suitcase under the bed. Iris, however, had no compunctions. She took the pig everywhere, dropping into its bloated stomach each half-dollar, quarter, and dime as it was won.

As Iris and I and the piggy bank started down the corridor, we were just in time to see Mimi Burnett's elfin figure slip into the room that was always kept for Chuck Dawson. Mimi was the sort of girl who would slip furtively into other people's rooms. But I did wonder dimly why Lover's fiancée should be having a private tête-à-tête with Lorraine's fiancé. Life was surely scrambled enough already without that.

When Iris and I reached the main hall, it was empty. We moved to the trophy room whose heavy wooden doors were closed. I opened the doors. Two people were standing at the far end of the room by the cabinet of poison darts—the Count Laguno and Dorothy Flanders, who looked even more luscious than usual in a white ermine wrap with long white leather gloves to her elbows. They looked startled when they heard us and swung round.

I said awkwardly, "Sorry if we broke in on anything."

"Broke in on anything?" drawled Dorothy. "What do you think the Count was doing? Making indelicate propositions?"

Count Stefano Laguno looked like an elegant lizard with a Continental education. He smiled, showing not very good teeth.

In a smooth, Oxfordish voice he said, "I was merely giving Mrs. Flanders a lecture on the Indians of the Amazon, Lieutenant Duluth. A bungling people. They have discovered one of the most deadly poisons in the world—curare. One drop of it in the blood stream will kill the strongest man or woman. And yet they use it unimaginatively—merely to kill deer or other Indians." His slant eyes slid to Dorothy, and it seemed to me that they glowed with a sly malice. "Curare has a certain nobility. It should be used with artistry—to kill only the most legitimate murderees. Don't you think so, Dorothy?"

Dorothy yawned. "Stefano, I'm sure you say the cleverest things if anyone had time to think them out. I never have the time." She looped her voluptuous gloved arm through his. "Come on or Lorraine will be honking horns at us."

The two of them moved out of the room. I stared at Iris. She stared at me.

"Well—" she said. And that was about all there was to say.

While the Count had been talking, I had moved up to the

cabinet that contained the Indian weapons. I stared down at the poison darts, evil little things with a reddish coating of curare still on their tips. They had been arranged in three groups, each group splaying out to make a fan design. Idly I counted the darts in the first group. There were six. There were six in the second group. I looked at the third group and my heart started thumping.

In the third fan there were only five darts. And, as I looked more closely, I saw indentations in the green baize between the darts, as if, quite recently, their positions had been changed. I counted the marks where the baize had been rubbed down. There were six of them.

That surely could mean only one thing. Someone must have removed the sixth dart and rearranged the remaining five to make the loss undetectable to a casual glance. I tried the lid of the cabinet. It was unlocked.

Iris was strolling toward me. "What are you looking at, dear?"

Hastily I turned my back on the table. What I was thinking was far too melodramatic to tell even Iris.

"Looking at?" I echoed. "Oh, nothing. Nothing at all."

Three

THREE CARS, with a Pleygel disregard for gas rationing, were waiting on the huge area of gravel in front of the house. Lorraine herself was at the wheel of the first, an old station wagon which she almost always used in preference to the glossier models at her disposal. She beckoned to Iris and me, and we bundled in, Iris in front with Lorraine and little Fleur Wyckoff, I in the back with Dr. Wyckoff and Dorothy. Screaming something to Lover in the automobile behind, Lorraine swerved the station wagon down the perilous drive with its breathtaking glimpses of the sleeping Lake Tahoe.

There was a full moon, shining bright as a brass button against a midshipman-blue sky. The drive to Reno over the vast hump of Mount Rose was a thing of uncanny beauty. As the car soared up toward the peak and our ears cracked at the altitude, lonely canyons toppled away on either side of us, giving place to high woodlands and mountain meadows of blue magic. A deer cantered across the road. The Nevada air was redolent of pine.

I was watching Dorothy Flanders out of the corner of my eye. Her beauty was as cold and inhuman as the night's. It was a beauty of line and curve, a surface beauty with nothing behind it except a magnificent digestive tract. Her blonde hair glistened like silver. Her profile was silver too, a cameo against the darkness.

No one spoke. We had brought our uneasiness with us, and the night did not relax it. I could see the back of Fleur's head, a little pool of stillness. But it was her husband of whom I was most conscious. He sat beyond Dorothy, rigid and unyielding. Once, when we swerved around a bend, Dorothy threw out a hand to steady herself against him.

That was the only time he showed a spark of life. The instant her fingers touched his knee, he dragged it away as if he had been bitten by a poisonous snake.

We had reached the peak of the mountain and were toppling down the far flank when a horn honked and a green coupé roared abreast of us. Chuck Dawson was at the wheel. Mimi Burnett, like a shabby pink butterfly, drooped at his side. Lorraine waved and shouted, but Chuck paid no attention. His cowboy face set in a grim mask, he shot the coupé past us, disappearing ahead in a reckless cloud of dust.

"That Chuck!" exclaimed Lorraine. "I could kill him a hundred times a day. Thinking he can race me!"

She jammed her foot on the accelerator. The old station wagon hurtled in pursuit. A twist in the mountain road loomed and Fleur gave a scream.

"Lorraine, please. Not so fast. Not on these roads."

Lorraine sighed. "Oh, I suppose you're right. Chuck's always making me do the craziest things. Mr. Throckmorton says I'll break my neck one day. But then Mr. Throckmorton's on the gloomy side although I adore him, of course." She slackened her pace and added suddenly, "He's cute, isn't he? I don't mean Mr. Throckmorton. I mean Chuck. He's my favorite fiancé in years."

Dorothy, who seemed to think any remark about a man was directed at her, stirred. "Very attractive, dear. But just what is he? Where's he from?"

"Who cares what people are or where they're from? Simply everyone in Nevada adores him."

"When are you going to marry him, dear?"

"Marry him!" Lorraine abandoned the wheel for a Gallic gesture. "Really, my dear, you're one to talk about marriage." She navigated another turn and gave a whoop of delight. "He's got a flat."

Chuck's green coupé was drawn up at the side of the road, its rear axle sagging. Chuck was tinkering with a jack while Mimi fluttered around him. When they saw us, both of them waved us to stop. But Lorraine merely poked her frizzy head out of the window and jeered, "Nyah."

She took a childish delight in her victory over her favorite fiancé. She was still humming under her breath as we plunged into the Washoe Valley and the lights of Reno, rowdy as a drunken duchess' tiara, sparkled in the blue darkness ahead.

There's something about Reno, a smallness, a cheerful strut, the vulgar tolerance of a Madam come up in the world. Unlike every other town in the country, there's no cleavage between the respectable and the disreputable elements. Housewives with steel-rimmed spectacles, glamorous divorcees from the East, soldiers, cowboys, judges, Indians, and hoboes all rub shoulders contentedly on the garish streets. They all eat at the same places, drink at the same bars, throw away the same silver dollars over the same gambling tables. You can be rich in Reno and lose. You can be poor and win. No one stays on the top or the bottom long enough for the mold to harden. It makes for a nice town.

Lorraine swerved into Virginia Street and under the brash electric sign announcing Reno, the Biggest Little City in the World. We turned past the Palace Club and down to where tall columns of neon light said: CHUCK'S CLUB.

We parked and scrambled out. Chuck's gambling place, although recently opened, followed the familiar pattern of Harold's, the Bank Club, all the others. It had even acquired its own raffish homeless dogs who lay sprawled across the threshold, hoping like the famous Curly to build themselves up into luck charms and wheedle T-bone steaks out of superstitious gamblers. We stepped over them and into the glare and smoke and chatter.

Saturday night was going full blast. Under a low mirrored ceiling, girl dealers with bows on elaborate coiffeurs flicked cards to society matrons and Indians across green baize Black Jack tables. The wheel of fortune creaked in a corner. A voice was blaring out the results of a Keno race, while, indifferent to it, military and civilian behinds bent over crap tables. Backless evening gowns, rags, uniforms and playsuits jostled each other, each with his or her own wishful and doomed system for coming out ahead of the house.

Chuck, I reflected, must be cleaning up.

I was apt to forget that Lorraine, as one of the richest girls in the world, was a nationwide celebrity. The combination of her and Iris made for a sensational entrance even in that hard-bitten throng. As we passed through the maze of tables, almost everyone turned to stare at them and whisper. Lorraine, used to nothing else, was completely unconscious of her news value. Iris tried bravely to be equally nonchalant. But Dorothy, who got her stares, too, was very different. She reacted, hip and bust, to each hungry male eye until I expected her to dislocate something.

Lorraine was saying, "I wonder where the others are," when the second party from the house trooped in—Lover French, the Lagunos, and Bill Flanders, hobbling on his crutch. Lorraine waved them over. They came, very glum. I imagined their drive had been as unsociable as ours.

Lover, looking prim, as if this vulgar atmosphere wasn't going to be suitable for his innocent fiancée, said, "Chuck and Mimi had a flat. We passed them. They'll be along any minute."

"Wonderful." Lorraine surveyed the circle of sour faces with a ravishing smile which was meant to sell them all on the idea of burying their individual hatchets. "Let's have fun, darlings. After all, I mean, there's nothing like fun. Let's have a drink."

She herded us all to the raucous, beer-stained bar and bought drinks for everyone, leaving the change from a twenty dollar bill as a tip for the grinning barman. She gulped her coke high.

"Everyone does what they want. It's much more fun that way. I'm going to play roulette." She slipped her arm through her half-brother's. "Come on, Lover. You're a stuffy old fuss-budget and you think gambling's a sin. But you're going to bring me luck. I feel it in my bones. Dorothy—" she grabbed Mrs. Flanders with her free arm—"there's something monumental about you. I think you'll be lucky, too. Eleven's the number, my pets. It's simply, absolutely bound to come up."

Iris, clutching her piggy bank, gave me a rather guilty smile and slipped over to the half-dollar slot machine by the roulette table. The rest of the party seemed most reluctant to join in the spirit of Lorraine's "fun." Studiedly ignoring each other, they started one by one to drift aimlessly after their hostess.

The roulette table was crowded, but the players parted like the Red Sea to give Lorraine Pleygel space. She pulled a hundred dollar bill from her frivolous purse and tossed it to the flashy female croupier, greeting her like an old friend. Bill Flanders had edged his way to the table between Dorothy and Lover. The Wyckoffs, keeping close together, but never looking at each other, pressed after him. The Count Laguno was hovering around Dorothy's back. Everyone was crammed tightly together.

The wheel was spinning. The green board with its black and red numbers was gaily sprinkled with red and yellow and blue chips. Lorraine had received a cluster of henna five-dollar chips. She pushed some to Dorothy.

"For luck, darling. Give a couple to Lover. It'll do him good to be dashing."

Dorothy scooped the chips up greedily. Lover watched with clucking disapproval.

Lorraine said, "Eleven's the number, angels."

Her hand hovered over her pile of chips. Somebody shouted, "Lorraine!" She turned from the table. Chuck Dawson and Mimi Burnett were hurrying toward us past Indians and dowagers and Chinamen and soldiers. They had another, unknown man in tow. Chuck, swaggering through friendly greetings, pats on the back, and the ravenous glances of divorcees, elbowed his way to Lorraine's side. He grinned.

"You rat," he said, "leaving us to rot by the roadside." He took her arm with rough affection. "Come on, baby. There's an admirer of yours who wants to meet you." His other hand gripped the startled Lover by the collar. "And you, my boy, ought to be ashamed. You know your girl friend says 'Naughty to gamble.' "

He grabbed the brother and sister away from the table. Lover struggled with outraged dignity. Lorraine protested, "But, Chuck, darling, I'm playing." But she did not make an issue out of it. She obviously liked having him treat her rough. "Play for me," she called to Dorothy.

Carried away like a couple of puppies in Chuck's husky grasp, Lorraine and Lover joined Mimi and the stranger. Mimi melted against Lover, twisting his lapels girlishly. The stranger, who looked very Spanish, was bowing over Lorraine's fingers as if she were a princess of the blood.

I turned to watch Iris. My wife was trying not to notice a little group of fans around her and was still pouring fifty-cent pieces into an apparently listless machine. I moved toward her. Suddenly the entire machine seemed to explode with a mad clanging, and fifty-cent pieces poured from its maw, like magic rain.

Forgetting her dignity as a movie star, Iris screamed in ecstasy and plunged to her knees, wallowing in Federal silver.

"The jackpot," she moaned like one possessed. "I've hit the jackpot."

The cluster of fans took it up. "Iris Duluth's hit the jackpot!" Their carryings-on caused a minor sensation. Everyone at the roulette table turned. Even Lorraine, Chuck, Lover, Mimi and their new friend came running over. There was complete confusion while people crept around under other peoples' legs, retrieving half dollars. Iris, her life's ambition satisfied, was kissing me tempestuously. Then, remembering her golden rule, she said, "The piggy bank. Where's the piggy bank?"

She had abandoned it on the floor. Chuck brought it for her. Beaming from ear to ear, she gathered her ill-gotten hoard and, piece by piece, plopped it into the horrible pig while people cooed and told her how wonderful she was and tried to get autographs.

While the confusion was subsiding, Lorraine, agog with a new enthusiasm, dragged the South American stranger forward.

"Everybody, this is Alvarez. He's doing a special rhumba act at the Del Monte and he saw me rhumbaing with Chuck last week and he says I danced a wonderful rhumba and he wants to rhumba with me. Isn't that divine? Gambling's dull, anyway. I'll tell you what. Let's all go over right away to the Del Monte and dance. Where's Dorothy?" She turned round to find Dorothy at her elbow. "Finished, dear?"

"Finished is right," drawled Dorothy, smoothing her white gloves and tucking her silver pocketbook under her arm. "I lost your all, I'm afraid. No elevens."

"That's wonderful." Lorraine, fitful as the wind, was already bored sick with roulette and hot on the trail of new "fun." She was naïve enough to be flattered that a professional dancer wanted to rhumba with her. That was Lorraine. It never occurred to her that there wasn't a gigolo in the world who wouldn't murder his mother for the chance of a crack at Lorraine Pleygel.

One arm through the dancer's, one through Chuck's, she started toward the door. Her party, sunk now in a mood of sullen resignation, trooped after her. In a few minutes "divine" roulette was a thing of the past, and we were all spaced stolidly around the best table on the best side of the dance floor in the Del Monte, while waiters, headwaiters, and even the manager hovered around to make sure that Miss Pleygel and Iris Duluth were getting the best of service.

The Del Monte was one of the very few places in Reno which made a stab at elegance and class distinction. With its subtle lights, its dark mirrors, its fancy rhumba orchestra, it aped New York with a shrewd eye on the pocketbooks of nostalgic Eastern divorcees. Even so, the brash exuberance of Reno had not been entirely excluded. Here and there among the evening gowns and the tuxedos, a cowboy's pink satin shirt or a rancher's denims showed up to take some of the chic out of the chi-chi.

Lorraine, who was doubtless as fed-up with her guests as they were with each other, was already on the dance floor, weaving her small hips around the South American's in blissful contentment. Ill luck had jammed me in a corner of the table, with Dorothy as a buttress between me and Iris, who was still clutching her piggy bank and talking animatedly to Lover. Before I could think out a reasonably polite way of leaning across Dorothy's bosom to ask my wife to dance, the Count Laguno sidled up with much bowing from the waist and whisked Iris onto the floor.

That definitely stuck me with Dorothy.

Drinks came, and with them a large chicken sandwich for Mrs. Flanders. Her eyes gloating at the sight of it, Dorothy peeled off her long white gloves and opened her large silver pocketbook to put them away. As the silver clasps broke, my eyes almost unconsciously glanced at the bag's interior. Instantly Dorothy jammed the gloves in, jerked her hand out as if it had been bitten, and, snapping the clasps shut, bundled the bag down onto the seat at the far side of her.

She had been quick, but not quick enough to keep me from seeing the henna chips, stuffed in edgewise between her compact and her handkerchief.

Dorothy did not improve with acquaintance. Expert in all the major vices, she was not above practicing the minor ones, too. She had lied to Lorraine about having lost everything at the roulette table. She had salted away a fistful of her hostess' five-dollar chips to be redeemed on a later, rainier day.

Since Dorothy knew I had seen and I knew she knew I had seen, the social situation between us was very strained. After a few moments of sick silence in which she took flustered snaps at the sandwich, I asked her to dance. It seemed the only thing to do.

With a smile that was meant to shatter the very soul of me, she rose in sinuous coils. Squeezing her rather too voluptuous hips through the narrow space between the table and the wall, she followed me out onto the dance floor. The orchestra was pouring forth its torrid South American noises. Dorothy Flanders extended her bare arms and engulfed me.

We moved in among the other couples without speaking, giving our all to the rhumba. Lorraine and her South American danced closer and then away again, Lorraine waving gaily. Mimi and Chuck, that unlikely partnership, also writhed near to us. I could just see Iris and Laguno at the other side of the floor. The softness and the heavy warmth of Dorothy Flanders in my arms would have sent most men into a tizzy of orchid and jungle fancies. But to me, as it happened, the only South American thing that reared its ugly head was the poison dart which either was or was not missing from the trophy room.

I glanced back at the table. I could see Janet Laguno flopped in her yellow dress, looking like a soufflé that had fallen. Lover was peering anxiously over Iris' piggy bank, searching the floor for Mimi. The Wyckoffs and Bill Flanders, his face strangely alight, were watching the dancers.

Lorraine, undulating by, waved again, her pretty pug face sparkling with enjoyment. As I reviewed that memorable and ugly evening, it seemed incredible that even the giddy Lorraine could have brought this dynamite collection of people together without realizing the probability of explosion. Had she been as naïve as she seemed? Had her plan been just one of her typical muddle-headed gestures of kindliness? Or was it possible that there had been in it some well-concealed and sinister malice? I had never in my life known Lorraine to be malicious before.

Back and forth, I pushed the exotic heaviness of Dorothy. The music and the rhythmic swaying of her body were having an anesthetic effect. The poison dart merged in my mind with an image of Iris as she said, *"Darling, you don't think Bill Flanders will try to kill her, do you?"* Then there was Laguno's voice, saying, *"Curare has a certain nobility. It should be used with artistry to kill only the most legitimate murderees."*

Legitimate murderees! If ever there was a legitimate murderee, I reflected, I had one right there in my arms.

I was as embarrassed by this thought as if I had spoken it out loud. Quickly I said, "Nice music, Dorothy."

The rhumba pounded on. Dorothy's hand on my shoulder had tightened its grip. She did not answer.

"Dorothy——" I began.

Then I stopped because the grip of her fingers on my shoulder had become so tight that it was painful.

Although she was in my arms, I had been too abstracted to look at her. I turned to half profile so that my face was almost touching hers. Her eyes were staring straight ahead, like a doll's, with no sense in them. Beneath the gorgeous blonde hair, her skin looked strangely blue in the dim light.

The hairs at the back of my neck stirred. My feet still went through the movements of the rhumba, but nothing seemed real any more.

"Dorothy——"

If I had leaned forward an inch or so, my lips would have been on hers.

And it was her lips that were so terrible now. Slowly, they were drawing backward, exposing her teeth like an ebb tide exposing white sand. It wasn't a smile. It was as if every drop of moisture was being drained away from her skin.

"Dorothy——" I said it so loudly that people turned to look.

Someone in the band started to sing in high, throbbing Spanish. The painted gourds hissed out their rhythm like trained serpents. Dorothy had given up following me. We stumbled. She was shaking all over. Suddenly her whole body writhed against me in one savage convulsion. Her face knocked against my shirt front and then sprang back, trickles of foam spattering from between clenched teeth.

"Dorothy——"

Her back arched. Then she collapsed, sagging, half sprawling toward the floor in my weakening grasp.

The man was still singing. The couples were still dancing. I stared down at the limp, unhuman thing that had been my partner.

And cold sweat broke out on my forehead.

Because there was no doubt then—no doubt at all.

There I was in the middle of the dance floor with Dorothy Flanders dead in my arms.

Part Two
JANET

Four

I TRIED to move her. I couldn't. I just stood there with that blonde dead thing which had been Dorothy Flanders limp in my arms.

The rhumba rhythm of the orchestra seemed to be throbbing inside my head. The couples near me stopped dancing. A crackle of chatter, ominous as a prairie fire, began to sweep the floor.

Men and women, pressing close, stared down at Dorothy. Their faces were caricatures, stylizing shock, curiosity, and horror. They did nothing to help. The thing was too violent for them. They could not quite take in the fact that here, in this elegant night club dedicated to frivolity, a woman could be sprawled unfrivolously and most inelegantly dead.

I was feeling that way myself. During two years of war in the Pacific, I had seen death in a dozen grim forms. But somehow this was worse. Dying belongs in battles. It didn't belong here.

Chuck and Mimi Burnett broke the spell. They pushed in from the periphery of the dancers, arm in arm as if they were still rhumbaing. Mimi saw Dorothy. Her gaze sprang away from the dead woman to Chuck. I saw the sham-elfin prettiness flee from her face, leaving it a prune-creased monkey mask. Then she screamed—one shrill, tilting scream.

I said, "Help me, Chuck."

Lorraine Pleygel's fiancé was looking down at Dorothy, too. There was none of the general horror on his handsome face. He seemed to be thinking about something complicated and quite different.

"Okay, Lieutenant. You take her shoulders."

We started carrying her. The dancers rustled a path for us, like dead leaves scattering before a wind. I caught a glimpse of my wife among them, her hand frozen on the Count Laguno's arm. Black-coated and agitated, the manager was beckoning us toward a door in the red leather paneling of the wall. We headed toward it. The orchestra was still playing, but the music sounded infinitely desolate like music played on a sinking ship.

The manager was holding the door open. Chuck and I carried Dorothy into an office. There was a couch. We laid her down on it. The manager shut the door.

My mind was spinning. I could only think that Lorraine had tried to reconcile three husbands and three wives. And now, only a few hours later, one of the wives was dead.

That was enough to think about—quite enough.

I said to Chuck, "She's dead. I don't think there's any doubt about that. But get a doctor. Get Wyckoff."

"Sure." Chuck started for the door.

I called, "You'd better get her husband, too."

Chuck left. The manager of the Del Monte came toward the couch on obsequious tiptoe. He looked at Dorothy. She wasn't something anybody would have liked to look at. The low evening gown was the worst part. There was so much naked bluish-white bosom.

The hair up-do had half crumbled. That made it a bit better. The trailing yellow hair concealed part of what the convulsive agony had done to her face.

"A terrible, terrible thing," the manager was moaning. "Dead. However did it happen?"

"I don't know," I said, which was true enough.

"And here in the Del Monte." Manager-like, his thoughts were largely on his own cash register. "A dreadful thing. I only hope it wasn't anything she was served. I hope——"

"You're not in the habit of serving Borgia highballs, are you?" I wondered why I had said that. Why was something in me already assuming that Dorothy's death had not been due to natural causes? After all, people do just—die.

Chuck came in again with Dr. David Wyckoff. Bill Flanders hobbled a little behind on his crutch.

Although I had been conscious of Dr. Wyckoff on more than one occasion that evening, his appearance had not particularly registered until then. He must have been around forty. Except for the stoop in his shoulders, he seemed younger. He was dark, with a nice, unassuming face, the sort of man's face that went with the pretty girl face of his estranged wife. He was trying to look cool and professional, but his eyes gave him away. The curious dread which had been lurking in them ever since his arrival at Lorraine's was still there—only much closer now to the surface.

He passed me without saying anything and bent over the couch. The manager fluttered to Chuck. His deferential attitude made me realize what an important figure Chuck Dawson must be in local life. The manager was twittering to him about the Del Monte and what a wonderful reputation it had and could Chuck help stop a scandal. Most of my attention, however, was on Bill Flanders.

The ex-marine stood close to me, his boxer's shoulders hunched sidewise, leaning their weight on his crutch. He was staring at what was visible of his wife behind Wyckoff's back. His face was tight and pinched. On the hand that gripped the crutch, the knuckles stood out bony and white. And yet it wasn't grief that was bothering him. I was almost sure of that.

He looked like a man who knew a fuse had been lit that

nobody could extinguish—a man waiting for an explosion.

I wished I hadn't asked Chuck to get him. It is the conventional thing to summon a husband at a moment like that. But Bill Flanders was hardly a conventional husband, even an about-to-be-divorced one.

Conventional husbands do not, as he had done only that evening, publicly threaten to kill their wives.

Suddenly he swung to me. Through lips stiff as wood, he asked, "Is she dead?"

"That's up to Wyckoff," I said. "I think she's dead."

He laughed then. It was a bad laugh, so rasping that the manager stopped his garrulousness to shoot him a shocked glance.

I didn't know what to do with him. I was afraid he might break down again the way he had broken down at dinner. And heaven alone knew what he might have to say this time. I certainly didn't want to hear it.

"You'd better——" I began.

The door burst open and Lorraine Pleygel came in.

This was certainly no place or moment for a woman, but none of us tried to keep her out. That was the way with Lorraine. Maybe it was her immense wealth or maybe it was just the indomitable spirit behind her frivolous exterior.

Lorraine Pleygel always got where she wanted to go.

She hurried toward her fiancé, half running on absurd high heels. "Chuck, darling. She can't be dead. It's not possible."

She saw Wyckoff at the couch and started toward him. Chuck grabbed her arm.

"No, Lorraine."

"But, darling——"

"No."

She let him hold her, but her gaze went to me. "Peter, angel, she was dancing with you. I saw her. People don't dance—and die."

All her life she had been insulated from unpleasantness by money. It seemed almost impossible for her to realize then that something distinctly unpleasant had happened and happened very close to home. She found a cigarette in her fantastic gray purse and lit it with a touch of bravado as if by lighting a cigarette she could get things back to being divine and fun.

"It's absurd," she said, "that's all. Just absurd." And then, "Oh, dear, if only Mr. Throckmorton were here."

Mr. Throckmorton had a way of popping up at the oddest moments. I still had only the dimmest notion of his function in Lorraine's life. Presumably he was some sort of guardian.

Lorraine's voice trailed away. Even the manager had stopped chattering. The silence was charged with the tension that radiated from Bill Flanders. I was watching Dr. Wyckoff's back as if it were the only thing in the world.

So were the others.

Any minute now Wyckoff would speak, would let us know how Dorothy had died. My own suspicions, built on so many little things which had happened on that impossible evening, made the period of waiting a jangle of nerves. As we stood, still as hypnotized birds watching a snake, David Wyckoff turned from the couch. His face was gaunt but he had a kind of artificial control that was compelling.

Lorraine jerked the cigarette from her lips. "Well——?"

Wyckoff looked down at his delicate, doctor's hands. "Mrs. Flanders was a regular patient of mine in San Francisco." His voice was so low it was hard to hear him. "For some time I have been treating her for a serious heart condition. I repeatedly warned her against any unnecessary excitement or undue physical exertion—such as dancing."

He paused. The silence dropped down on us again like a collapsed pup-tent. I could scarcely believe that was what he had said. Dorothy Flanders, the healthiest looking hunk of woman I had ever met, a regular patient of his suffering from heart disease!

Dr. Wyckoff moistened his lips. "I told her that unless she was willing to take a long rest her condition might assume very serious proportions." He turned then so that his dark gaze was fixed steadily on Bill Flanders. "Her husband will confirm that. I told him the same thing some weeks ago. Didn't I, Flanders?"

As I looked at Bill Flanders, it seemed to me that for one instant his face showed dazed incomprehension. But the expression vanished—if indeed it had ever been there—so quickly that I felt I must have been imagining things. He gave a shrug.

"Why, sure, doc," he said. "Sure. That's what you told me."

The tension in the room should have relaxed then. It didn't. Everyone seemed even more strung up, except the manager who was having difficulty keeping a smug smile of relief from showing.

He said, "You mean, doctor, that this lady died from a heart attack?"

"Knowing her history," said Doctor Wyckoff, "it is my opinion that certain—er—excitements of the day, combined with overindulgence and the exertion of dancing, brought on a cardiac attack which proved fatal."

The manager's fingers were fluttering all over his black tie. "Then there won't be any need for—for publicity, the police——?"

"I am a Californian," said Wyckoff. "I don't know the correct procedure in this State, but I'm prepared to——"

Chuck Dawson broke in. Looking very big and tough and alert, he said, "You were her regular physician, Wyckoff. You've been treating her. As far as I've got it figured, it's perfectly okay for you to sign the death certificate, and that's all there is to it. You're ready to sign the certificate, I guess?"

"Why, yes, naturally."

Chuck glanced at the body on the couch. "We'd better make sure though. I've got a lot of friends down in the police department."

He went to the phone on the manager's desk and dialed a number. Soon he was telling the receiver what had happened. Put in the way he put it, the whole thing sounded as innocent as a lamb chop. A lady in the party of Miss Lorraine Pleygel had just died at the Del Monte. The physician who had been treating her for a heart condition was present and, after an examination, was ready to sign a certificate of death from heart failure. Chuck sprinkled his account lavishly with the Pleygel name, which was enough in itself to intimidate a police official; he threw in Iris for full measure, adding that the manager of the Del Monte was eager to avoid any unpleasant notoriety for his establishment. He listened and then put down the receiver.

"It's okay," he said. "Wyckoff signs the certificate. They're not sending up a police doctor. They understand how Miss Pleygel and Iris Duluth and the Del Monte feel and they promise to keep the reporters off. No inquest, no anything. There won't be any stink."

That was all there was to it. In less than fifteen minutes Dorothy Flanders was well on her way to a respectable coffin.

The manager was almost purring now. Chuck turned to Lorraine.

"Listen, baby, there's nothing you can do. Get Flanders and the others home. Wyckoff and I will attend to everything, see she's taken to a funeral place. When we're through, I'll drive Wyckoff back and sleep at your house. Okay?"

"Why, yes, darling. Yes, of course." Lorraine's face,

which was so naïve for all its sophistication, was puckered like the face of a little girl who'd just seen a puppy run over. "But poor Dorothy. How perfectly ghastly. Who ever dreamed Dorothy would die of a weak heart?"

Lorraine, Bill Flanders, the manager, and myself were hustled out of the office. The manager scurried away, presumably to soothe his customers. Lorraine linked her arm through mine.

Her words were still echoing in my ears.

Who ever dreamed Dorothy would die of a weak heart?

Who indeed? Maybe Lorraine believed in that heart attack. Lorraine could believe anything she put her mind to. Maybe the manager believed in it too, it was so obviously to his advantage to do so.

But did Wyckoff? Did Flanders? Did Chuck Dawson? Did I?

Five

IRIS HAD LOCKED her piggy bank with its hoard of ill-gotten half dollars in the dressing-table drawer which served as her private Fort Knox. She slipped out of her black evening gown and sat, very decoratively, at the mirror, combing her dark hair. It was a relief to be over with the noisome evening and to be alone with my wife again.

I was hanging my uniform in the closet when Iris remarked, "So Dorothy Flanders died of a heart attack."

"That's what they say." I started to unbutton my shirt. "Incidentally, never rhumba with someone who's going to die of a heart attack. I don't recommend it."

Iris went on combing her hair noncommittally. I grabbed

up my pajamas, a fancy blue silk pair bought largely to impress Lorraine's domestic staff, went into the bathroom, and started brushing my teeth.

My wife's voice sounded again in competition with the running water. "Considerate of her, wasn't it?"

I knew she was sending up a trial balloon. I grunted a guarded, "Sure," through toothpaste.

My wife appeared in the door of the bathroom, slender and beautiful, and watched me brush my teeth.

"Darling, you want your leave to be a nice leave, don't you? Nice and peaceful?"

"Sure."

"And you like being alone with me?"

I'd have kissed her if it hadn't been for the toothpaste. She looked so exactly like something you wanted to kiss.

"Being alone with you's the only thing I like without reservation," I said.

My wife's forehead puckered. "In that case, we leave here tomorrow. We'll live in a tent in the desert if necessary. And—" she paused "—and Dorothy Flanders died of a heart attack."

She withdrew to the bedroom, leaving me with my teeth and my thoughts. My thoughts gave me more trouble than my teeth. By every law of reason, I should have been panting to exchange the unappetizing situation here for a brief period of peace and quiet with my wife. And yet, in the old frivolous days before I joined the Navy and Iris became a movie star, we had been mixed up in a couple of murders. We had always maintained that we had hated every moment of them. But somehow, whenever a chance came to become embroiled again, there we were. Something happened to us —something funny and tingling in the spine. I was tingling now.

I scrambled into my very civilian pajamas. Hardly knowing I had said it, I called, "Darling, remember that old drunk with a beard in Frisco who warned you that Eulalia Crawford was going to be murdered?"

"Yes." My wife's reply was prompt.

"And remember Fogarty in the strait-jacket at Dr. Lenz'?"

Iris was at the bathroom door again. She had changed into a Magnificent Pictures black negligee which had almost certainly shocked the staider members of Lorraine's domestic staff. Her eyes were shining with a gleam I knew of old.

"So you do want to stay too, Peter. We are going to find out what really happened."

I watched her. "Remember, baby. You're Iris Duluth of Magnificent Pictures now. You belong to the world. If there was any scandal, what would Mr. Somethingstein——"

"Don't call him Mr. Somethingstein, Peter. He's Mr. Finkelstein. And who cares what Mr. Finkelstein thinks? If there is a scandal and if Will Hays finds me unsavory, they can rustle up someone else to belong to the world."

Having disposed of her movie career, my wife grabbed my hand and pulled me down onto the edge of one of Lorraine's wildly modernistic beds.

"Darling, with her husband threatening to kill her and everything, Dorothy couldn't have died of a heart attack. It's too much of a coincidence. Besides, you just had to look at her to see she was as healthy as a water buffalo. Tell me— exactly what happened in the manager's office?"

I told her. She said, "Then, if Dorothy was murdered, Wyckoff risked his entire professional career making a false diagnosis. Why?"

"There's a lot of whys about Wyckoff anyway. Why did he come here in the first place? Certainly not to get reconciled with his wife. He hasn't even spoken to Fleur since he arrived."

"If he was faking, he took a terrible risk, passing the buck like that to Bill Flanders. Bill might have denied knowing about Dorothy's weak heart."

"He had to take that risk. No one would have believed his story unless it was backed up by Dorothy's husband. Besides, he was at dinner. He'd have known Bill had everything to lose if it came out that his wife had been murdered. Bill's the obvious one to have murdered her anyway. And if he did, I can't say I'd blame him much."

"Neither would I." Iris paused. "But what about Chuck Dawson? Do you think the two of them managed to fool Chuck?"

"As a matter of fact, he seemed as eager as they were to sell the heart attack theory. He was actually the one who made it possible, using his influence to keep the police from investigating. It doesn't make sense, his helping to hush up her murder. So far as I know, he'd only known her the week she'd been here."

"A week of Dorothy'd be enough for anyone." Iris crossed her knees and clasped her hands around them. "Peter, if she didn't die of a heart attack, how did she die?"

"I guess she'd have to have been poisoned. And if she was poisoned, I have a hunch where the poison may have come from." I told her about the curare-tipped Indian dart which might possibly have been missing from the cabinet in the trophy room. "I didn't tell you when I noticed it. I didn't want to worry you."

"Curare!" Iris whistled. "The Count Laguno made that crack about curare to Dorothy this evening."

"Exactly."

"Peter, what do you know about curare?"

"Just what you read in detective stories. It doesn't hurt you if you swallow it. Dorothy wolfed down a chicken sandwich at the Del Monte. But I guess that couldn't have been poisoned. It has to get in your blood stream. But one prick with a pin's enough to kill you."

"Dorothy certainly had enough naked areas to prick. It works quickly, doesn't it?"

"Yes. But I don't know how quickly. Anywhere from three minutes to twenty minutes, I think."

"That cuts out Chuck's club then. We were in the Del Monte more than twenty minutes. But it doesn't help. Anyone could easily have stuck her when we were all crowding to the table." Iris looked puzzled. "Darling, somehow I don't see Bill Flanders doing something as wild and imaginative as sticking Dorothy with a poisoned dart. He wanted to kill her, yes. But he's the sort who'd have bashed her over the head or——"

"Or chased her with a steak knife," I put in. "But it doesn't have to be Bill. The Lagunos and the Wyckoffs knew the Flanders in San Francisco. Lorraine knew her too. Anyone who knew Dorothy might have been proud to murder her."

Iris' face was determined. "Come on, darling. Let's get our teeth into this. Let's begin at the beginning and reconstruct everything that happened this evening."

We were still reconstructing in our individual zebra-striped beds an hour later. Iris' reconstruction got more and more vague until it faded in a sigh and she was asleep.

But I was not sleepy. I lay in bed, smoking in the dark, thinking. Our rehash of the evening had made it clear that, apart from vague suspicions, there was no evidence of murder. We couldn't even be sure that a dart had been taken from the trophy room. Only an autopsy could tell whether or not Wyckoff had been lying. And Iris and I were hardly in a position to barge around demanding autopsies on other people's wives.

Around two, Chuck Dawson and Dr. Wyckoff came back. I heard them outside my door. Chuck said a low

"Good night, Wyckoff," and two sets of footsteps sounded as they moved off to their rooms.

Dorothy, presumably, had been safely stowed in a Reno funeral parlor.

I found myself sliding into an uneasy doze, dominated by a grisly vision of Dorothy's bluish-white corpse, with its tumbling blonde hair, laid out on a marble slab in a bleak room.

I must have slept, but only lightly because, suddenly I was wide awake again, sitting up in bed, my heart racing. The luminous dial of my watch showed three-thirty. I tried, in a sleep-confused way, to think what had wakened me. Then I understood.

Outside my door, audible against the bare cedar of the corridor floor, sounded the faint tap of footsteps.

Footsteps, even at three-thirty in the morning, should not have been particularly disturbing. But these were, because they were so furtive. A gentle shuffle, then a tiny squeak. A shuffle, a squeak. . . .

It was as if someone were passing my door on tiptoe, his heart in his mouth.

I lit a cigarette and lay back in bed as the footsteps grew dimmer and then quite inaudible. They had been going down the passage toward the head of the stairs. I smoked the cigarette to its butt, thinking about them. It was none of my business who was going where, but, as a self-appointed investigator, my curiosity was more than I could bear. About five minutes later, when the footsteps hadn't returned, I tumbled out of bed, into slippers and robe, and eased my way into the corridor.

The moon must have set. The darkness in the passage was thick as tar. I stood a moment, getting my bearings. Then I saw a faint streak of light fanning out from under the door of a room on the other side of the passage, between me and the stairs. As I watched, it snapped out. I heard the rattle of a cautiously turned doorknob. Then the footsteps were there again, coming straight toward me from the room which had been lighted.

Shuffle, squeak. . . . Shuffle, squeak. . . .

It was an odd feeling, standing in the darkness, having that unknown person creep closer and closer. In the early desperate days in the Pacific I had sharpened my instinct to associate any stealthy creeping sound with danger.

The footsteps were almost abreast of me now, on the far side of the corridor. I could have reached out and touched the person, whoever it was. But I didn't. In a millionairess' mansion, house guests don't pounce on each other without provocation.

Instead I said, "Who's there?"

There was a second of utter silence. Then, with a scurrying like the Rabbit in *Alice in Wonderland*, the invisible presence darted past me. Almost before I had time to turn around, I heard a door open and shut behind me. Again there was nothing in the corridor but the darkness.

It was impossible to tell into which room my invisible fellow guest had vanished, and obviously I couldn't follow. I turned back toward the stairs. The geography of the house had fallen into place in my mind now. There were only three rooms between myself and the head of the stairs. Chuck Dawson and Janet Laguno had the two rooms on my side.

But the single room across the corridor, the room from which the prowler had just come, was the room that had belonged to Dorothy Flanders.

I hurried to it. The door was ajar. I slipped in, closing the door behind me. I stumbled around for a lamp, found one, and turned it on.

Dorothy had been given one of the few sedate rooms in Lorraine's crazy house, a sort of Early American affair. Its condition, however, was far from sedate. The drawers in the antique highboy had been tugged open. The exotic dresses in the closet were in confusion. Empty suitcases were sprawled all over the carpet.

I made a brief survey of the place. Rings and necklaces were lying in full view on the vanity. I found a pile of silver dollars in one of the open highboy drawers. It was only too plain that the person who had just ransacked the room so feverishly had been no common or garden sneak-thief.

This seemed to be one up for the murder theory. People don't play havoc with the rooms of women who die from respectable heart attacks.

But what had the burglar been after? I looked around. There was nothing to give me a clue. I was mad as a hornet for having let him or her slip through my fingers in the passage. The lamp I had lighted was by the window. I crossed, turned it out, and stood a moment, staring into the night and wondering what to do next. Immediately below, the edge of the terrace was dimly visible in the starlight. Something else was visible too—the red tip of a lighted cigarette.

Anyone up at that hour of the night was worth investigating. I slipped out of the room into the corridor and down the stairs. Passing through the great living-room, I pulled open one of the plate-glass windows and stepped onto the terrace.

It was lighter outside than in. Stars were gleaming with a high polish in the Nevada sky. The red tip of the cigarette was no longer where it had been. For a moment I thought the terrace was deserted. Then, further up, beyond the huddle of potted shrubs, I saw its gleam. Behind it, I could just make out a shadowy silhouette.

I strolled up the terrace, making no attempt to conceal myself. I was just someone who couldn't sleep taking a walk in the starlight. The figure in front of me was a man. I could see that now. He was sitting, hunched forward, in a white wooden chair. Something was propped against the chair. A crutch.

At least I knew one thing. It hadn't been Dorothy's husband who had rifled her room.

I went right up to Bill Flanders. He was fully dressed, the way he had been dressed that evening. He was staring out across the faint shimmer of Lake Tahoe, unconscious of me and everything else.

"Hello," I said.

He started. The cigarette dropped from his hand. "Who——? Oh, it's Lieutenant Duluth, isn't it?"

"Couldn't sleep," I said. "Guess you're having the same trouble."

"Sleep! Did you expect me to sleep?"

Somehow I felt like a heel. I half suspected him of murdering his wife, and here I was spying on him. I turned away, but surprisingly the ex-boxer-marine grabbed my arm.

"Don't go, Lieutenant," he said hoarsely. "I gotta have someone to talk to or I'll go nuts."

I didn't say anything. I just perched myself on the balustrade of the terrace, close to him. Although I couldn't see his face, I could tell he had worked himself up to a pitch where his nerves had almost gone.

"I gotta tell someone this, Lieutenant, because it's weighing on my mind. Last week, before she quit to go to Reno, I tried to murder my wife."

So much that was startling had happened in so short a time that this very remarkable confirmation of what Dorothy herself had claimed neither surprised nor shocked me.

He was glaring up at me, his hands twisting together. "Maybe you'll think I'm a maniac or something and oughtta be put away. Maybe you're right at that. I don't know any more. In the old days, I was always kind of a peaceable guy.

I was a boxer. But when I was up there in the ring, I didn't feel like it was fighting. It was just my job, see? I was just working like any other guy, salting money away because all I wanted was to settle down some place with Dorothy, settle down quiet and have kids. Then the War came, and Saipan. And there it was kill or be killed. But all the time I was kind of dreaming how it would be different someday and I'd be back again with Dorothy. I knew she was much smarter than me. She'd been married before, been around with society people and all. But after all, she'd married me and I thought——"

His voice choked. I didn't like having to listen.

"Then I lost my leg and I came back, Lieutenant. And—well, you know what I found. She'd run through all my dough. She'd been carrying on with every 4F in sight. And I got to figuring. I'd been out there fighting the Japs for her and what had she been doing? How was she any better than the Japs? And she started throwing all those bills at me she expected me to pay and—— Oh, what's the use? I couldn't never make you understand."

"Sure," I said quietly, "I understand. If I'd come back to a wife like that I'd probably have tried to kill her too."

"You mean that?" He sounded pathetically eager. Then his voice went flat again. "But that ain't all, Lieutenant. Day before yesterday this Lorraine Pleygel calls and invites me to come up here, to get reconciled with my wife, she says." He laughed. "That struck me as funny, that did. Reconcile with Dorothy. But scarcely before I knew I'd done it, I was saying, 'Sure. Sure I'd like to come.' And I did come, and for only one reason." He added huskily, "I accepted that invitation and I came here just for another chance to give Dorothy what was coming to her."

I didn't speak. We were on far too dangerous ground.

Bill Flanders stirred in the white porch chair. "I had it all figured out. I was going to kill her tonight, strangle her in her bed, and I was going to give myself up to the police. It was just something I had to do because I couldn't live on any longer and not do it. But it's just like there's some power, some power bigger'n us that takes things out of our hands. Because I never got a chance to kill her. She just up and died like that—from her weak heart."

It was very hard, after that, to believe that Bill Flanders had murdered his wife.

Warily I said, "You're sure that she did die from a heart attack?"

His voice harsh as a buzz-saw, he said, "What d'you mean? You're not saying you think I killed her after all?"

"Not that you killed her, Bill. Just that——"

"But Wyckoff looked at her. He's a doctor. He knows. He——"

"What if Wyckoff hadn't been telling the truth?"

"You mean about Dorothy having a weak heart? You're crazy. Of course she had a weak heart. You heard me say so, didn't you? Wyckoff told me about it weeks ago." He laughed. "I should know. There's been enough money paid out on it. Here——"

He was fumbling in his breast pocket. He pulled out a sheaf of papers. With a shaky hand, he lit a match and started leafing through them.

"These are some of the bills Dorothy never paid. I brought 'em with me just to keep me mad. There's a couple from Wyckoff. Here, see for yourself."

He handed me three pieces of paper. Feeling rather dizzy, I lit a match myself. Each of the papers had Wyckoff's letterhead at the top, and each of them was a bill for professional services, addressed to Mrs. Dorothy Flanders.

"And, if you don't believe me, Lieutenant, you can look up Wyckoff's files——"

Bill Flanders went on talking, but I didn't listen. My

whole murder theory rested on the fact that Dorothy hadn't died of a heart attack.

Now, unless things were far more complicated than they seemed, she had died of just that.

Flanders and I stayed there on the porch. He wanted to talk some of the tangled nightmare things out of his mind. I was sorry for him, doubly sorry because I was feeling such a fool myself. The great peaks of the Sierras had started to loom through the dawn when I left him and went upstairs.

As I passed Dorothy's room, I decided to give it another once over. After all, even if our murder theory had been given a body blow, at least the robbery had still to be explained. I opened the door, remembering the confusion as I had last seen it. Faint gray daylight from the window made it bright enough to see.

All the drawers in the highboy were closed. The dresses were hanging neatly in the closet. The suitcases stood in a tidy pile at the foot of the bed. There was not the slightest hint to show that the room had ever been searched.

No murder. And now—no robbery. That was too much for me.

I stole back to our room. Iris was still asleep. I slipped into the bed next to hers, trying not to feel like a gibbering lunatic.

I suppose I slept.

Six

"I'VE BEEN thinking and thinking, my angels, really I have. And there's only one thing to do and that's not to think." Lorraine Pleygel brandished that remark at us across the sun-splashed breakfast tables on the terrace. "Mr.

Throckmorton would say we should all go about in long black veils. But then, Mr. Throckmorton's from Boston and everything's so depressing in Boston. After all, thinking and being morbid won't help poor Dorothy. So let's just go on having fun. I'm sure I'd want people to go on having fun if I died."

Putting this typical piece of Pleygel philosophy into practice, Lorraine was wearing the most frivolous garment I had ever seen. It was a swimming suit built exclusively from dazzling silver scales. It made her look like a pedigree bull terrier disguised as a mermaid.

In spite of Lorraine there wasn't much fun on that terrace. Iris and I, having thrashed out my experiences of the night before, were both subdued. David and Fleur Wyckoff, as usual, were sitting side by side, ignoring each other as completely as two strangers who had happened to pick adjacent seats on the subway. Bill Flanders, Janet Laguno, Lover French, and Mimi Burnett had not put in an appearance. Chuck, who had brought up the subject of Dorothy with a curt announcement that the funeral had been set for the next day, seemed to be in a disgruntled mood. In old denims and a red hunting shirt, he was striding up and down, glowering at the tranquil beauty of Lake Tahoe.

Only the Count Stefano Laguno appeared content with existence. He was wearing a loud sports coat and slacks, with a blue silk scarf knotted around his throat. He probably felt he looked Western. He didn't. He looked like something shady in one of the less reputable resorts of the Riviera. He was watching everyone from sardonic black eyes and, at the same time, eating everything the hovering butler provided.

A few minutes later Lover and Mimi appeared from the living-room, hand in hand for a change. Lorraine's half-brother and his fiancée did not add to the festivity. Lover shed the gloom of a professional mourner. And Mimi, in trailing gray, was girl grief itself, as if all the fairies at the bottom of her garden had died during the night.

"Lorraine dear." She gave Lorraine's brow a feathery kiss, while her sly eyes, trying to look soulful, darted around not missing a trick. "I know how all you poor things must be feeling. I didn't sleep a wink. Neither did Lover, did you, Lover?"

Lover shook his head glumly: "Why, sure, Mimi."

Having snuffed out whatever spark of gaiety there might have been, they settled down to breakfast.

"This morning," said Lorraine suddenly, "we'll all go dashing about Lake Tahoe in the speedboats. It's divine, really it is. And then tonight there'll be a moon. We'll all go down the hill and swim in the hot springs. You haven't been in my hot swimming pool. I can never make out why it's hot. I mean, coming straight out of the ground like that. But it's divine." She beamed at Dr. Wyckoff and then at Fleur, as if, insanely, she still had reconciliation on her mind. "So romantic. Everybody says so. I adore it."

It was at this moment that Janet Laguno erupted onto the terrace. Erupted was the only word. I had never seen so volcanic an entrance. In a twisted gray skirt and a screaming magenta sweater which made her face sallow as celery, she plunged out of the French windows, glaring down at us.

"I," she announced, "am a woman of few, short words. I am about to say one short word and say it to my so-called husband."

She whipped round to the Count, her pearl necklace swinging pendulum-wise across her magenta bosom.

"Rat," she said, "Rat, rat, rat!"

Stefano Laguno wiped an imaginary crumb from his mouth with his napkin. He gave his wife a languid smile.

"Good morning, my dear. I gather you didn't sleep well last night."

"Sleep! I'll never sleep again, so long as I'm under the same roof with you."

Janet Laguno started scrabbling through a large, scarlet market-bag sort of pocketbook, spilling compacts and cigarettes on the terrace. She produced a letter and flourished it.

"A letter," she said, "written in the untutored hand of a man laughingly calling himself the Count Laguno."

Stefano stared, his face suddenly flat and sharp as a trapped fox' mask. He sprang from his chair, making a lunge for the letter. Janet pulled it away, and he sank back, looking foolish.

"As a child," said Janet ominously, "I was praised for my recitations. I trust I haven't lost the knack. Listen, while I read this masterpiece verbatim, correcting the spelling as I go. It is addressed to the happily deceased Mrs. Dorothy Flanders."

In a voice dripping with mock sentiment, she began:

Dorothea, mia carissima,

Who have I been dreaming of all day? Need I say? You. I spent such a terrible evening pushing The Monster around the dance floor in some expensive, vulgar night club. Only the vision of your wonderful, wonderful face kept me sane. Darling, I thought I was a cynic, world weary, woman weary. Always after a week or so, I have tossed a woman aside like a squeezed lemon. But I have met you—and what is cynicism? A word—something that means nothing. Beloved, I am in a dream, a dream of heaven. I planned a little present for you, but The Monster guards her jewels like a dragon. There are eyes in the back of her neck. You must not be impatient, my dove. I am poor now. But The Monster has left me everything, as you know. I mourn each night that she should be so healthy. Would that could be changed. Ah, mio tesoro, with The Monster out of the way, we could make our sweet music sing to eternity, you and I.

My precious, I kiss the pillows and think of you. Addio, Dorothea of my dreams.
Your loving
Pumpkin.

By the time that extraordinary reading was over, the Count was flushing to the thinning roots of his hair. I think it was the word "pumpkin," delivered with all of Janet's concentrated venom, which crumpled the last defense line of his poise. The others just sat around the tables, openmouthed, staggered out of speech.

That letter, with its preposterous literary style, had staggered me, too. Although Iris and I had decided that some sort of relationship might have existed between the Count and the man-eating Dorothy, I had never imagined anything as sordid as this.

In the blade-sharp silence, Janet folded the letter back into its envelope. Crossing her arms over the magenta sweater, she watched her husband.

"The Monster!" she snapped. "Thank you, Stefano. I'm probably one of the few wives in history to appear in her husband's love letters as—The Monster."

The embarrassed color was fading from the Count's cheeks. Most of his insolent composure was back. "I'm sorry, my dear, if you find the title unattractive. You weren't intended to read that letter, you know."

"So I imagine. And for your information, Pumpkin, The Monster doesn't have eyes in the back of her neck unless they're myopic. I knew Dorothy was as rotten as an overripe cantaloupe. And, heaven knows, I have no illusions about you. But I never dreamed you'd been getting your rottennesses together."

As usual when confronted with unpleasantness, Lorraine was trying to pretend it didn't exist. She was fluttering around Janet.

"Angel, there must be some mistake. I mean, people just don't write letters like that. Pumpkin! It's a forgery. Your husband's name isn't pumpkin. Where did you find it anyway?"

"It was pushed under my door when I woke up this morning. Some kind friend must have thought it would make good pre-breakfast reading. But it's certainly in my husband's fine Italian hand. So who cares where it came from?"

I cared. Dorothy was the type who would have kept compromising letters, just the way she had snitched Lorraine's five-dollar chips, against a rainy day. Almost certainly the person who ransacked her room the night before had found that awkward document and, either from malice or for some other purpose, had slipped it under Janet's door.

Janet was staring at the Count again. "When I left for Reno, I was prepared to divorce you, Stefano, lick my wounds and call it a day. Things are very different now. That letter hints that you were playing with the idea of murdering me and living on the proceeds with your burly blonde. 'I mourn each night that she should be so healthy,' indeed! Of course, I know it was just a phrase, you'd never have had the courage to go through with anything. But, not having been married to you, the police won't know that. And I'm going to call them immediately. A little rugged prison life would do you the world of good."

The Count smiled back at her almost blandly. "I doubt whether you or anyone in this house will call the police, my dear."

I perked up. Janet said, "And why not?"

"Really, Janet, don't be stupid. That's one thing you seldom are." The Count found a cigarette and lit it with exasperating elegance. "I had been hoping not to bring up an unpleasant subject. But your attitude leaves me no alternative. If you call the police, I shall have no compunction in letting them know that Dorothy Flanders was murdered last night. Then all the good work put in by Wyckoff and the rest of you will go for nothing."

That was by far the most electrifying remark of that very electrified breakfast. I darted a look at Iris. Here was our murder theory coming back on us like a boomerang. Wyckoff sprang to his feet, his face gaunt as a ghost's. Mimi, all angel child, cowered into the protective plumpness of Lover's arm. A spurt of chatter flared and faded. Chuck Dawson swung from the terrace and barked:

"Dorothy murdered? Are you out of your head?"

"Now, now, don't get alarmed." The Count flicked ash into the saucer of his coffee cup. "So long as Janet doesn't dabble in criminology, there's nothing to be afraid of. That most indiscreet letter was written by me. I admit it. I haven't any idea how it came into my wife's possession, but that's neither here nor there. What is both here and there is that Janet omitted to mention the date. It was written over a month ago. I'm afraid my ardor for Mrs. Flanders was not of a very long duration. In fact, at the end I was distressingly bored with her. So you see, in my quiet little way, I was as glad to be rid of her as the rest of you."

So the Count's squeezed-lemon policy had caught up with Dorothy. I made a mental note of that although there were so many more things to be noted. Fleur Wyckoff was staring at her husband. She looked so pale that I thought she was going to faint. Wyckoff himself didn't look any too steady.

"I would like to know, Count," he said quietly, "if you are accusing me of deliberately falsifying the death certificate. I have given it as my diagnosis that Mrs. Flanders died from a heart attack."

Stefano Laguno showed his slightly yellowed teeth. "It didn't look like a heart attack to me, Doctor Wyckoff. Of course, I'm not a highly paid specialist like you. But in my misspent youth I lived for a while up the Amazon, on a very soggy and unappetizing jungle rubber plantation. I have seen a man die from curare poisoning. I had no chance to examine Mrs. Flanders last night. I scarcely saw her at all. But I would be interested in your opinion of death by curare."

I was clinging to the arms of my chair. Lorraine gave a gasp. "Curare!"

Wyckoff didn't say anything.

The Count went on, "Of course, I have no idea who killed her or why or how. I haven't the slightest idea why you, Wyckoff, should have decided to hush it up, or why several other people have been so eager to help you. I'm not even interested enough to find out. I have made my point clear, I believe. If my wife behaves herself, I shall take no action whatsoever. If my wife, through most unladylike spite, tries to make trouble for me—" he shrugged "—I shall make trouble for you."

Though he lacked all other virtues, Count Stefano Laguno was at least frank. And his frankness seemed to have been too much for everyone except his wife.

Janet had been listening with astounded fury.

Suddenly she said, "Don't be fooled by him, anyone. It's all a preposterous sham. He knows I could have him jailed for attempted robbery and, probably, for conspiracy to murder too. He's just faking all this to scare me. He hasn't a jot of evidence."

"Of course I have no evidence, Janet, my dear." The Count turned in his chair to give her the benefit of his most Continental smile. "But there's one simple way to prove me right, isn't there? All I have to do is to express my suspicions to the police. An autopsy would do the rest."

He was looking once more at Wyckoff, who was gazing back at him with a steadiness which showed either confidence or immense control.

"And are you going to demand an autopsy, Count?"

"Nonsense." It was Janet who broke in. "Don't let him trick you, David."

"There's something else." The Count Laguno was playing with the fringe of the tablecloth. "Once they find out that Dorothy was murdered, they will start looking for motives. When they see that letter, Janet, my dear, you will have the best motive of all. Spurned wife kills rival in fit of jealous rage."

Janet's face was stained scarlet, a shade that clashed with the magenta sweater. "Spurned wife—" she spluttered.

"Think about it, my dear." The Count put down his napkin and rose. "I have a feeling you're going to be sensible."

He gave Lorraine a formal bow and strolled away from the terrace.

Seven

AFTER her husband's departure, Janet stood speechless for a moment. Then she glared at Lorraine. "Well, my dear, it boils down to this. Either you throw Stefano out of your house or I pack up and go back to Reno. Reconciliation, indeed! Someone should take your divine ideas, tie them in pink ribbons, and give them away to the poor."

With that, she flounced away down the terrace in the opposite direction from Laguno.

Lorraine was staring at the French window through which the Count had disappeared. "What a simply horrible man!" She turned to Wyckoff, her pug face crinkled with earnestness. "David, darling, of course Janet was right. I mean all that absurd talk about murder—he just made that up to try to keep her from calling the police, didn't he?"

David Wyckoff's shoulders were hunched. He looked much older now than his forty years. In the face of the evidence, I still had to believe Flanders' story that Wyckoff had been treating his wife. But a new thought had come. Perhaps Dorothy had had a weak heart and, even so, had been poisoned with curare.

No one moved as we waited for Wyckoff to reply.

Without looking up, he said, "You heard him, Lorraine. And last night you heard me. It's my word against his."

Lorraine, easily reassured, was all smiles. "Then there's nothing to worry about. I knew there wasn't. And that frightful man—I suppose Janet's right. But then he is a guest. I mean, you can't just invite people to your house and then throw them out. I'll have to talk to Janet. Oh, if only Mr. Throckmorton would hurry up and come. And—but let's forget it all for a while, children." There she was whooping us up again. "I've had picnic lunches and things prepared. We can all go off in the speedboats over to the California side of the Lake. That's what we'll do. Have a lovely long day in the sun."

And we did—that is, Chuck, Lorraine, the Wyckoffs, Iris, and I. Mimi and Lover didn't come. They had planned, said Mimi, to spend the morning with Edna St. Vincent Millay. Poetry was a great healer. The sun and the superb beauty of Lake Tahoe should have been great healers too. We dashed about the Lake, ate a sumptuous Pleygel lunch at Emerald Bay, swam, and lay on the soft silver sand. Iris was with me. I had everything a war-weary husband could have desired. And yet I could not relax.

Although Janet had pooh-poohed it, the Count's incredible letter had carried an implied threat on her life. That threat had linked itself in my mind with a remark Laguno had made to Dorothy the night before when Iris and I had interrupted their tête-à-tête in the trophy room. *Curare has a certain nobility. It should be used with artistry to kill only the most legitimate murderees.*

Iris and I had interpreted that as a malicious thrust at Dorothy. What if we had got it wrong, and some sort of conspiracy had existed between the Count and Dorothy to do away with Janet and make their "sweet music sing to eternity" on the proceeds of "The Monster's" estate?

What if there had been some plan of that sort which had gone wrong? Or if somebody else had got in ahead of them and murdered Dorothy before she and Laguno. . . .

As our little speedboats flashed us home across the green velvet lake, I felt a mounting anxiety over what had already happened and what might yet come.

When we reached the dock, Mimi Burnett, all Wendied up in gingham, was waiting for us without her plump Peter Pan. She hurried to Chuck Dawson with some talk about a long distance call which had come in for him. As she looped her girlish arm through his muscular one and drew him away, I watched her, wondering. Lorraine was watching too.

Suddenly she snapped, "She's got my poor wretched brother roped. Does she think she can corral my fiancé too?"

I had never before heard Lorraine make a spiteful remark. Her face was flushed with indignation. I reflected that Lover was penniless while Chuck Dawson seemed to have all the money in the world. Was Mimi deciding to change lovers in midstream? Was that the lesson she had learned from her day with Edna St. Vincent Millay?

Back in the privacy of our own room, Iris and I, unshackled at last, started gabbing each other's ears off about the episode at the breakfast table. I wasn't surprised to discover that my wife had reached much the same conclusions as I. She had, in fact, gone me one better.

"I've been thinking, Peter. What if Laguno and Dorothy had planned to have Dorothy stick Janet with the curare and then by mistake Dorothy got stuck herself? Of course, nothing fits with anything. Wyckoff's a heart specialist. He'd have known right away if Dorothy had been poisoned. If she was, he's got to be tied into it somehow. And what about Chuck? And is Bill Flanders telling the truth? And then, the Count—he's a right royal rat all right. But, even with Dorothy to egg him on, do you think he has the spunk actually to try to murder Janet?"

"I don't—" I began, and stopped as a knock came on the door.

Iris said, "Come in," and Janet Laguno herself stalked into the room. She was still wearing the tousled gray skirt and the magenta sweater. A cigarette drooped from her broad mouth. I was getting to like her for her defiantly unalluring appearance; just as I had liked the savage candor of her behavior at breakfast. Janet Laguno had a certain stature. She was afraid of no man.

She was holding a piece of paper. "Well, children, I'm still here. Lorraine went Emily Post about evicting Stefano, and I called every hotel in Reno for a room and there wasn't one. So I stay on till tomorrow."

She perched herself on the arm of one of the zebra chairs and patted her knee with the paper.

"Surprise, surprise, my dears. This document is, of all things, a will. A new will. I want the two of you to witness it." She grimaced. "Of course, you'll think I'm a silly neurotic female. I probably am. No one in their right mind would ever have married Stefano anyway. I haven't made this will for any melodramatic reason. I know Stefano hasn't the guts to try to do anything to me. But Destiny has an evil sense of humor. It's just conceivable that I might fall and break my neck in the bathtub or trip over a croquet hoop. If my beloved Pumpkin ever got a cent of my money, I'd spend the rest of eternity in an apoplectic fit."

Iris and I exchanged a rattled glance. Although Janet was making light of it, this fitted too well with our anxieties. The Countess Laguno unfolded the paper and handed it me, spilling a long caterpillar of ash from her cigarette.

"You'd better read it," she said. "I don't believe in having people sign things they don't read."

Iris read the will at my elbow. It was short and simple. It invalidated all former wills; it emphatically cut out Stefano; it left her entire estate to—Bill Flanders.

We both looked up astonished. Iris said, "Bill Flanders? But—but I didn't know he was an intimate friend or——"

"He isn't. Not particularly." Janet crushed her cigarette into some strange glass thing which either was or wasn't an ash tray. "But I don't have any family of my own, except for one nauseating aunt in Seattle. I was talking to Bill this afternoon. He's a nice guy; he lost his leg fighting for us; and he's been left penniless thanks to Dorothy. I'm sorry for him. And I can think of nothing that would make Stefano more furious than to have Dorothy's widower supplant him. So——" She threw out her hands. "Sign will you, babies? Here's my pen. People never have pens in moments of crisis."

Iris and I both affixed rather shaky signatures to the bottom of the document. Janet rose and gave the will back to me.

"I suppose I should have made two copies. But I didn't. So you keep it, just to be safe." She crossed to the door and paused, grinning sourly over her shoulder. "And don't look so ominous, my dears. Nothing's going to happen to me. The Monster never felt healthier in its life."

As the door closed behind her, Iris muttered, "I only hope she's right." We locked the will away in the drawer that served as a safe for Iris' piggy bank. In a definitely jittery mood we got ready for dinner and went downstairs.

Sunset and cocktails had started on the terrace. Janet and Bill Flanders, together on a love seat, were gazing out at a crimson sky, split by the giant peaks of the Sierras. Lorraine, Mimi, and Chuck Dawson, ignoring the beauties of nature, were drinking Martinis under a yellow umbrella.

As Iris and I joined them, Chuck, very handsome and cowboy in corduroy pants and a leather jacket, was kidding Lorraine about her citified clothes and saying her silver-scale swimming suit made her look like a haddock. At this, Mimi gave a tinkling laugh and threw a whimsical smile up at him. Lorraine snapped, "All right, Chuck, if you don't like it, I'll throw it away." Mimi's hand slipped down Chuck's arm and settled on his fingers. Lorraine, her face blazing, whipped round on her and said, "For God's sake, stop pawing Chuck."

Chuck looked uncomfortable. Mimi's deep-set eyes glinted. I was startled at the violence of the tension between the two women.

But Lover appeared then, archly jovial, with Fleur Wyckoff on his arm. Mimi ran to him, crying, "Naughty Lover to leave me and look at the sunset with someone else. Lorraine's been saying the most awful things."

Clinging to Lover's sleeve, she found refuge in engaged bliss.

Wyckoff came next. After him, contemptuously indifferent to hostile stares, the Count Laguno strolled out of the French windows and poured himself a Martini. Forgetting her worries, Lorraine started being the high-power hostess again. By the time we moved inside for dinner, she was as chattery and gay as ever.

Dinner was monopolized by the hot swimming pool and how divine it was going to be to swim there by moonlight. For some reason her guests were more rebellious than usual. Chuck grumbled and most ill-advisedly suggested a trip to Reno instead. Janet announced she had no suit. Even little Fleur raised her mousy voice. But Lorraine, in magnificent form, carried all before her.

An hour or so later the whole peevish bunch of us went upstairs for our swimming things, then congregated on the drive. There were two cars. Lorraine went first in the old station wagon, with Iris and me, Bill Flanders, Janet Laguno, and Fleur. The moon had not yet risen. We plunged down the hill in murky gloom. Crickets were scraping; tree frogs were cheeping. There was a heady tang to the country darkness. Lorraine brought the car to a halt before the glimmering silhouette of a poplar grove.

"Here we are."

We scrambled out and passed through a white gate. Lorraine found a light switch and the darkness leaped into illumination.

The towering poplars had been planted in a rectangle with flowering shrubs at their feet. In the center of the glade stretched an immense swimming pool with a broad stone border. Dressing-rooms, built like individual cottages, made little villages on the two long sides. Ropes of multicolored lights twinkled above the gleaming water.

"It's rather nice, isn't it?" said Lorraine. "I don't know why I don't use it more. Peter, Bill, men go over the other side to change."

The dressing-rooms were as luxurious as everything else that belonged to Lorraine. Each had its little sitting-room with waterproof upholstery on the chairs, a closet that could be locked, and a shower-room. Bill and I were the first to be ready. In his swimming trunks, Bill Flanders' chunky, boxer's physique made the useless stump of his leg even more pitiful. He hobbled with the crutch to a flight of steps in the center of the pool and rolled into the water. I dived in after him.

It was a voluptuous sensation, diving into water as warm as a warm bath. I lazed over onto my back, sniffing the faint medicinal odor of sulphur, letting the heat seep into me. The rainbow lights glittered like crazy stars. Beyond them, above the vaulting mountain peaks, I could see an opalescence in the sky which heralded the rising moon.

Bill was splashing around, happy as a polar bear. Janet appeared from the women's side. Her swimming suit deficiency had been remedied by Lorraine's discarded fish-scale number. She dived in and came toward us, looking like some frightening, phosphorescent monster of the deep.

Iris came with Fleur and Lorraine, all in sober black. They dived in and soon we were sporting around in the velvety warmth. Some minor catastrophe happened to Fleur's brassière top and, with much giggling, Lorraine and Janet whisked her away into a dressing-room to fix it. Iris, Bill, and myself were alone in the pool when the second carload arrived. Mimi, the only girl, tripped like a slightly aging sylph over to the women's section, and the male dressing-rooms rang with stamping feet, snatches of dialogue, and even an unidentifiable and off-key rendition of "Home on the Range."

The party was brightening up.

Iris and I were lolling in the shallowest and warmest part of the pool when every light in the grove went out. Iris gripped my wrist. Grunts of disapproval sounded from the pitch blackness around us. Someone called out. Then Lorraine's voice came, gay and high. "Darlings, the lights are fused. Isn't that divine? It's much more fun in the dark. Don't try and fix it, anyone. The moon will be up in a second anyway."

I heard a splash, saw a glimmer of white, heard other splashes. Everyone, apparently, agreed with Lorraine that it was divine to be in the dark. As a matter of fact, it was quite a sensation, swimming through that caressing warmth in anonymous blackness.

People were calling to other people. There were little half frightened, half excited screams from the women. I completely lost track of Iris and was swimming blind. Every now and then I bumped against another hot, wet body. Once I heard Chuck Dawson's voice. "Lorraine, baby. Is that you?" And Lorraine's, "Yes, darling. Isn't this fun?" I swam on. I collided with someone else. Tense hands were gripping my arms, and Mimi's voice whispered, "Chuck, I've been looking for you all over. I'm scared. I'm——" "It isn't Chuck," I said before she gave herself away any more. Quickly I swam on to save her the embarrassment she ought to be feeling.

After a while, the warmth of the water and the unrelieved blackness became stifling. The radiance in the sky was the only visible thing. Floating on my back, I watched it grow stronger and stronger. Then, with a jerk like a jack-in-the-box, the full moon soared up into the sky. You could see the poplars again, and the white dressing-rooms gleaming. A path of silver spread across the water. I could even see individual heads bobbing here and there in the pool.

In those few seconds the Stygian darkness had been changed into a fairyland.

I saw Iris and swam to join her. Chuck and Lorraine came crawling to us. Lorraine seemed annoyed about something.

"Too hot," she said. "Let's get out of here before we're boiled."

We were near the steps. She climbed out. Chuck followed. Iris and I went too. I wanted a cigarette.

"There's a bar down here," said Lorraine. She called over the water, "Come on, angels, we're all going to have a drink."

The guests started splashing out of the water. Lover came

first, helping Bill Flanders up the steps to his crutch. Then Mimi came, her arm around Fleur's waist. Wyckoff pulled himself up at the far end and came padding toward us, while the Count Laguno, self-consciously ignoring the fact that he was being ignored, slicked back his black hair and clambered up at our feet.

Lorraine glanced around. "Are we all here?"

"Janet," said Fleur. "Where's Janet?"

"Janet!" Lorraine called the name indifferently. "Come on out, Janet."

There was no reply. My pulse quickening, I gazed out over the moonlit expanse of water. Nothing broke its calm surface.

"Janet!" Mimi called it then. "Janet, where are you?"

"Maybe she got out before the moon came up. Maybe she's in the dressing-rooms." Iris grabbed Lorraine's arm. "Come on. Let's find out."

They ran around the pool, disappearing into the cottages on the far side. The rest of us stood in growing uneasiness while the two women's voices trailed eerily through the moonlight.

"Janet . . . Janet. . . ."

Suddenly Chuck dived into the pool. That was the signal. One by one we tumbled after him. No one said anything. That was what made it so ominous. Mimi swam past me. Laguno, his eyes very bright, paddled by. Even Bill Flanders was in again, thrashing the water with his powerful arms.

The moonlight seemed unbearably bright now. Someone muttered close to me. There was a splashing. I could still hear Lorraine and Iris calling.

Then, at the far end of the pool, a woman screamed. It was Fleur Wyckoff. I recognized her voice.

"Janet—she's here. I can see her—she's under the water—she's drowned——"

Part Three

FLEUR

Eight

Fleur Wyckoff stopped screaming. There was a fragment of silence, then babel broke out. Everyone in the pool started splashing and thrashing toward Fleur. I had the farthest to go. The dark heads in front were converging into a circle. They looked grotesque in the moonlight—bodyless heads floating on the black, traylike surface of the water.

I reached them. The water was deep at this end, at least ten feet. Everyone was milling, twittering, not doing anything. In the center of the circle, Fleur was whimpering softly. I swam to join her. Chuck Dawson, big and easy in the water as a seal, rolled at my side.

I said, "What is it, Fleur? Where did you see it?"

Her little hand clutched my arm. "Look. Look down. You can see her suit—see it gleaming."

I peered down. She was right. Something was there under the water, silver, quivering like a reflection of the moon.

Chuck said, "You and me, Lieutenant. Dive."

He arched forward in the water, his athlete's legs flailing up and then sliding down out of sight. I went after him.

It was weird sinking through the warm water toward that glimmering something which seemed to have no shape, no meaning, but which I knew must be Janet Laguno. I kept my eyes open. The sulphur in the water made them smart. My arms were stretched ahead of me. My hand made contact with a thing that was smooth, solid—an arm.

I grabbed with both hands until I had some sort of grip on a shoulder. Chuck was at the other side. Kicking with our legs, we started to lift that reluctant shape to the surface. The hot water felt cloying as glue. But at last I was free of it, able to breathe again.

I shook the wet hair out of my sore eyes. Chuck's face was only a little way from mine. I found myself staring straight at him. Then my gaze shifted to what lay between us.

Under the water, it hadn't been so bad. There had been something to do. But now, as I looked at that floating thing, the horror of what had happened beat in on me. Janet Laguno's face was grayish green in the moonlight. Her open mouth was a shadowy, foolish hole. Her hair, which had always been so unmanageable, trailed along the surface of the water in writhing tentacles.

Chuck, gasping air into his lungs, mumbled, "The steps. Behind you. Get her to the steps."

The others were scattering like clumsy, frightened ducks. Chuck and I towed Janet to the steps, tugged her up them, and laid her down on the chill stone border.

Lorraine and Iris were running toward us from the dressing-rooms. Iris called, "Peter, what is it?" Then Lorraine saw and screamed. Everyone was swarming around, bodies hot and wet from the pool.

I shouted, "Keep back."

One of the men, in black swimming trunks, pushed to my side. It was David Wyckoff. "Let me look at her, Lieutenant." He called, "Lorraine, get some blankets, anything, from the dressing-rooms. Something to keep her warm."

There was a scurrying. Wyckoff dropped to his knees and eased Janet over onto her front. Lorraine, Iris, and Lover came dashing back, carrying slipcovers, cushions, a random assortment of warm things. Wyckoff slid some under Janet, spread some over her, and started artificial respiration.

Chuck and I hovered. Chuck said, "Lorraine, get everyone away. They can't do any good. Get them dressed. Take them all to the bar and give them a drink. But get away from here."

There was an obedient patter of wet feet on cement. In a few moments only the three of us were left on the moonlit edge of the pool. Chuck turned to me. "You needn't stick around, Lieutenant. I'll relieve Wyckoff when he gets tired."

"Thanks," I said. "But I'll stay."

Yesterday, when Dorothy had died, Wyckoff and Chuck had taken over. I didn't trust them any more.

Chuck stared at me, shrugged, and swung back to Wyckoff, who was working in grim silence. After fifteen minutes or so Chuck slipped into his place. I relieved Chuck, and then Wyckoff relieved me. We kept it up for over an hour. Iris came out with robes for us, which was just as well, for after the warmth of the pool we were blue with cold.

At last Wyckoff stood up. "It's no use," he said. "We'll never get her back. She's dead."

I'd never really expected anything else.

"Let's get her into one of the dressing-rooms where we can take a look at her."

The three of us carried her into the nearest dressing-room and laid her down on a studio couch. After the moon, the electric light was dazzling. It glared down on the bluish gray skin, the staring eyes, the pitiful, tangled hair.

The words Janet Laguno had spoken to me early that evening came back.

Don't worry. Nothing's going to happen to me. The Monster never felt healthier in its life.

Don't worry!

Wyckoff, deep lines around his mouth, was examining the bare arms and legs. He didn't say anything. But it was obvious that he was looking for scratches, for any signs of a struggle.

There were none that I could see.

He stepped back from the couch, stripped off his bathrobe and laid it over the body.

"I need a drink," he said grimly. "Let's get to that bar."

We got dressed and joined up again. Chuck led us along the moon-splashed edge of the pool toward a lighted bungalow. Chuck and Wyckoff walked very close together as if there were some unadmitted alliance between them. The smooth city heart-specialist and the rough Nevada man of mystery made an incongruous team. I would have liked to know what was in their minds.

We stepped into a luxurious modernistic bar which only the Pleygel madness and millions would have tossed down beside a swimming pool. The rest of the party was all assembled. A bright fire was burning in the fireplace. Lorraine, Iris, Fleur, and Mimi Burnett were crammed together, as if there was comfort in nearness, on a long chartreuse couch. Bill Flanders sat hunched in a gray arm chair, his crutch propped against the back. Lover, like a gloomy barman, was perched on a stool behind the glass, half-moon bar, while Count Stefano Laguno, apparently unconscious of the others' hostility, was pacing up and down, his sleek reflection throwing itself back from the black mirrors on the walls.

They all had drinks.

Nobody spoke as the three of us went to the bar and mixed ourselves highballs. Then Iris caught my eye. In the thin voice of someone who hasn't spoken for a long time, she asked, "Peter, she's—she's dead?"

"I'm afraid so," I said.

The Count Laguno came to Wyckoff, smiling a toothy smile which was half uneasy, half insolent.

"Well, doctor," he said, "what's the verdict this time? Did she just drown, or was she murdered?"

His cynical frankness cracked the silence like a whiplash. Fleur Wyckoff, twisting her little hands together fiercely, was staring straight at her husband. So was everyone else. Wyckoff carefully avoided his estranged wife's eyes.

He said very quietly, "Lieutenant Duluth and Chuck examined your wife's body with me, Count. I think they'll both agree that there were no visible signs of a struggle."

Stefano's smile was a lot easier then. "What a relief for all of us," he drawled. "Particularly for me. Thanks to Janet's lack of reticence in reading that letter out loud at breakfast, I might have been in a most uncomfortable position." He paused. "However, I had the foresight to slip into her dressing-room just now and extract this from her pocketbook."

From the breast pocket of his loud sports coat he produced the letter he had written to Dorothy with its implied threat on his wife's life.

"Since none of you saw it except my wife, no one can testify to its contents." While we all watched in thunderstruck silence, he strolled to the fire and pushed the letter deep into the flames. "There. Just to be tidy." He turned back, still smiling. "Now, even if there should be any unpleasantness, there's nothing conspicuously suspicious about me except that I am the sole beneficiary under poor Janet's will. A natural enough state of affairs for a married man."

If people came scummier than the Count, I had yet to meet them. I could see from their faces how the others were feeling about Stefano Laguno. I turned to him, giving him back his own bland smile.

"I hope for your sake you didn't murder your wife, Count," I said. "If you did, I'm afraid you wasted your time. You see, this evening Janet made a new will. My wife and I witnessed it. It cuts you off without a nickel."

All the swagger went out of him. His face turned the muddy white of vichysoisse.

"Janet—" he spluttered.

"Yes," I said. "She made a new will. My wife and I have it safely in our possession. It'll be quite legal, I'm sure. She left everything to Bill Flanders."

Dorothy's widower turned in his chair. Every eye shifted to him. His face was blank.

"To me? But that's crazy. I hardly knew her. I——"

"I know," I said. "She just figured that Dorothy and Stefano between them with their shabby little affair had given you as raw a deal as they'd given her. She felt that by leaving you all her money she could put her husband very neatly in his place. And I think she has." I turned back to the crumpled Count. "Of course, she had no idea that she was going to die so soon."

Conversation was fizzling now like a damp fuse. Mimi Burnett had completely forgotten her "Nature-I-Love-And-Next-To-Nature-Art" pose. Her shoe-button eyes were darting from face to face as if she were watching a lightning-quick ping-pong match. Lorraine's voice finally subdued the others.

"But, angels, all this talk, this unpleasantness. Who cares who poor Janet's money goes to? David says that she—she just drowned. There was nothing terrible." Her eyes were popping out under the long lashes, desperately trying to help her muddled words make us understand the way she wanted life to be. "The lights fused. That might happen any time. Everything was dark in the pool. Something happened to poor Janet, a cramp or something. The water's too hot, much too hot. I've often felt faint myself. Maybe she fainted. Maybe she tried to call for help. But we wouldn't have noticed because we were all shouting and laughing. It's frightful, of course. Dorothy, and now poor Janet. And the Count's a horrible man and I'll probably throw him out of my house and I'm glad he doesn't get Janet's money. It was so lucky she made that will. I think everyone should make a will. I'm going to have Mr. Throckmorton make one for me when he comes. But that isn't the point. I mean, the point is that poor Janet's dead, that there's been an accident."

I said, "It'll be up to the police to decide that, Lorraine."

Wyckoff and Chuck Dawson moved a little closer together. Everyone swung round to stare at me, almost as if I were an enemy.

"The police!" Lorraine gulped. "But, Peter, dearest, David says—I mean, don't you trust David?"

"It isn't a question of trusting or not trusting anyone," I said. "All accidents that result in death have to be reported to the police. There'll have to be an inquest. Chuck will tell you that."

Lorraine's fiancé was watching me with a strange wariness. His tongue came out between his teeth. "Sure. Of course." He glanced at Lover behind the bar. "You've got the telephone, Lover, over there. Call the police. Call Genoa City. It's nearer, and I guess we're under their jurisdiction here anyhow."

Lover tried to look hearty, and muttered his inevitable, "Why, sure." He called the police, gave a jumbled version of what had happened, and put down the receiver.

"They're coming as fast as possible," he said and poured himself a straight Scotch.

It was a dreary, protracted wait. Practically no one talked. Every now and then somebody went over to the bar and mixed another drink. I tried to think how we would have been acting if we had been ten ordinary people whose friend had just been drowned in a swimming pool. Surely not like this.

But then we were so far from being ten ordinary people.

We were ten people bound together with a dozen intricate chains of suspicion and fear; ten people left out of twelve.

Of course, Janet could have drowned accidentally. In this case even more than in the case of Dorothy, there was nothing to arouse legitimate suspicion except the tawdry character of Janet's husband and the strained coincidence of two "natural" deaths in two days. But I was sure that Janet had been murdered; just as I was sure that Dorothy had been murdered. I was sure that the lights had been fused deliberately so that in the ensuing darkness someone could hold Janet's head under the water until she was dead. Who had done it, and why, I did not know, any more than I knew who had killed Dorothy, or even how she had been killed. But I liked Janet and I dislike murderers on principle. I was determined to bend this one's ears back even if it took every moment of my precious leave.

I had enough wit, however, to realize that, at this early stage, I had no shred of evidence to offer. If I raised a stink when the police came, I would only make a fool of myself. The police would investigate. If they were satisfied with the accident theory and an inquest backed it up, it would be my job and Iris' to plod on as best we might until we were in a position to explain to the authorities why eight reasonably respectable people were all, for a cryptic variety of reasons, banded together to obstruct justice.

Because that's just about the way things stood, so far as I could see.

At last the police came, three of them, led by a small man with alert eyes whom Chuck introduced as Sergeant Davis. Chuck and Wyckoff took them off to see the body. They were gone quite a long time. When they came back, it was obvious that the Sergeant, after an examination, had found nothing to warrant suspicion. He knew about Dorothy's death the night before and mentioned it, but only as an unfortunate coincidence. After a thorough but routine questioning, during which he copied our answers into a notebook, he announced that he would turn in his report to his superior, who would probably arrange the inquest for the following morning. He said that only Laguno, as husband of the deceased, Chuck, and Wyckoff would have to attend. He understood that Miss Pleygel and Iris Duluth would prefer to have the proceedings carried out with the minimum of publicity and promised to do his best to see that everyone was inconvenienced as little as possible in his period of grief.

"Frankly," he said in conclusion, "when I heard about the other lady dying last night, I kind of wondered. And if Mrs. Laguno had been a strong swimmer, we'd have to go into this a little deeper. But, what with the confusion, the darkness, it would have been easy enough for her to lose her bearings and once she was in the deep end——" He paused, turning to Wyckoff who stood silent and stooped at his side. "The doc here tells me he was her physician in Frisco and that he and his wife were friendly with her. As he remembers, she couldn't scarcely swim at all." He glanced at Laguno. "I guess that's correct, isn't it?"

Laguno said quickly, "Yes, yes. My wife was a poor swimmer."

The Sergeant's alert eyes shifted to Fleur. "You confirm that, Mrs. Wyckoff?"

Fleur had been staring straight at her husband. She seemed unconscious of everything around her. But she said, "Yes, my husband was Janet's physician. And I've known her all my life."

"And she couldn't swim?"

Fleur's lips were very pale. She hesitated and then said, "No, I don't think Janet swam very well."

The Sergeant left then, taking Wyckoff and Chuck with him. It had all passed off as uneventfully as I had expected.

"Well, that's over." Lorraine got up and went to pour

herself a drink. "You see what I mean? I'm sure that man was very sensible and understands about inquests and things. He said it was all all right." She turned to Fleur, her face as guileless as a child's. "But, Fleur, angel, there is just one thing that strikes me as queer. Do people forget how to swim? Don't you remember, pet? When she was a girl, Janet was always winning prizes and cups and things. She was the champion swimmer of the school."

For a moment Fleur stood very straight, staring in front of her.

Then, like a puppet with its strings snapped, she crumpled into a limp heap on the floor.

Nine

MIMI, FLUTTERING AROUND like a wood sprite with a Red Cross diploma, brought Fleur out of her faint. When she came to, Mrs. Wyckoff made feeble remarks about the heat in the room. Overheated rooms often made her faint, she said. It was most unconvincing.

Lorraine started gathering everyone together to drive them up to the house. Iris and I said we would walk. When the others zoomed ahead in the car, we started on foot through the shadowy poplars along the moonlit drive.

My wife slipped her hand in mine. "Well, that's torn it, Peter."

"It certainly has," I said.

"I was dying to scream out to that policeman to use his wits, but it would have been hopeless. Janet was murdered, of course she was. And the bad part is that they're all siding with the murderer. Even Lorraine. I don't think she realizes it, but she's so determined to keep life divinely gay that it comes to the same thing. Peter, it doesn't make sense. She was killed so simply, so cleverly, but so pointlessly. I can't see who could have wanted to kill her or why."

"There's Laguno. He didn't know Janet had changed her will. You could tell that from his face when I broke the sad news."

"I know. This afternoon we had the theory that Laguno and Dorothy had been planning to kill Janet and then Dorothy got killed by mistake. But I've been thinking. This morning Dorothy's death was neatly accounted for as a heart attack. Laguno was the only one of the bunch who brought up the question of murder. He'd have been crazy to do that if he'd murdered her himself—completely crazy if he'd also been planning to murder Janet tonight."

"There's Bill Flanders," I said. "He had every reason for wanting to kill Dorothy, and he benefits under Janet's will. Maybe Janet told him she'd changed her will and——"

"But, darling, Bill Flanders couldn't have murdered Janet. He was the only one in the pool with us when the lights fused. There can't be two murderers crawling all over the place. The person who fused the lights must be the person who killed Janet."

"Unless the lights fused by accident and the whole thing was unpremeditated, just someone taking advantage of the darkness."

Iris squeezed my hand. "You can't bring accidents in, darling. That's cheating."

"Well, there's Wyckoff and Chuck. Between them, they managed to make Dorothy's death look respectable. And they did their best on Janet tonight. Only I can't see how either of them link up with Dorothy, let alone Janet."

"Dorothy and Janet were both Wyckoff's patients in San Francisco. Maybe he's one of those movie mad-ghoul doctors who go around murdering their own patients."

"If he does, it's a lousy way to make a living. In Janet's

death, it's this swimming business that's the crux. That policeman would never have been so casual if he'd known Janet was a champion swimmer. Wyckoff was the one who said Janet couldn't swim. Laguno backed him up. But Laguno would have lied anyway. He's so scared of his own hide. It's Fleur——"

"Exactly. Fleur knew Janet could swim and yet she lied in her pretty little teeth. Then, when Lorraine called her on it, she fainted. I've wondered about her from the start. She goes around so mousy quiet with that look in her eyes as if everything's a trap. She treats her husband as if he didn't exist. But then Janet was supposedly her friend. Why should she lie to help her murderer?"

"Why is everyone lying to help the murderer?"

Iris said bleakly, "Oh, Peter, this is hopeless. We're just talking around in a void."

For a moment we walked up the winding drive in silence. My wife's profile gleamed, pale and lovely, in the moonlight. I felt a sudden longing to take her away, to get out from under and have the sort of leave a husband and wife ought to have.

I said, "Honey, shall we quit? After all, there's your movie career to consider and——"

"Peter, don't be silly!" Iris turned to me almost fiercely. "We liked Janet. We're not going to let someone murder her and live happily ever after." She paused. "Besides, two women have been killed in two days. How do we know what's going to happen next?"

She looked so young and stubborn. I kissed her. "Okay, baby. We stay."

Her fingers slipped back into mine. "If only there was something concrete to work on."

"There's the burglary in Dorothy's room. We know it happened. But that's about all."

"We don't even know whether a poison dart was taken from the trophy room or not. If only we could prove that one was stolen—Peter, I've never seen that cabinet. Let's go now and see what we can see."

When we reached the formal gardens that stretched up to the terrace, the ground floor of Lorraine's crazy house was in almost complete darkness. Lights in upstairs windows indicated that our fellow guests were going to bed. We slipped into the living-room through the French windows and down the corridor which led to the trophy room. It was in darkness, too. I turned on a light. It was unnerving the way all the animal heads on the walls sprang into view. With elks, zebras, bears, and crocodiles leering out of glass eyes at us, we moved to the cabinet that contained Lorraine's Amazonian blowpipes and darts. The monstrous portrait doll, on its throne, sat staring at us with its fixed, imbecile smile. I pointed down at the three fan-shaped designs of darts whose tips were coated with the sticky, reddish brown poison.

"You see," I began, "the first two fans have six darts, while the third——"

I stopped, feeling very silly, because the third fan, which had had only five darts the night before, now had six. There was no getting around it. I tried the lid. Yesterday it had been unlocked. Now it was locked.

Iris, looking down, said doubtfully, "Peter, are you sure?"

"Of course. Someone must have put the sixth dart back today."

I was staring at the fan of six darts. Each dart had its point smeared with the reddish substance.

"It was stolen all right," I said gloomily. "But every darn dart's got its poison still on it. It couldn't have been used." I peered more closely and gave a little grunt. "Wait a minute.

Look at the second dart from the left. The stuff on its tip—it's a slightly different color, isn't it? It's redder and it looks newer."

"Yes, it is. Peter, then we're sure now. We're sure that Dorothy was killed with curare." Iris spun round to me. "If only we knew more about curare, the way it works and—darling, let's try the library. Lorraine must have an encyclopedia or something. Quick."

We hurried into the library. Lorraine had the oddest selection of books. But there was an encyclopedia of sorts. Eagerly we read the paragraph on curare. It was neither full nor very scientific. It told that the poison was derived from the same plant as strychnine, something called *Strychnos ignatii*. It said how deadly a poison it was. There was one sentence, however, which brought me up with a jerk. After curare has been injected under the skin, I read, actual death may not occur for ten to fifteen minutes. But complete muscular paralysis sets in much more quickly. To all intents and purposes, the victim would be a living corpse in three minutes.

"Three minutes!" I exclaimed. "Then someone must have pricked Dorothy either with the dart or with some kind of curare-tipped needle three minutes before she collapsed in my arms on the dance floor. She probably wasn't dead then. She probably died while we were carrying her into the office."

Iris stared at me. "You were dancing for almost three minutes. It must have happened on the dance floor. Who came near you?"

I thought back. "Lorraine and her South American friend came quite close a couple of times. But I'm pretty sure neither of them touched Dorothy. Neither did anyone else. I mean, no one else from our party."

"Then it must have happened just before you went dancing. Who was sitting next to her?"

I grinned weakly. "I was on one side of her. You were on the other. Later, when you went dancing with Laguno, Lover was next to her. But there was a big gap. And I know he didn't even look our way. He was talking to Janet." I shrugged. "We're brilliant. We've solved the case. Either you or I poisoned Dorothy. Wait!" An idea suddenly came. "Of course, I see it now. Just before we started to dance, Dorothy took off her gloves and stuffed them in her pocketbook."

I told her what had happened. "That must be it, baby. No one had to be near her to kill her. It was the smartest trick in the world. Someone fixed her pocketbook so that she'd stick herself when she opened it. My God, where is that pocketbook! I wonder if Bill Flanders has it."

"No. I thought about it this afternoon. I asked him. They never gave it to him."

"Then it was probably left right there on the seat under the table in the confusion. We're going to Reno tomorrow for the funeral. Maybe we'll be able to get it."

Iris' eyes were shining. "At last," she said, "at long, long last we're getting somewhere."

We felt almost elated as we went up to bed. We were still speculating some half an hour later when there was a tap on the door. I called, "Come in." The door half opened to reveal the small figure of Fleur Wyckoff. When she saw we were in bed, she looked confused and started backing out, but Iris said, "No, please come in. Don't mind us. Come sit on my bed and have a cigarette. We're not sleepy."

After a moment's hesitation Fleur stepped in, closed the door, and padded across the carpet. She was dressed in a smoky-blue housecoat, tiny red leather slippers peeping out below its full skirt. With a flimsy smile, she sat down on the extreme edge of Iris' bed.

"I couldn't sleep," she said. "I hate being alone anyway. I felt I had to have company—just for a little while."

Iris and I, both agog to know why she had really come, tried to hide our curiosity. Iris handed her a cigarette.

"I know," she said. "When Peter's away at sea, I get frightfully sorry for myself."

Fleur lit her cigarette with a great deal of puffing. Her childish hands were quite uneasy, too. We waited, saying nothing, not helping her.

"It's terrible about Janet," she said suddenly. "The shock was so bad that when that policeman talked to me, I couldn't remember anything. I found myself saying Janet couldn't swim." She gave a small, inappropriate laugh which was sheer nerves. "Of course I knew Janet could swim. I realized it just a few moments later and—and it was too late. I was so rattled I suppose I fainted."

Was this why she had come? To give us this official and obviously inaccurate reason for her fainting spell?

Iris made sympathetic cooing sounds. Fleur seemed to be gaining confidence.

"That's really what I'm worried about. If I had told that policeman Janet could swim, you don't think it would have made any difference, do you? I mean you don't think anything——"

"I think it would have made a great deal of difference," I said quietly but firmly. "After all, does it seem reasonable to you that a champion swimmer would drown in ten feet of water just because the lights went out?"

Fleur's lashes fluttered. "You mean you do think somebody killed her? You think that frightful Count killed her?"

I let her have it then. "I think she was murdered by the same person who murdered Dorothy Flanders last night."

The cigarette was quite out of control then. "But Dorothy wasn't murdered. That's just some beastly lie the Count made up to try to shield himself. You can't believe that. Dorothy died because of her weak heart."

"You knew she had a weak heart?"

"Of course I did. David—my husband had been treating her for it."

"Your husband had been treating Janet, too, hadn't he?"

"Treating Janet? Why, no. Certainly not. There was nothing wrong with her. Oh, in the past, yes, she's been to him. Janet was our friend. She always went to David if she was sick."

"What sort of a doctor is your husband?" I said that quickly, trying to keep her rattled.

"David? Why, he's a heart specialist." She was defiant then. "One of the best heart specialists in San Francisco. You can look him up in the Medical Directory."

"He examined Dorothy last night. He would have been in a position to know for certain if she had died of a heart attack?"

"Naturally."

"He could have told right away if she had been poisoned?"

"Of course he could."

"With a rare drug like curare, for example?"

"Why, yes, yes."

"He would know all the symptoms and everything of curare poisoning?"

"Of course he would."

"Then he might easily have poisoned her with curare and given out that she had died from a heart attack."

It was as if I had tossed a monkey wrench at her. She doubled forward on the bed, throwing up her arm to cover her face. Then, in a swirl of housecoat, she jumped up, her eyes blazing.

"So you're accusing my husband of murdering Dorothy and Janet and using his position as their physician to protect himself? That's a filthy, beastly——"

I saw I had gone too far. So did Iris. My wife got out of bed and went to her.

"Fleur dear, Peter didn't mean that. But you've got to understand. We believe that Dorothy and Janet were murdered. We honestly believe that. You can't expect us to do nothing about it, can you? We've got to try to find out the truth. We've got to suspect everybody, got to try every possible line."

Fleur tried to drag her arm away from Iris' hand. "What's it to you? What business is it of yours anyway?"

Iris said, "Fleur, would you be willing to let someone kill two women and get away with it?"

Mrs. Wyckoff gave a helpless shrug. "I'm sorry. If you think that, then, of course—I'm sorry." She slipped onto the edge of the bed again. "All those things you've been saying, are you going to tell them to the police?"

"We're not telling anything to the police until we're sure," I said. "If we're wrong, if there haven't been any murders, we don't want to raise a stink just for the fun of it."

Fleur sat quite still. Suddenly she said, "You don't suppose I'd try to protect my husband if I thought he was guilty, do you? After all, I'm divorcing him. He means nothing to me."

Iris said, "Fleur, I don't want to pry, but just in case it helps, why are you divorcing your husband?"

"Oh, just because. He's so busy. Working night and day at the hospital, at his office. I never saw him." She looked up, her lips quivering. "What's the point of being married to a man you never see?"

I was watching her guardedly. "Your husband knew Dorothy, didn't he? I mean knew her socially—not just as a patient."

"No." The word came quick as a pistol shot. "No. He didn't know her at all. Even I hadn't seen her—not since we left school."

I took a shot in the dark. "So I'm wrong. I thought you

were divorcing your husband because he'd been having an affair with Dorothy."

Fleur sprang up again. "That isn't true. That's absolutely not true."

"You're sure?"

"Of course I'm sure." Her flowerlike face was flushed and furious. "And I'll tell you something else. I don't know who killed Dorothy or who killed Janet. I don't even believe they were killed. I think you're both of you just cruel, cynical, sensation seekers trying to make everyone suffer so's you can have a cheap thrill. Well, you're not going to be able to have a thrill at my husband's expense."

She paused, glaring at both of us. "This evening in the pool, David couldn't have killed Janet. All through the time when the lights were out, my husband was—with me."

She swung round toward the door. I sprang out of bed.

"Fleur——"

She reached the door, threw it open, and slipped out into the dark corridor. I hurried after her. I opened my mouth to call her back, then I shut it again because I could hear her footsteps pattering back to her own room.

A shuffle and, above it, like an overtone, a very slight squeak—the squeak of her red leather slippers.

Shuffle, squeak. . . . It was not the first time I had heard that sound.

I went back into the room. Iris was watching me.

"Well, Peter. Just what do you make of that?"

"I don't know," I said. "But I do know something. I just heard Fleur scurrying away down the passage. Her footsteps are the footsteps of the person who passed me last night in the corridor."

I went to my wife. "Fleur's the one who pushed the Count's letter to Dorothy under Janet's door. Fleur's the one who ransacked Dorothy's room."

Ten

LORRAINE WAS EXUBERANT at breakfast, as though nothing had happened. She was being particularly sparkling because she had received a communication that Mr. Throckmorton was on the Clipper and would arrive that night. Mr. Throckmorton would make everything all right, my dears, I mean everything. She herself would go to the airport to pick him up and dinner might be a little late but we'd simply adore Mr. Throckmorton who was a lamb and so clever even though he came from Boston. Mr. Throckmorton, it seemed, was sufficiently godlike to be able to raise both Dorothy and Janet from the dead.

We were fed Mr. Throckmorton all through breakfast.

The rest of us unhappily had no Mr. Throckmorton to buoy us up. After breakfast Chuck, Wyckoff, and Laguno went off to attend the inquest on Janet. Those of us who remained had nothing to look forward to but their return with the verdict and the dubious pleasures of attending Dorothy's funeral that afternoon in Reno. Bill Flanders had received a telegram from Dorothy's only living relatives in the East, expressing condolence and regretting inability to attend the funeral. I gathered from its tone that, so far as Dorothy's near and dear ones were concerned, her death was no occasion for an overwhelming display of grief.

After Fleur had left us the night before, Iris and I had decided to search her room in an attempt to find out what it was she had stolen or tried to steal from Dorothy's belongings. We had worked out an elementary if unscrupulous plan. Under the guise of apologizing for our impertinent questions of the night before, Iris was to engage Fleur in conversation downstairs, while I slipped up to the room. The plan worked smoothly but produced no results. A thorough and discreet search of Mrs. Wyckoff's possessions revealed nothing that seemed in any way suspicious. Fleur remained as enigmatic as ever. All our deductive hopes rested now on retrieving Dorothy's pocketbook when we went to Reno.

Chuck, Wyckoff, and Laguno came back from the inquest about eleven-thirty. Lorraine, Mimi, Fleur, Iris, and I were waiting for them on the terrace. We were a rather disagreeable group because of the thinly disguised tension which existed between Mimi and Lorraine. The hostility came to a head when Chuck strode out from the French windows with the expected news that the inquest jury had returned a verdict of accidental death. Both Lorraine and Mimi rose to greet him.

Mimi, all girlish smiles, went to him, laying her hand on his sleeve. "Poor boy," she cooed, "after that dreadful morning you need a drink. Come and I'll get you one."

Lorraine's face darkened. "He's perfectly capable of getting a drink for himself if he wants one."

Chuck's handsome face registered discomfort, but Mimi, clinging to his arm, drew him into the house. He raised no objection, and, as they went, I heard Mimi murmuring sweetly, "Dear boy, you deserve to be pampered once in a while."

For the second time in two days Mimi had won a complete victory over Lorraine.

Iris' and my chance to retrieve Dorothy's pocketbook came with surprising ease. The two Pleygel carloads of us, all dressed in sober hue, were half an hour too early when we arrived at the obscure little church where the funeral was to be held. My wife muttered something about the Post Office and airmail envelopes and we ducked off, hurrying along the vulgar bustle of the Reno streets toward the Del Monte. We passed the Bank Club, the Palace Club, and Chuck's own club. Business was going full tilt. Although it was only two-thirty, people were winning and losing at the tables, drinking coke highs and having themselves one hell of a time. The festive rowdiness of the place was a welcome change from the jittery tension of the Pleygel mansion.

The manager of the Del Monte remembered me and was impressed by a visit from Iris Duluth. Yes, indeed, he said, one of his waiters had found Dorothy's pocketbook on the red leather seat where we had been sitting. He had been planning to send it up to Lorraine's that very afternoon. He assured me that no one had opened it since the waiter had seen Dorothy carrying it earlier in the evening and had known it to be hers. The manager's willingness to hand it over to us showed that the sooner he relieved himself of anything connected with Dorothy and her embarrassing death the better pleased he would be.

With the large silver pocketbook tucked under my arm, I hurried out into the street with Iris at my heels. We saw a small deserted alley and slipped into it like conspirators.

Iris hovered tensely. "Darling, for heaven's sake be careful. If we're right, it's a trap. There'll be a needle with curare or——"

I didn't need to be warned. Very gingerly I squeezed the clasp, and the bag split open. Staring up at us were the long white gloves I had seen Dorothy put away that night. I eased them out and handed them to Iris. I peered at the remaining contents of the pocketbook. I saw the henna chips which Dorothy had lifted from the roulette table, a jeweled compact, a comb, a lipstick, a mirror, some loose dollars, and a handkerchief. Everything looked innocent enough.

Suddenly Iris gave a squeak of excitement. "Peter, look!"

She was holding out the right-hand glove. Smeared across the tip of the middle finger was a faint reddish stain.

"It must be curare, Peter. She touched it—touched something with her finger when she had her gloves on."

"But she had her gloves off when she opened the bag," I said. "She opened the bag to put the gloves away."

"Then maybe the gloves just smeared against the needle or whatever it was when she stuffed them in. We must be on the right track, Peter. Look, but be careful."

Very cautiously I began to pick objects out of the bag one by one, examine them, and hand them to Iris. I can't imagine what the people passing the mouth of the alley thought of us. At last we had examined everything with the utmost care, each chip, the inside of the lipstick, everything. We almost pulled the lining out of the bag. But we had to face the fact that if at one time the pocketbook had been a death trap, it was a death trap no longer.

Iris looked at me disconsolately. "At least we've got the glove. That's something. That—oh, lord, it's late. Come on or we'll miss the funeral."

The service had already begun when we tiptoed into the bare little church. Lorraine and her seven other guests were grouped together in two central pews. With them was a bored looking man who was presumably Dorothy's divorce lawyer come to mourn a vanished fee. The minister, indifferent to the presence under his roof of one of the richest girls in the world, was droning on in a musty voice. Fleur Wyckoff, small and intent, was at the end of the second pew. I slid in next to her and Iris came after me.

As the service progressed, I grew more and more conscious of the irony of the situation. Almost certainly one of those eight discreet mourners had murdered Dorothy. Certainly several others had been more than thankful to get her out of the way. I started to think of the reddish stain on the finger of Dorothy's glove, trying to guess its secret.

It was while these godless reflections were sneaking through my mind that I glanced down and saw Fleur's large black pocketbook lodged on the shiny surface of the pew between her elbow and mine. Why hadn't I thought of it before? We had searched Fleur's room for the thing she had stolen from Dorothy, but it had never occurred to us that little Mrs. Wyckoff might be carrying the object—whatever it was—around with her.

This case seemed to be developing into a tragi-comedy of pocketbooks.

Fleur was staring at the minister, absorbed, it seemed, with the melancholy course of the service. The pocketbook, like Dorothy's, had a block clasp which had only to be pinched to jump open. Feeling rather guilty, I reached my hand down until it hovered over the clasp. Fleur did not move. I gripped the clasp between two fingers and squeezed. The pocketbook sprang open and slid toward me on the pew, revealing its pink lined interior. To me the faint snap of the clasp sounded as deafening as a fusillade. But Fleur did not seem to hear. I peered down into the open bag and my heart began to thump.

Because, inside it, sticking up between a handkerchief and a little suede purse, was a letter. And on the front of the envelope, I could just make out, in ink, the words:

Mrs. Dorothy Fland . . .

With an agility that became a pickpocket rather than a naval lieutenant, I flicked the letter out of the bag and into my own pocket. I reached back to snap the clasp and, as I did so, the organ started playing and people began rustling. Fleur half turned. The pocketbook was still open. There was only one thing to do. Making a clumsy grab for a hymn book, I managed to tilt the pocketbook off the pew with my elbow so that it flopped to the floor, disgorging its contents out onto the bare stone. It happened so quickly that I was pretty sure Fleur had not realized the clasp had been open before the fall.

Grinning sheepishly, I bent, stuffed the things back into the bag, shut it, and handed it to her. She was lost in some gloomy reverie. She just took it absently and slipped it under her arm.

It looked very much as if I had found the mysterious object which Fleur had stolen from Dorothy Flanders' room.

A letter written to Dorothy—by whom?

Chuck had business in Reno and did not come back with us. Iris and I drove in the station wagon with Lover, Mimi, and Fleur.

When we reached home, Lover went to put the station wagon away, Mimi and Fleur drifted off together, and Iris and I became tangled up with Lorraine who had driven back in the other car. She was brandishing a telegram and bewailing the fact that Mr. Throckmorton's priority had collapsed under him and he had been thrown off the plane at Cheyenne. He would not be arriving until tomorrow.

Making vague sympathetic noises, I managed to brush Lorraine off and bundled my wife upstairs to our room, where I proudly produced the letter with the necessary explanations. Iris was flatteringly impressed with my theft.

"Quick, darling. Let's read it. Quick."

Ignoring the delicate ethics of the situation, I pulled the envelope out of my pocket and extracted from it a single sheet of note paper, covered with a blunt, masculine handwriting.

With Iris eagerly at my side, I read:

Dorothy,
    At least you've achieved something. You've opened my eyes once and for all. I see now what sort of a person you are and what a monstrous fool I've let you make out of

me. I don't understand what you want. Surely it can't be marriage. I suppose it's money. Well, blackmail is blackmail, however daintily you express it, and I will not be blackmailed. So go on. Do your worst. Shout from the housetops that Dr. Wyckoff, the favorite son of a hundred ailing dowagers, made unwelcome advances to you when you visited him as a patient. As I remember it, the advances were not altogether on my side. But if it gives you pleasure to ruin my career out of spite—go ahead. I deserve nothing better. I am making plans to see that you can hurt no one but myself. This will be the last communication between us. I shall remember you till the day I die—or you do.

David Wyckoff

I looked at Iris. She looked at me and grimaced. "Wyckoff, too! The more we find out about Dorothy the less attractive she becomes, if possible."

"Sure. She cheats on Flanders, runs through all his dough, has a tawdry affair with Laguno at Janet's expense, sneaks five-dollar chips from her hostess, has a tumble with Wyckoff and tries to blackmail him with threats to ruin his career. The sort of girl any man would be proud to murder."

" 'Till the day I die—or you do,' " mused Iris. "It looks as if Wyckoff had murder on his mind, doesn't it?"

"Exactly," I said. "Which brings us to Fleur."

Fleur's position seemed as obvious now as it was pitiful. Clearly she had lied to us last night about her reason for divorcing her husband. She must either have known or suspected about Dorothy. And then, when Dorothy died and Wyckoff diagnosed the death as heart failure, Fleur must have jumped to the conclusion that it was murder and that her husband was hushing it up because he was guilty. She knew Dorothy was the careful homebody type who keeps incriminating letters tied up in pink ribbons. So she had sneaked into Dorothy's room to make sure there was no evidence against her husband floating around. She had found this letter and Laguno's letter to Dorothy which she had slipped under Janet's door. Since then she had been lying herself black in the face to protect Wyckoff.

One thing was certain, Dorothy or no Dorothy, divorce or no divorce, Fleur was still in love with David Wyckoff.

"The poor kid," said Iris, "she must have been suffering the tortures of the damned." Her face clouded. "But what do you think? Wyckoff's by far the most likely one to have murdered Dorothy. Everything fits that way."

"But why kill Janet?"

"Don't you see? Wyckoff knew Janet had Laguno's letter to Dorothy. He assumed that Janet was the one who had ransacked Dorothy's room and that therefore Janet had this letter which incriminated him."

"Could be." I folded the letter back into the envelope. "But before we stick our necks out, we'll give Wyckoff a chance to talk. Once he's confronted with this letter, he'll have to talk willy-nilly."

Iris, greedy for action, said, "Shall we go find him now?"

I kissed her. "Not we, darling—I. This is going to be one of those delicate talks with sex and things rearing their ugly heads. I think it'd better be carried out on a man-to-man basis."

I left her, taking the letter with me, and went in search of Wyckoff. I tried his room first and he was there.

Dr. Wyckoff had one of the most startling of Lorraine's many startling rooms. Built on a corner, it was dominated by two huge plate-glass windows, each of which took up an almost complete wall. The afternoon light was fading, and the two views were as flat and unreal as gigantic photo-murals. One stretched all the way to the hump of Mount Rose with Lorraine's steep, zig-zag drive tumbling precipitously in the foreground. The other showed the walled-in approach to the house and the gleaming expanse of Lake Tahoe with its brooding sentinel mountains beyond.

This Wagnerian setting made David Wyckoff seem small and forlorn, although he was over six feet. He gave me a makeshift substitute for a smile.

"Oh, hello, Lieutenant Duluth. I've got a bottle of rye somewhere. Have a drink."

"No, thanks." I could have done with a shot, but it didn't seem cricket to gulp down a man's liquor when you were planning to accuse him of double murder. "I've just come in for a chat."

"Chat?" He echoed that sissy little word with surprise. "You mean—about something in particular?"

"Something very particular."

"I hope I'll be able to help you." His voice was changed. It was all dressed up with society doctor charm. "Just what is it?"

"It's this," I said. "I think Dorothy Flanders was murdered and I think Janet Laguno was murdered. I know a dart tipped with curare was stolen from the trophy room some time before Dorothy died and I know it was put back again the next day with its tip faked. I'm pretty sure Dorothy was poisoned with curare by a trap set in her pocketbook. I'm pretty sure you know she was poisoned, too." I paused, giving that time to sink in. "That's what I want to chat about."

Wyckoff bore up very well under my blitz. Very softly he said, "I shall ask you what I asked Count Laguno when he made a similar accusation. If you believe what you say you believe, Lieutenant, why didn't you demand an autopsy before Dorothy was buried?"

"Because I'm Lorraine's guest here. I didn't want to mess everyone up in a scandal before I was sure."

"You're accusing me of giving a false diagnosis in order

to hush up a murder. What reason would I have for jeopardizing my entire professional career?"

Wyckoff had a nice face really, open and good-natured. That supercilious expression didn't suit it.

I said, "Your entire professional career was so nearly jeopardized already. Just a little mud slung in the right places can ruin a doctor. Dorothy, alive, going around accusing you of having made attacks on her virtue when she visited you as a patient, was dangerous enough. Dorothy murdered, with a good chance of everything breaking, was a thousand times more dangerous. You stood to gain everything if a little professional lying could whisk her respectably into a coffin with no questions asked."

Dr. Wyckoff was gripping the back of one of Lorraine's interior decorator's apologies for a chair. Against the great Nevada backdrops of the windows, he seemed a gaunt shadow with no substance.

"What are you trying to tell me?" he managed to say.

"I don't like reading other people's mail as a rule, but this was just one of those things."

I produced the letter from my pocket and handed it to him. He took it with shaking fingers, staring down at it like a man staring at his own death warrant. He looked old and beaten.

"You're going to the police, Lieutenant Duluth?"

"I'm afraid I don't believe in getting sentimental about murderers."

He handed the letter back to me. He stood up straight, trying to square his shoulders.

"All right. We might as well get this over as quickly as possible. I killed Dorothy and I killed Janet."

Eleven

THAT HAD ME STAGGERED for a moment. I had evidence against him, yes, but certainly not enough evidence to make a murderer throw in his hand that wholeheartedly.

Firing the question at him, I said, "What was the trap to kill Dorothy?"

"I—I—" he floundered. "I just——"

I saw then. "Don't bother. Things are complicated enough without your getting noble. You didn't kill her, did you? You think your wife did. That's your trouble."

He flared. "That's a lie. If you think you can——"

"This is all rather funny. Here you are ready to take the rap for Fleur while she's been running around in a swivet—faking alibis for you, making up stories, breaking into people's rooms, stealing things—just because she thinks you're guilty."

I told him all I knew about Fleur's carryings-on then. It was amazing how he changed. He looked boyish again, excited, almost gay. And when I had finished, he was pathetically eager to talk.

His story was pretty much what I had expected it to be—a sordid tale about a woman who needed a sound kick in the pants and a man who forgot for a few heady moments that you can't have your cake and eat it too.

Wyckoff and Fleur had been married for eight years and for eight years they had been devotedly in love with each other. Then one day Dorothy had showed up in Wyckoff's office, referred to him by another physician for a slight heart ailment.

"She did have a slight systolic murmur, but it wasn't transmitted, wasn't serious at all. After I'd examined her, she stayed on. We got to talking. And—oh, well, you knew her. I don't have to go into the grisly details of those unwelcome advances, do I?"

Dorothy, apparently more than satisfied with the unwelcome advances, had continued to pay him regular visits. To give their sessions an air of professional respectability, she had insisted on his sending her periodic bills which she merely left for the still hospitalized Bill Flanders to face on his bitter homecoming.

In spite of Dorothy's heady fascination he was still in love with Fleur, lived in constant terror that she would find out, and felt more and more of a heel as the weeks dragged tawdrily on. It was the same old story with the same old sting in its end. At last, Dorothy, bored with his scruples and self-recriminations and on the loose again with Laguno, had turned nasty and tried to hold him up for money. In a fury of disgust he had written her the letter. Soon he received a reply, pointing out that the letter had admitted her charges and that it would come in handy if she chose to bring a law suit for damages. She would give him a couple of weeks, she said, to make up his mind whether to settle the matter or not. He realized that he might as well kiss his career goodby. By then he felt he deserved anything that came to him anyway.

But he wasn't going to have his beloved Fleur dragged through the mire with him. Before anything could break, he had gone to her, told her nothing about Dorothy but asked her to divorce him, giving her no explanations. She had been terribly shaken but had asked no questions.

"She's as proud and stubborn as they come," he said, a note of pride in his voice. "I never dreamed she'd known about Dorothy all the time. She never let me guess. She wanted to spare me that final humiliation."

And so Fleur went off to Reno with her little heart breaking while David Wyckoff waited at home, expecting the worst every day. He thought it had come when Bill Flanders showed up at his office. But all Flanders was worrying about was his wife's bills. Wyckoff told him the half true story of Dorothy's weak heart, and Bill fell for it. During the interview Flanders let it slip that Dorothy had gone to Reno.

"She had to," I put in. "Flanders had got wise to her. He'd started chasing her around with steak knives. San Francisco wasn't healthy for her any more."

David Wyckoff's lips were still pale. "It was a few days later that Lorraine called me with her crazy invitation. I accepted. It wasn't because I ever hoped for a reconciliation with Fleur. After what I'd done, I wasn't even worthy to tie her shoes. I dreaded having to see her again. But I did come because Lorraine said that Dorothy was here, too. I was terrified of what might happen with Dorothy and Fleur in the same house, terrified of what Dorothy might tell my wife. I was half crazy with worry by then anyway. I had a mad idea that if I came, maybe I could argue with Dorothy, persuade her to give me back my letter—something. I knew she'd probably just laugh at me. But, well, it was a last desperate chance to save something from the wreck."

"And when you got here, you did talk with Dorothy?"

"I never had the chance. But I did see Fleur. She came to my room just before we all went in to Reno. She was very quiet, very cold. She just said, 'It's Dorothy, isn't it?' And then, when I didn't say anything, she laughed and said, 'It's funny really, funny that my whole life's ruined and it's all because of Dorothy—something any drunk sailor could pick up on a Saturday night. I suppose you're going to marry her. Well, I wish you happiness.' Then she was gone, running down the corridor. She never gave me a chance to speak to her again."

That same evening Dorothy had died at the Del Monte.

David Wyckoff's face lived again some of the torture he must have gone through when he examined her body in the manager's office. He had seen at once that she had died from heart failure. But there were symptoms of paralysis, and he was pretty sure that heart failure was secondary to the anoxia of respiratory failure due to paralysis of the diaphragm and the thoracic muscles. Everything pointed to the fact that death had been the result of a poison working on the respiratory system.

"You talk about curare, Duluth. It's not much in my line but I've seen it used at the hospital in tetanus cases and I must admit the idea of curare crossed my mind. But—well, you can imagine how I felt." He watched me intently. "I knew that if any other doctor saw the corpse, he would discount a diagnosis of simple heart failure. I thought of my letter. Dorothy had it in Reno. If the police knew she'd been murdered, they'd be bound to find that letter which would mean the end of me. And then Bill Flanders was there in the room. I knew what he felt about Dorothy. If he had murdered her, who was I to blame him? But that wasn't all. It was Fleur. She thought I was in love with Dorothy, thought I was going to marry her, knew her life had been ruined by her. What if Fleur had—— That's what decided me. It was a mad thing to do, but there was just a chance of my getting away with it since I had been Dorothy's personal physician, and both Flanders and the doctor who sent her to me honestly believed she had a weak heart." He pushed the dark hair back from his forehead. "Heaven knows what would have happened if I hadn't convinced Chuck. It was his influence with the police that made the whole dirty thing possible."

Later that night, when he came back from Reno with Chuck, he had gone to Dorothy's room in search of his letter. He found the room in disorder and the letter gone. He did not know, of course, that it was Fleur who had taken it. He had straightened the room because he knew if it were found that way next morning people would start wondering.

That explained the miraculous fashion in which the room had tidied itself during my midnight talk with Flanders on the terrace.

"About Janet," said Wyckoff, "I don't know. She wasn't poisoned with curare. I can tell you that. But—I suppose you must be right. I suppose she must have been murdered, too—held under the water—though I can't imagine why unless Laguno——" He came to me, gripped my arm. "I've told you the truth. I swear it. What I did was a criminal thing for a doctor to do and I'm ready to take the consequences. But you've told me yourself that Fleur's been thinking I did it. That means you can't possibly suspect her, can you?"

That made sense. He thought Fleur had done it and Fleur thought he had done it—which should cancel them both neatly out. For one cynical moment it occurred to me that between them they might be putting on a colossal piece of double bluff, but it was hard to believe such a thing as I looked at Wyckoff's gaunt face.

So the Wyckoff saga was complete—a tragic little tale of a man and wife still in love with each other, one too proud, the other too humble, to admit it.

I moved away from him to one of the windows, trying to think. I stared down idly. The old station wagon was parked in front of the pillared entrance to the house. It hadn't been there when I last looked out.

I said over my shoulder, "If I went to the police and demanded an autopsy on Dorothy, you'd be through as a doctor, wouldn't you? You'd even be arrested as an accessory after the fact?"

He joined me at the window. Huskily he said, "Of course. I realize that. But there's nothing I can do to stop you."

"Maybe there is." I turned to him and held out the letter

he had written to Dorothy Flanders. "I'm ready to make a bargain."

He stared at the letter as if he couldn't believe his eyes.

"This letter's the only thing that incriminates you and your wife. I'll let you have it if you'll promise to go with me to the police tomorrow morning and ask for an autopsy on Dorothy yourself."

He still stared blankly. "Myself?"

"That's the only way to save you and the easiest way to get an investigation started. If I went to the police, they might think I was a crackpot. But you're the doctor who signed the certificate. If you handle yourself right, you can sound perfectly innocent. Tell them Dorothy had a weak heart and that you'd never have become suspicious if I hadn't come to you with a tale about a stolen dart tipped with curare. I'll tell you about the dart later. Say there's a possibility she might have been poisoned and that you're no longer satisfied with your own diagnosis. The post-mortem will show the curare, the police will get on the job, and we'll have done all we have to do." I still held out the letter. "You'll run the risk of having them dig up your affair with Dorothy, anyway. But at least you'll be able to destroy this."

He took the letter. I could tell what he was thinking from his face. I'd not only been able to show him that his wife still loved him. I was even giving him a chance to pull himself out of one of the messiest situations in which a doctor had ever floundered. It was just too much of a good thing.

"Of course I'll go to the police with you." He added, "But I'm afraid an autopsy will not clear things up as easily as you think. I doubt whether there's a pathologist in the country who could prove that curare had been administered."

I hadn't banked on that. I said, "You mean the police would have to show definitely how the curare had been administered before they had a case?"

"I rather imagine so. They would probably have to produce the murder weapon—the needle or whatever it was. And also prove the suspect had access to curare. It's not an easy drug to come by."

"It is in this house. Lorraine's got that trophy cabinet full of it. That won't bother us. But the murder weapon——"

I told him then my half-formed theory that someone had set some sort of death trap in Dorothy's pocketbook. I asked his opinion.

He said, "It's the popular belief about curare that even the smallest dose injected into the blood stream by a prick will prove fatal. That's not strictly true. In academic circles you'd be told that no dose less than twenty-five milligrams could be depended upon to be lethal, and that the dose would have to be injected deeply, intramuscularly. The truth lies somewhere in between. There are so many incalculables to consider—the general health of the victim, idiosyncrasies, etcetera. If you asked me if anyone could be killed by the prick of a needle tipped with curare, I'd say yes, particularly in a case like that of Dorothy where a heart condition already existed. But it couldn't be relied upon. Someone might easily be stuck once or twice and not die."

"Then the person who murdered Dorothy took a big risk?"

"Not necessarily. It's much more likely that, as a layman, he assumed that one prick would be deadly, and he was lucky. Most people know next to nothing about curare except what they read in sensational fiction."

"And that includes me." I grinned. "Well, if I want to impress the police, I guess it's up to me to find that murder weapon. Or at least figure out more definitely how Dorothy could have been killed with curare. Thanks, Wyckoff. You've been a big help."

He stared at me incredulously. "You're thanking *me*. It's I who should thank you. How can I ever begin to——"

I felt self-conscious. "If I were you, I'd go find your wife and start getting your stories together." I smiled. "Maybe Lorraine isn't such a giddy girl, after all. The Lagunos and the Flanders didn't respond to treatment. But it looks as if the Wyckoffs are in for a slap-up reconciliation with trumpets blowing."

His face lit up. "Yes, I must find Fleur. I——"

He stopped. He was staring out of the window. I turned just in time to see the small figure of Fleur Wyckoff run down the steps of the house and jump into the station wagon.

"Where's she going?" said Wyckoff sharply.

"I don't know."

He tried to tug the plate-glass window down so that he could shout to her. It wouldn't move. He tried again feverishly. Fleur was in the station wagon now. It lurched forward and started down the drive. She reached a sharp bend, swung around it, and disappeared from sight.

There had been a recklessness about the way she was driving that somehow infected both of us. We ran to the other window which showed the lower part of the drive careening dangerously down the flank of the mountain toward the foothills of Mount Rose. It was a strange sensation staring out through the plate-glass window of that upstairs room. It was like watching something on a movie screen, something that was not quite real.

Two figures were strolling up the drive. I could just make them out as Mimi and Lover. Fleur's car hadn't appeared yet. Wyckoff was close against the window, watching with white anxiety.

"What's the matter, Lieutenant? She was driving like a crazy woman. She——"

The station wagon came into view. And it was a horrible sight because it wasn't acting like a car. It was hurtling and staggering down the precipitous drive like a rudderless ship in a high sea. Although it was utterly impossible for his wife to hear him, Wyckoff shouted, "Fleur! Fleur!"

I was watching in horrified fascination. Completely out of control, the car was heading straight for Mimi and Lover. I saw Mimi scuttle up the stony bank to safety. Lover made a move to follow her and then turned back, waving wildly at the oncoming car. It almost reached him. With a disregard for danger that made me wince, he made a futile attempt to leap onto the running board. The car flashed past him and he fell forward onto the rocky gravel of the drive.

There was a sharp bend ahead with a naked drop down into the canyon. There was no fence, no anything to guard it. Lover scrambled to his feet, waving again. The car roared on.

Wyckoff had gripped my shoulder. His fingers were digging into my skin.

"Fleur. . . ." he cried, and the word faded into a whimper.

Because the car reached the bend and did not turn. It went right on into nothingness.

It plunged out of sight—over the edge of the canyon.

Part Four

MIMI

Twelve

DAVID WYCKOFF gave a single cry. It was a horrible sound to hear from a man—thin and shrill as a dog's yelp. He spun from the window and ran out of the room, disappearing headlong into the corridor. I ran after him. The sight we had just seen through the window sent questions racing through my mind. Fleur Wyckoff had dashed out of the house and jumped into the old station wagon. Why? The car had careened down the drive, completely out of control. Why? In spite of Lover's efforts, the car had plunged over into the canyon, carrying Fleur to almost certain death. How had it happened? I knew no hows or whys.

I just knew, with a sinking sensation, that for the third time in as many days an "accident" had brought disaster to another of Lorraine's guests.

Dorothy . . . Janet . . . Fleur . . .

This wasn't just a murder case any more. It was a mass slaughter. The thing in Lorraine's house was running amok as insanely as the car that had just toppled over into the canyon.

David Wyckoff had already reached the stairs. As I started after him, the door of our room opened and Iris ran out. My wife stared down the corridor at Wyckoff and then came to me, her lovely face pale with foreboding.

"Peter, what's the matter with David Wyckoff?"

"Quick," I said. "Come on. Quick. It's Fleur."

"Fleur?" Iris ran at my side. "What's happened to her?"

We reached the great staircase. "The car," I said. "Something went wrong. It plunged off the drive. Wyckoff and I saw it from his window."

"Peter! But what was Fleur doing in a car? Where was she going?"

"I don't know. Mimi and Lover were coming up the drive. Lover tried to stop it. At least they'll be there if anything can be done."

The broad wooden stairs swept to the right. I could see the enormous hall stretching below, opulent and without personality, like the very latest thing in picture galleries. Wyckoff was running toward the front door. Bill Flanders was down there, too, sitting with his crutch propped against him, on a low settee. He was reading a magazine and glanced up idly as Wyckoff dashed past.

It seemed impossible that anybody could be sitting stolidly and reading a magazine at a moment like this.

Wyckoff was through the door. As Iris and I came panting into the hall, the Count Laguno appeared from the trophy room, his lizard face bright with curiosity.

"What's all the fuss about?"

"Fleur." I said.

"Fleur? She asked me to get a car for her from the garage. About fifteen minutes later she came rushing downstairs and leaped into the car without so much as a civil thank you. What's the matter with her?"

I stared at him. "Was the car all right when you brought it round?"

"All right? The brakes seemed a trifle weak. What is this, anyway?"

There was a clattering of high heels behind us. I turned to see Lorraine hurrying from the living-room, all fancied up for the evening in a trailing black raspberry creation.

"My angels, what goings-on! What is this? Some divine new game or——"

Iris said, "Fleur's gone off the drive in the station wagon."

Our hostess' eyes popped with horror. "Off the drive! But it's a drop—almost a sheer drop into the canyon!"

I had started toward the open door. The others clattered after me, all except Bill Flanders. It would have been foolish for him to come, anyway. He couldn't make any time on his crutch.

The light was fading as we sprinted out into the wide, walled-in approach to the house. Iris and I were ahead. There was a desolate grandeur to the mountain peaks. Here and there in the huge view stretches of evergreens stood out black and smudgy as trees in a woodcut.

I said grimly, "There we were muddling along trying to catch up with yesterday's murder, and all the time today's murder——"

"Murder!" echoed my wife.

"Of course it was murder. That car had been tampered with. No one could have kept it on the drive. Someone fixed it so Fleur would plunge over the side."

I had said it now. It was out.

Lorraine, for all her high heels and her swirling evening dress, was running with the best of us. She caught up with Iris and me, her curls flying, her elegance absurdly out of place.

"Peter, darling," she panted, "why on earth did Fleur want to go to Reno anyway?"

"To Reno?" I said. "So that's where she was going."

"Yes. I mean, it seemed so weird. She positively hurtled into my room when I was changing for dinner. She said she had to go to Reno to get something. Could she take the station wagon? Was there enough gas? I told her Chuck was in Reno, she could call him and get him to bring whatever it was she wanted. But she insisted on going herself. I couldn't understand. I——"

Her monologue rambled on. I gave up listening. With a crawling sense of guilt, I was beginning to realize just what had happened to Fleur. When we got home from Reno, she must have discovered the loss of her husband's damning letter to Dorothy. She didn't know I had stolen it but she did know that her pocketbook had fallen and burst open on the church floor. Naturally she assumed the letter was still there in the church, and naturally she would have had only one idea—to rush and retrieve it.

It it hadn't been for my attempts at so-called investigation, she would never have dashed off on that wild-goose chase. In a sense I was responsible for whatever it was we were going to find.

I was half sick with anxiety. We came to a sharp bend. A fresh segment of the drive came into view, clinging like a huge, winding serpent to the precipitous flank of the mountain. The spot where the car had plunged over into the canyon was about two hundred yards ahead.

We could see Mimi Burnett running from it along the drive. Ahead of us, David Wyckoff was hurrying toward her. The sight of his lonely figure brought the pitiful irony of the situation into focus. A few minutes after he had learned from me that Fleur still loved him, Wyckoff had had to see his wife and the station wagon reel off the drive before his very eyes.

Wyckoff was paying a bitter penalty for his past indiscretions.

He reached Mimi. The two of them stood together for a moment. Then Mimi turned and they started back to the point where the car had disappeared. They came to it. Mimi pointed. Recklessly Wyckoff swung himself down from the bare edge of the drive and disappeared, leaving Mimi fluttering on the brink.

I was the first to join her. She was wearing a pseudo-medieval evening gown with long trailing sleeves. It was creased and strewn with scraps of dead sage. She was wringing her hands like a demented Lady of Shallot. She threw herself into my arms, hiding her head against my shoulder.

"Lover shouted to her to open the door and jump," she sobbed. "The car toppled over. She opened the door. It threw her free. She's lying down there. Lover's with her. And the car, it went on and on, rolling, rolling, rolling——"

I was still panting, trying to get my breath back. The others crowded up. I stared over Mimi's quivering head, down into the canyon. The slope at this point was not sheer, but it was steep and bare except for a few jutting rocks and an occasional tangle of straggly sage bushes.

Hundreds of feet below us stretched a dry, boulder-strewn river bed. Sprawled in it, looking scarcely larger than a toy and blazing like a beacon, lay the ruins of the station wagon.

Some thirty feet down the slope from the drive, Lover was clinging plumply and precariously to a sage bush. Wyckoff was scrambling and sliding down the treacherous mountainside toward him. Lover was stooping over something, invisible to me, which lay in an outcropping of sage above a flat slab of rock.

Relief poured through me as I realized that Fleur was not in the flaming wreckage of the car. She had been sufficiently in control of her wits to obey Lover's desperate yell to open the door. She had been thrown free. She might still be alive.

Mimi was almost hysterical. Lorraine and Iris hovered at my side with Laguno behind us. I maneuvered Mimi over to my wife.

"Take care of her, darling. Laguno, see whether you can find a rope in the house. They'll need one to get her up. I'm going down to see if I can help."

Lorraine said, "There's a rope in the garage, Count."

Laguno ran off. Iris put her arm around Mimi. Her eyes were frightened.

"Peter, do be careful."

"It's okay. I've got rubber soles."

I eased myself over the edge and started slithering down the slope, catching at sage to support myself. Wyckoff had already reached Lover. He had dropped to his knees at his side and was stooping over the thing I couldn't see. Soon I came down to them. My heart was thumping from the exertion. I grabbed a sage bush next to Lover and stared down over his shoulder.

I saw Fleur then. Wyckoff, his own face white as a corpse's, was running his hands over her little body. She lay on her back, her dress ripped half off her, her arms tossed limply over her head. Her hair was tangled around her flower face. Her eyes were closed and there was blood, gaudy as paint, staining the ivory skin of her cheeks.

I couldn't tell from looking at her whether she was alive or dead.

Lover, swinging round on his sage-bush anchor like a clumsy, bespectacled sloth, stared at me. There was nothing hearty about him now. He looked shot to pieces.

"The car," he said hoarsely. "We saw it coming, Mimi and I. There was something wrong with the car, Lieutenant."

Behind the shock, you could see his dazed mind stumblingly putting two and two together.

"I don't understand. I drove the station wagon back from Reno this afternoon. It was all right when I put it away in the garage. And then—then it came careening down the drive as if it had no brakes at all. How d'you figure that?"

I was pretty sure I knew what had happened to that car, but I didn't want to say it then in front of Wyckoff.

I muttered, "At least you had the sense to shout to her to jump. If she's alive, I guess she has you to thank for it."

A smile flickered dimly over his face. "I—I tried to stop it. But what could I do?"

Wyckoff was still bending over his wife. His eyes were the eyes of a man in a nightmare. Slowly his hands slipped from her body. He squatted a moment, staring at nothing. Then in a strangled whisper, he said, "The sage—the sage must have broken her fall."

I felt as if an enormous weight had been lifted from my shoulders. "You mean she's all right?"

Wyckoff turned to me. It was obviously an immense effort for him to concentrate on what I said. I think he even had trouble remembering who I was. Enunciating each word separately in a travesty of a professional voice, he muttered, "There are no broken bones. I do not believe there are any internal injuries. There are bruises, cuts. She's unconscious. She——"

He stopped then and threw his hands up to cover his face.

I could tell he had used up all his reserves of strength getting himself prepared to find her dead. Now that she was miraculously alive, there was nothing left in him to cope with good fortune.

A voice above us shouted, "Rope, Lieutenant."

I looked up to see Laguno dangling a long rope down the slope to us. He had harnessed one end to a small mountain mahogany. The three of us with the help of the rope managed to carry Fleur up to the drive. Once we were there, Wyckoff didn't speak a word to anyone. He just picked his wife up in his arms and started to walk back to the house.

The rest of us trooped after him. Mimi in her sham medieval get-up was still sniveling. Iris walked with her, her arm around her waist, trying to encourage her. Lorraine and the Count Laguno, chillily ignoring each other, followed. Lover and I came last.

Although he trundled along in silence, I could tell from his face that Lover was still struggling with uneasy deductions. After a while he turned to stare at me as if trying to make up his mind whether or not I was a dependable confidant. I must have passed the test for he said, "I'm worried. I've been worried for some time. I haven't wanted to say anything. Poor Mimi's so highly strung, so sensitive. I'd cut my finger off before I'd upset her and everyone without a good reason. But now—Lieutenant, I'm sure that car was tampered with."

I made a noncommittal sound.

"Maybe," he continued, "if Mimi and I hadn't actually been there, hadn't actually seen it happen, people might have just figured it was an accident. Another accident." He stressed the word *another* ironically. "But I know that old station wagon. I've been driving it for Lorraine for weeks now. It wouldn't have come down the hill like that—not unless the brakes had been fooled with." He moistened his lips. "It's an old model with a cable brake. It would have been easy for someone to sneak into the garage and file half way through the cable. Just coming down that steep, winding drive would do the rest."

I had been thinking that, too. There would have been time enough for someone to have filed through the cable between the time Fleur expressed her intention of driving to Reno and the time she actually left. But who?

Voicing my thoughts, Lover said, "I wonder whether Fleur got it out of the garage herself."

"Laguno got it out for her," I said.

"Laguno?" Lover walked on, his pudgy face pale. Impulsively he added, "Dorothy died of a weak heart. Janet was drowned. And yet Wyckoff, Chuck, and everyone took it in their stride. None of them seemed to think it was odd, two women dying like that in two days. I've been trying to tell myself I was just imagining things. But now——" He lowered his voice although there was no chance of the others ahead overhearing him. "I think something's wrong, Lieutenant, badly wrong."

It was a relief, after the zany optimism to which I had been submitted for so long, to hear someone taking a reasonable and gloomy view of the situation. Until then I'd always thought of Lover as just a stooge for Mimi. His stock was beginning to rise.

I looked back at him and said, "Sure something's wrong. Two murders and one attempted murder—that's quite wrong enough for me. Three wives in three days. If this keeps up, we'll all be widowers soon."

I had meant that to be funny, something to ease the tension.

But once I'd said it, it didn't sound funny at all.

Thirteen

WHEN WE REACHED the house, Wyckoff had carried his wife upstairs. Only Bill Flanders was in the great hall, standing propped on his crutch below a huge, flagrantly indecent canvas which one of the "divine little artists" of Lorraine's art-crazy epoch had done in Mexico and was "really so attractive, my dear." Flanders hadn't turned on any lights. As we entered, there seemed to be a blight on that high, shadowy room.

It wasn't just the gloomy twilight. Houses are funny. They absorb the mood of their occupants like blotting paper absorbs ink. We were all slightly afraid now. There was no getting around it. Even the prosaic Lover had come out and admitted that murder, cunningly disguised as Chance, had struck three times in three days. Our fear was mirrored by the house. The doors which led to the dining room and the library loomed like flimsy barricades against nameless terrors. And the great staircase, which had been merely something to go upstairs by, now led upward to a realm of impalpable dangers.

Lorraine shivered and said, "Let's have some light. It's a tomb here." She trailed around in black raspberry taffeta, tugging at lamp chains. As the light came, she exclaimed, "My dears, what a disheveled spectacle we are." Her eyes focused on Mimi, narrowing into the malice which seemed reserved exclusively for her half brother's fiancée. "Mimi, my pet, you look as if you'd been ravished by the Paiutes. Come on upstairs and patch yourself up."

Lorraine, Mimi, and Iris went upstairs. Laguno sidled off into the living-room after a drink. Bill Flanders hobbled up to Lover and me and started shooting questions at us about what had happened to Fleur. I told him the story, but I wasn't really listening to myself. Things were getting so hopelessly out of control. Dorothy's murder had been reasonable enough. Anyone in his right mind might have wanted to murder Dorothy. Even for Janet's death there had been some shred of motive. But why on earth should anyone want to kill little Fleur Wyckoff?

Perhaps when she rifled Dorothy's belongings she had found something we did not know about, something that, maybe, hadn't seemed important to her but which was vitally important to the murderer. There was a germ of sanity to that theory. But, infected by the insidious atmosphere of the house, I was beginning to abandon any attempt at a sane solution.

Three wives had been about to divorce three husbands. Two of those wives were now dead and the third had avoided death only by a miracle.

It was as if some strange power was loose in Lorraine's chilly mansion, dispensing death to divorcees.

I wanted a drink much more than I wanted to satisfy Bill

Flanders' curiosity. I left him and followed the Count into the living-room. Stefano Laguno had withdrawn into a corner with his highball. He was looking both uneasy and self-righteous.

As I poured myself a straight Scotch from a decanter which stood on a Queen Anne buffet at the far end of the room, Lover French joined me and made a drink for himself. Casting a conspiratorial glance over his plump shoulder in the direction of the Count Laguno, he breathed, "You weren't kidding, Lieutenant? You mean what you said just now? You do think Dorothy and Janet were murdered?"

I was in no mood to pull punches and I needed all the allies I could get. I told him exactly what I knew and what I suspected. He seemed more relieved than surprised. He'd been feeling much the same way himself, he said, only he'd figured he must be crazy. It was nice knowing he wasn't crazy. He was eager for action. In spite of the spectacles and the graying hair, he looked absurdly like a little boy all agog over a game of Cops and Robbers.

"We've got to call the police right away," he said. "And this time you and me are doing the talking, not Chuck and Wyckoff."

That was just what I had planned, only I wanted Wyckoff to be in on it too. I explained it to Lover by saying that, as Dorothy's physician, he was the correct person to demand an autopsy. I also said that we should warn Lorraine before we plunged her household into a triple murder investigation. Lover seemed doubtful when I mentioned Wyckoff. It obviously wasn't his idea of Cops and Robbers for the Cops to take one of the potential Robbers into their confidence. But he raised no objections. In fact, he seemed relieved that I was willing to take the responsibility. It would give him more time for Mimi. Poor Mimi, he said. It was going to be a terrible shock for her sensitive nature when she heard there was a murderer at large.

Personally, I felt that at this stage of the game even a moron would realize a murderer was at large without having to be told, and Mimi Burnett, for all her airy-fairy posturing, was about as sensitive as a bar of pig iron.

But then I wasn't blinded by love.

Lorraine, Mimi, and Iris came in, resplendent again after sessions with their individual mirrors. They all got drinks, but two deaths and a narrowly averted third were enough, apparently, to snuff out even Lorraine's vivacity. The three women sat around looking much too dressed up. Laguno and Bill Flanders each sulked in his own particular fashion, while Lover hovered solicitously around his fiancée, who had decorated her medieval bosom with a solitary white rose.

The blight which had been in the hall was spreading here. No one mentioned murder, but you could tell it was the only thing in everyone's mind.

As they sat there trying to keep up a façade, you could almost see the fear gaining ground in their eyes.

After a while I announced into the sticky silence that I was going upstairs to find out how the Wyckoffs were. Lorraine, in a threadbare attempt at playing hostess, said, "Oh, yes, darling, and do ask them if there's anything we can do."

Iris rose and said, "I'll come with you, Peter."

My wife followed me into the hall. She was looking very beautiful. Outshining Lorraine's elaborate gown and Mimi's Marianna of the Moated Grange creation, she was sheathed in her newest dress, creamy white with long lines, something bought especially for my leave. I could tell she had put it on for morale.

She slipped her hand through my arm. "Peter, it's been ghastly not knowing. Tell me everything that happened since you left me to talk to Wyckoff."

As we ascended the stairs, I gave her a general outline of the whole thing.

"And Fleur was driving to Reno in search of the letter we stole from her." Iris grimaced. "Fine couple we are. Between us we almost managed to do her in."

"Which is one of the many reasons I'll have for rejoicing when the police take over."

Iris paused at the head of the stairs. "Peter, I can't tell you how glad I am we don't have to struggle on any more on our own. This thing, it's like that station wagon, hurtling down the hill, gathering speed all the time."

I could see from her eyes that she was frightened. I hated having to see her that way. "We were crazy not to pack up and quit yesterday," I said. "It's too late now. No one'll be able to go. I could kick myself for messing up our leave."

"You didn't mess it up, darling. I was as determined to stay as you were. And how could it be messed up so long as we're together anyway?" Iris smiled but the smile faded. "Even the house is beginning to scare me. With a murderer who hides behind sly little accidents, you don't feel anything's safe. You feel maybe you'll be killed walking into a room or lighting a cigarette or—or brushing your teeth." She gave a harsh little laugh. "He's run through the discontented wives now, Peter. I only hope he doesn't start on the contented ones next."

There she was saying the same thing I had said to Lover in a different way. It hadn't sounded funny when I had said it. It sounded infinitely less funny now.

We went to Fleur's room. Wyckoff came out when we knocked. He looked blissfully happy. Fleur had regained consciousness, he said. He could still scarcely believe she was uninjured. The sage had broken her fall. If it hadn't been for Lover calling out, and the sage, she wouldn't have had a chance. With a shy glance at Iris, he told me he had taken my advice and confessed everything to his wife. She, in turn, had confessed her motive for stealing the letter. Reconciliation, it seemed, was complete.

I told him that I had decided to break the case wide open and give it to the police. I explained. "I want you to be in on it so you can cook up your own story about Dorothy's death certificate and the autopsy."

He watched me strangely. "You're giving me a sporting chance to save my career. I still can't understand why you're being so generous."

I shuffled. "Oh, well, someone might as well try to help someone."

He said I could talk to Fleur if I didn't stay too long. She was lying in the bed by the window. I moved to her side while Wyckoff and Iris stood by the door. In spite of the scratches and cuts, Fleur's face was radiant. She gave me a broken little speech of thanks for my part in bringing her and her husband together again. Since I had almost got her murdered, I felt that was big of her.

"And it was so kind of you to give David the letter. I should have destroyed it when I first found it. But somehow I couldn't bring myself to, not until David had explained everything to me." She smiled. "We've destroyed it now."

I said, "That station wagon—it had been tampered with, hadn't it, Fleur?"

The memory of horror showed on her face. "Yes. The moment I swung the car around the first bend in the drive I was sure. The brakes had been all right. And then, suddenly, there were no brakes at all—as if the cable had snapped."

"Then you've got to tell me something. Who knew you were going to Reno? I mean, who had time to file through the cable while you were upstairs talking to Lorraine?"

"Why—I asked the Count to get the car for me."

"You didn't tell anyone else?"

"Why, no. At least, Bill Flanders was there when I spoke

to Laguno. He was reading. He didn't seem to be listening. There wasn't anyone else. You three were upstairs. Mimi and Lover were out walking. And Chuck was in Reno."

"Okay," I said. "And just one thing more. That night when you ransacked Dorothy's things, did you take anything else except your husband's letter?"

"I found that other letter, the one Laguno had written to Dorothy." Fleur's eyes were unsteady. "Maybe it was terrible of me to have slipped it under Janet's door, but—well, it seemed only fair to let her see it."

"Apart from the two letters, you didn't take anything?"

"No. Nothing."

"You're sure? Not even some little thing, something that seemed of absolutely no significance to you?"

She stirred in the bed. "I'm sure I didn't, Peter. What are you trying——"

I grinned and patted her small hand. "Never you mind. We don't want you worrying that pretty bruised head of yours."

Wyckoff and Iris came over. While Iris spoke a few words to Fleur, Wyckoff took his wife's hand and gazed down at her with reverent adoration as if he half expected her to sprout a halo and float away up through the ceiling.

We left. Outside in the corridor Iris said, "So only Laguno knew she was going to use the car, Peter."

"Only Laguno, and maybe Flanders."

"But it couldn't have been Bill Flanders. He couldn't have gone sneaking around poking under cars, with only one leg."

"No," I said. "I guess he couldn't."

The others were streaming in to dinner when we reached the hall. I spoke to Lover and we decided to break the news to Lorraine after the meal and then call the police.

For some reason it had been decided that we should eat by candlelight that evening. Candlelight is supposed to be intimate and chummy. It wasn't in that bare, dyspeptically modern room. The cones of flickering light illumined faces with an eerie glow.

It was one of Lorraine's most elaborate dinners, but that didn't help. Strangely enough, in spite of the myriad crosscurrents of tension, it was the hostility between Lorraine and Mimi that dominated the room. It wasn't anything they said. In fact, they hardly spoke to each other. But every now and then Lorraine would glance across the table at Mimi, and the candle flames would catch an ominous gleam in her eyes. Mimi was less transparent. The soft light was flattering to her. In the low cut maroon gown with the Merovingian sleeves and the white rose at her bosom, she looked almost as picturesque as she thought she did. She took birdlike pecks at her food, stopping occasionally to caress the rose. But there was a smugness about her that could not be missed—a sort of inward triumph.

I assumed it all had something to do with Chuck Dawson, but I didn't understand. Mimi's relationship with Chuck was beyond my comprehension.

I glanced at Lover to see whether I could get a clue from him. But he was bumbling unimaginatively through his dinner. He didn't seem to be noticing anything.

After dinner Lover and I told Lorraine we wanted to talk to her alone, and she took us into a small room off the library which I had never seen before. It was very French, with an Aubusson rug, yellow brocade chairs, and a lot of good Sèvres china. A fire was burning on the hearth. One of Lorraine's better interior decorators must have thought it up.

Lorraine pulled one of the yellow chairs to the fire and sat down. She looked rather wonderful, with her small, quick hands, her tousled hair, and her black raspberry gown. There was an elegance about her that went with the room.

Lover sat down on a couch looking plump and pontifical. I stood by Lorraine at the fire.

"Well, darlings," she said. "What is it?"

I had a feeling this was going to be difficult. From the beginning Lorraine had given a superb imitation of an ostrich. I didn't blame her for it. It was just that she had too much money. There had always been Mr. Throckmorton and his minions to keep her from making contact with a world where anything as ugly as murder could flourish. Having to tell her there was a murderer in her house was like having to tell a princess in a fairy story that her godmother's magic wand was on the blink, and that the toad, instead of turning into a prince as scheduled, would have to go on being a toad.

To my surprise, however, when I started talking about the station wagon, Lorraine took the end of the sentence right out of my mouth.

"You're trying to tell me someone filed through the brake cable. I know. I realized that myself right away. I'd had the wagon's brakes overhauled only a week ago." The firelight played over her pale, piquant face. "I may seem a fool, darling. But I'm not that much of a fool. Someone tried to murder Fleur this evening." She looked up. "That means Dorothy and Janet were murdered too—in spite of everything. That frightful Count Laguno was right all along. You're going to call the police, aren't you? That's why you brought me in here to break the news gently as if I was a nasty old beridden woman with a bedjacket and a pink satin boudoir cap."

I said, "I'm glad you're taking it this way, Lorraine."

"What way did you expect me to take it? I believed David and—and Chuck about Janet and Dorothy. Why shouldn't I? There wasn't anything to make me suspicious. But now—Peter, what is it? What's happening?" Her gaze flickered, pleading from me to her half-brother. "I invited them here. I invited their husbands. I suppose I was an idiot. But I had my reasons. I wanted everyone to be happy. I—I never dreamed—— Peter, I invited them here and—and they're dead——"

Her eyes were shadowed with fear. I went to her and took her arms. "Baby, it wasn't your fault."

She rose, drawing away from me, staring at me. "Peter, who is it? Who's doing this?"

"I only wish I knew."

Lover got up too. "Don't worry, Lorraine. I guess the police will find out. It's up to them now."

Lorraine said, "You're going to call them immediately?"

"The sooner the better," I said grimly. "You don't know what's going to happen next around here."

"If only Mr. Throckmorton hadn't been thrown off his plane!" Lorraine clutched my arm. "Peter, darling, please wait till Chuck gets back from Reno. He should be here any minute."

His voice tinged with hostility, Lover said, "Why should we wait for Chuck? You admitted yourself he was one of the ones who's been trying to hush this up."

"I didn't say that." Lorraine swung round to me. "He's implying Chuck deliberately kept the police from knowing. That isn't true, is it?"

"Not necessarily," I said. "He just followed Wyckoff's lead. Wyckoff's the one who started the hush-hush. And he admits now that he was mistaken. He admits Dorothy was probably poisoned. He's going to ask for an autopsy." And then, because I could see from her eyes that she loved Chuck very much and that it would kill her to have to be suspicious of him, I added, "Don't worry about Chuck. You know him better than any of us. You know what he would and wouldn't do."

Lorraine turned back to her half-brother. "Lover—that ghastly name! Why do I call you Lover? Walter's the name mother gave you. It's a good enough name. Walter, please wait for Chuck to come back."

Lover shuffled and looked at me. "Well——"

"Please." Lorraine crossed to him. "Walter, don't you see? You've never been rich. Oh, I know it must be tough having me your sister and one of the richest girls in the world. But I am just that and it means I'm news. Everything that ever happens to me gets plastered over every scandal sheet in the world. Think what it's going to be for me—going everywhere for the rest of my life with people staring at me and whispering, 'There's Lorraine Pleygel. My dear, I've always wondered about those women who were murdered at her house. You know, they say. . . .' Chuck knows all the policemen in Nevada. If he called them, talked to them, they'd be more sympathetic. They'd try and help me, see things weren't blasted all over the front pages. Don't you see?"

Lover gave her hand a clumsy pat. "I guess it's all right to wait for Chuck, isn't it?"

"Sure," I said.

"Thank you, dears. Thank you so much."

Lorraine took a cigarette from a small cloisonné box and lit it. She moved back to the fire. None of us spoke. As I looked at Lorraine's slim, elegant figure standing in front of the quivering flames, I started to think about her. I had known her and rather loved her for years, but she was still a mystery to me. Why, for one thing, had she never married? Since I had first known her, she'd been engaged at least five times and then something had always happened. Why? Was it her money? At the last moment had she always discovered that it was the Pleygel fortune rather than herself that had brought on the admirers? I wondered about Chuck, too, the elusive gambler about whom so little seemed to be known. That Lorraine was crazy about him, I was pretty sure. I had seen it just now in her eyes when she spoke of him.

But I had seen something else in her eyes, too. The specious little face of Mimi Burnett fluttered through my mind, Mimi with her white rose and her medieval gown, Mimi with her sickly sweet gushings over Lover and her sly glances at Chuck. Was Mimi the cause of that other look in Lorraine's eyes?

The fragile yellow room was very quiet. Then, from outside the window, I heard the throb of a car swinging up to the front door.

Lorraine stiffened. "That'll be Chuck now."

"Come on," said Lover. "Let's get him."

We all went out into the library. Laguno was sitting there, reading glumly. We hurried past him and out into the hall. The front door was ajar. Lorraine slipped through it. I came next, bumping against her as she stopped dead in her tracks.

I stared over her small frizzy head. Chuck's car was parked outside. But I had no time to look at it because Chuck and Mimi were standing in front of it. And Mimi was in Chuck's arms.

They were locked together in a close, passionate embrace.

Fourteen

CHUCK AND MIMI sprang apart. It was much too late. As usual, Chuck was wearing tight cowboy pants and a tartan lumber jacket, open at the neck. But all the customary swagger that went with them was gone. Mimi had the unexpected decency to be embarrassed, too. Her lips were half parted in something that was meant to be a dear-little-girl smile but which looked more like the snarl of a trapped weasel. The white rose was still at her bosom. It was crushed now. One of its petals slipped loose. We all of us, stupidly, watched it twirl to the ground.

All of us, that is, except Lorraine. She was watching Mimi. In spite of the frivolous curls, the frivolous face, the frivolous sweeping gown, there was a stillness about her that was impressive.

She said, "You can pack your things, Mimi. You'll be leaving immediately."

Her tone was magnificently contemptuous; she was a mistress firing a slatternly maid.

Lover had been staring at his fiancée and at Chuck with astounded incomprehension. Now, his plump chin quivering, he turned to Lorraine.

"There must be some—some explanation."

"Of course there's an explanation," said Lorraine. "If you hadn't been so infatuated, you'd have seen this coming on for days. She worked it so's she drove into Reno alone with Chuck that night we all went down. In the car she no doubt demonstrated how clinging and feminine she could be. Then she had him rhumbaing with her. That was to show how glamorous and sexy she could be. Then she started poking fun at me, pointing out how crazily I dressed. When Chuck kidded me out of wearing that swimming suit, for example, that wasn't his idea. It was Mimi. She was making him see how flighty I am, just to point up how artistic and otherworldly she is herself. Then, later on, she started cooing over him and getting him drinks when he was tired. That was to show what a lovely, lovely wife she could be. Slippers in front of the fire every night." She gave a weary shrug. "The whole thing's been so obvious it's made me sick."

Chuck was looking down at his feet. Mimi still didn't say anything. Lover, pitifully at sea, stammered, "But, Lorraine, she's—she's engaged to me."

Lorraine put her hand on his arm. "Dear, I haven't wanted to interfere in your life, haven't wanted to say anything. I suppose I was wrong as usual. You're so easy to fool—it's taking candy from a kid. Heaven knows where you picked her up. Las Vegas, wasn't it? Why do you imagine she got engaged to you? You're not exactly an Adonis, my poor dear. Don't you see? Because you were my half-brother, you looked like a good catch. But when you brought her here and she started to realize that the money hadn't been left to you, it was a different matter. And there was Chuck, the big-time gambler with his own club in Reno—a much more promising victim, even though he was engaged to me. Oh, the switch was done slyly, of course. You were kept on a string just in case."

Lover blinked. Lorraine turned to Mimi.

"You!" she said. "You with your Edna St. Vincent Millay, your 'Sonnets from the Portuguese,' your 'Lover picked me a white rose tonight'! Wherever you've gone, there've been fairies and pixies dancing in your wake. Phooey on the fairies and the pixies. Wherever you've gone, you've been a slut."

That was telling her. Mimi's face was as white as the crushed rose. She took half a step toward her fiancé. "Lover," she began.

Lover gave a weak smile. "I'm sure it's all right, Mimi. There's been a mistake. There must——"

Lorraine laughed. "You'd better make up with Lover, Mimi. I don't know how far you've gone with Chuck, but I'm afraid you're wasting your valuable time. In the first place, he hasn't a cent except what I've given him. In the second place, he's not in the market for wives."

She paused. We were all watching her. In a quiet voice that was almost a whisper, she added, "Chuck has been married to me for almost six months."

That set me back on my heels. Lover's mouth popped open. Mimi sagged in her maroon evening gown as if her knees had given way. Chuck, beads of sweat on his chiseled upper lip, exclaimed, "Lorraine——!"

Lorraine swung round to him. "What does it matter now? We were planning to tell Mr. Throckmorton anyway." She turned to me. "That's why I asked Mr. Throckmorton here. We were planning to tell him first because he's my guardian. Then we were going to announce the marriage and possibly have another wedding, a real wedding. And I asked all my schoolfriends here because I was so happy, because I thought being married was so nice and I wanted them to make up with their husbands and be happy too." She laughed suddenly. "That's funny now, isn't it? My schoolfriends aren't reconciled—they're dead. And my husband's been cheating on me before the marriage has even been announced."

Chuck's handsome face was agonized. He took a step toward her.

"Lorraine, baby, just listen———"

Lorraine ignored him and turned to Mimi. "I don't want a scene, Mimi. So please go at once. Pack up and go."

"Certainly I'm going," Mimi said primly. "I'm not going to stay in this house and be insulted—not another minute."

Trying to bring them all back to earth, I put in, "But we're going to call the police. When they hear what's been going on around here, I doubt whether they'll let anyone leave."

Mimi whipped round to me. "So you're all finally breaking down. You're admitting two of Lorraine's snooty guests have been murdered. Fine. All the more reason why I'm crazy to get out from under. If the police want me, and I can't imagine why they should, I'll leave an address. They'll be able to reach me."

Picking up her trailing skirt, she rustled past us, heading for the front door.

Lover started after her. "Mimi———"

She paused on the steps, throwing him a spiteful glance. "Any man who can stand and watch me insulted like that is no use to me. I'm through with you, too. Through.

T-h-r-o-u-g-h." She gave a harsh laugh. "And don't think it ain't been charming, Lover."

With that she swept into the house.

Lover hesitated a moment, clucking nervously. Then he turned on Lorraine. "My dear, I think you were very harsh with her, very unjust and inconsiderate." He trundled off into the house, calling, "Mimi, Mimi," like the tenor in the last act of *La Bohème*.

Chuck was paying no attention to Lover or Mimi or me. He was staring at Lorraine, his lips very tight. Suddenly he strode to her and put his husky arms around her. She struggled but he wouldn't let her go.

"Baby, I know it looks bad," he said hoarsely. "But I can explain. God knows, I should have explained the whole dirty business before. I——"

"What is there to explain?" I could tell that part of Lorraine wanted to stay there in his arms, that she was fighting not only him but herself. "You kissed Mimi. You can't explain that away. Not that one kiss and one Mimi matter. It's that you could waste your time playing around with a dreary little fake like that."

"But, Lorraine, just listen——"

"Oh, I understand now. I'd be a fool if I didn't. You said you wanted the marriage to be secret because you were poor and you'd be embarrassed to have people know you'd married Lorraine Pleygel. I believed you. I lent you that money to open the gambling club because you said you wanted to make a success of something on your own before we announced the marriage. Oh, you've made your success all right. But you're just the same as the others. You married me because you were after the Pleygel dollars. And you wanted to keep the marriage a secret so you could strut your stuff down at Chuck's Club, the attractive young buck of a bachelor with money to burn and no strings, the hick Lothario. Just how many of those Reno divorcees have been your Mimis?"

Chuck's eyes were flashing. "I love you, Lorraine. And you're the only one. I——"

Lorraine tugged herself free. "Don't lie to me. What's the use?"

"It isn't a lie."

She stood there, looking very wispy and pathetic. Her lips were trembling. She pulled out a frail black raspberry handkerchief and blew her nose.

"It'll never be the same," she faltered. "Never, never."

Quickly, her skirt swirling around her, she ran away from us up the steps into the house.

Chuck made no attempt to follow her. He just stood as if he'd been stunned. I was fairly stunned myself. How anyone in his right mind could have carried on with Mimi Burnett was hard enough to understand. That Chuck should have been doing so when he was the accepted husband of Lorraine was beyond the realm of belief.

My sympathy for him was not as deep as it might have been. Not without irony, I said, "Let me congratulate you on your marriage."

He started and stared at me. He gave a sickly grin.

"Women!" he said. "Whatever way you look at it, women are women."

After that penetrating observation, he seemed to have nothing more to say for himself.

Things had gone far away from the business in hand. Chuck's intricate love life might be important to him but it was not as important as the fact that we had two murders on our hands. I felt it was time to bring Lorraine's secret husband up to date on what had happened. Bluntly I told him of the attempt on Fleur's life which had happened while he was in Reno. I also told him that Wyckoff, Lover, and I were going to wrap the whole affair in wax paper and hand it to the police.

If I had hoped to shock him into some sort of guilty admission, I was doomed to be disappointed. When he heard Wyckoff was going to ask for an autopsy on Dorothy, he snapped, "Why in hell can't that guy make up his mind? He's the one who said she died of a heart attack. If I hadn't listened to him, I'd never——"

He paused, staring at me closely. "I've been a sucker. I've been kidding myself. I see that now. I figured something like murder just couldn't happen here, not here in this fancy house with Lorraine's fancy friends. I guess I was wrong."

"I guess you were," I said.

He whistled. "Dorothy, Janet, Fleur—what is it, Lieutenant? What's the racket?"

"You'll have to ask me something easier than that."

"You—you don't think there'll be any more of them, do you?"

"I'll be a lot happier when the police come," I said. I told him that Lorraine wanted him to be the one to call the police.

"Sure." He was brisk and competent now. "Inspector Craig's the guy. Smartest man they've got. A lot of pull with the press, too." He started toward the house. "Come on. We've wasted enough time already."

Chuck Dawson seemed to be an adaptable young man. Only that morning he had been the champion of the everything's-going-to-be-all-right school. Now he was screaming for action.

I followed him into the empty living-room, where he was talking into the telephone. He slammed the receiver down.

"Craig'll be up in about an hour and a half. I didn't tell him anything. Just said to come."

"Fine," I said.

He gave me another of his sickly grins. "And, Lieutenant,

I'd appreciate it if you didn't mention our marriage or this Mimi business to the police. For Lorraine's sake, I mean. Mimi didn't amount to a row of beans. I guess I'll go up now and put things right with the little woman."

He said that with a certain bravado. And yet, as I looked at his face, I wondered just how easy putting things right with the little woman was going to be.

Fifteen

THAT HUGE LIVING ROOM was as bleak as a morgue. The house was beginning to give me the jitters. Only two days ago we had been a reasonably gay party. Look at us now. Dorothy and Janet were dead. Bill Flanders and the Count were widowers. Fleur, having escaped death by a hair's breadth, was a patient under her husband's care. Lover, plain Walter French again, nursed a broken romance, while Lorraine, her secret marriage perilously close to the rocks, was probably shut up in her room refusing to listen to Chuck's so-called explanations. And here were Iris and I in the thick of it.

The casualty rate in that luxurious mansion was as high as the casualty rate on a stormed Pacific atoll.

Probably no naval lieutenant in history, I reflected, had dreamed up a worse way of spending a leave.

I poured myself a drink because I needed one, and started thinking about Iris. I had reached a stage where I worried if she was out of my sight. I was going to search for her when Bill Flanders hobbled in on his crutch. The ex-marine came up to me. He looked uneasy.

"Lieutenant, there's something I want to ask you. I—well, I happened to be out in the hall just now when Chuck called the police. They're coming tonight, aren't they?"

"Yes," I said. "They'll be here in about an hour."

He looked down at his boxer's hands. "I've been wondering. I mean, are they coming just on account of this accident of Fleur's this afternoon?"

There wasn't any point in keeping things dark any longer. "We're calling them," I said, "because someone tried to murder Fleur this afternoon and because someone did murder Dorothy and Janet."

That didn't seem to surprise him. "I guessed as much, Lieutenant. I figured Dorothy must have been murdered after all when that thing happened to Janet."

Arbiters of elegant behavior might have expected him to register shock at the fact that his wife had been murdered, but I knew Bill had been more than glad to see the end of Dorothy and he knew I knew. We understood each other on that point at least.

"I've been thinking," he said suddenly. "That crazy will Janet made leaving all her dough to me, you've got it, haven't you?"

"Yes," I said, wondering.

"I don't like it." His voice was gruff. "She didn't hardly know me. She just left me everything on a kind of fancy. I don't feel I've got a right to it. Lieutenant, I want you to do me a favor. I want you to tear that will up and forget it."

"Tear it up? Bill, I can't tear it up. Janet left it to me in trust."

He stared at me stubbornly. "I don't want her dough."

"Listen, Bill, you're crazy to feel that way. Janet left you her estate because she wanted to make up to you for what Dorothy had done and because she didn't want her own husband to get it. If I tore up that will, Laguno would inherit the whole works. Do you imagine Janet would have liked that?"

He smiled faintly. "I guess she wouldn't—not much." The smile faded. "But it's a ritzy woman's dress shop she had, wasn't it? Lieutenant, I can't go fooling around in a woman's dress shop."

"You can sell it. It's quite a place. What with it and the rest of the money, you stand to be comfortably off for life." I glanced down at the flapping end of trouser where his leg should have been. "It's not going to be easy for you to get a job—not to begin with. Don't be a sucker. Take what's coming to you. And if you find yourself getting too high-minded, you can always endow a home for superannuated welterweights or anything you like."

He seemed puzzled. He stared at me and then shook his head. "Well, I guess—if it's that way, I'm sorry. Sorry I brought it up. Forget it."

He turned on his crutch and started limping away.

I called, "Seen my wife, Bill?"

"Yeah. She's in the library—reading."

I hurried past him into the hall. As I did so, I saw Chuck Dawson stalking down the stairs. His face was dark and stormy. He reached me and I said, "So Lorraine isn't listening to explanations yet, eh?"

He didn't say anything. He just scowled, swung past me to the front door, and went out, slamming the door behind him.

Iris was alone in the library, sitting under a fan light, a ponderous tome on her lap. She put it down when she saw me, stood up and came toward me. Just walking across a room, she could do something to you. No wonder Hollywood and Mr. Finkelstein had made a star out of her.

"Peter, whatever's been happening? Everyone's been running upstairs looking sour. Mimi, then Lover, then Lorraine, then Chuck."

"Plenty's happened," I said.

"You called the police?"

"Yes. They'll be here fairly soon. What have you been reading?"

"Oh, I've been trying to find out some more about curare. I'm sure the whole solution lies in that beginning thing. If only we could once get it straight how Dorothy was poisoned, I think the rest of it might make some sense." My wife shrugged dispiritedly. "I haven't been getting anywhere, though."

"There's no need to get anywhere any more, honey. It'll be up to the police now."

"I know." My wife didn't look particularly pleased. "It'll be a relief having them here. There won't be that feeling of danger. But, Peter, I guess I have a tidy mind. I hate leaving things in midstream."

She looked so earnest that I bent and kissed her. "Iris Duluth, the glamorous Hollywood sleuth now under contract to Magnificent Pictures."

"Peter, don't make fun of me. It just makes me mad having people murdered to left and right and not being able to figure out why. We've got Dorothy's glove with the smear of curare on it. I've been thinking about those gloves and they're leather, darling. I don't believe she could have pricked her finger through them. They're too tough. That means the glove must have been smeared when she put them away in her pocketbook. But we've got the pocketbook and there's no curare in it. If the bag was fixed as a poison trap then someone must have gotten at it later and taken the trap out. But then anyone could have gotten at the pocketbook after Dorothy died." Iris looked indignant. "Oh, dear, it's all so exasperating."

She was right about the poison trap. Wyckoff had made that plain. An autopsy was not going to be enough to prove that Dorothy had been poisoned with curare. And if they couldn't prove that Dorothy was poisoned, they were going to have a tough time proving that Janet's death wasn't accidental.

My wife tossed her dark hair defiantly. "Peter, if I don't find out how Dorothy was poisoned, I'm going to become frustrated and my neck's going to shrivel. You wouldn't like that, would you?"

"No," I said.

"Then don't give up just because the police are coming. Go on helping me. And, to begin with, tell me what's been going on." She sighed. "It isn't fair. You get in on everything. I'm always left out."

"All right, honey. I'll tell you everything, on one condition."

"What's that?"

"That we get out of this grisly library and go upstairs to our room where I can kiss you whenever I feel so disposed."

Iris slipped her hand into mine and we moved out into the hall. It was deserted. Once the house had been too full of people. Now Iris and I seemed to have it to ourselves.

As we started up the great stairs, however, the figure of Mimi Burnett appeared, hurrying down from the second floor. She wore a ratty fur wrap over the medieval gown. She was carrying a suitcase.

When she came to us, her little black eyes fixed on me coldly. "I'm taking Chuck's car. If anybody wants me, I'll be at the Riverview in Reno."

She swished past us and hurried out of the front door, leaving it open. Iris stared after her.

"What on earth is she doing?"

"That's one of the things I'm going to tell you," I said.

We reached our room and flopped down on the beds. Everything else in the room was too angular and modernistic for comfort. I gave my wife a colorful account of my brief encounter with Bill Flanders over Janet's will.

"That's the works," I concluded, "except that Chuck's got an Inspector Craig coming up. Apparently he's a good man and he'll try to keep things quiet—if anybody can keep three murders quiet."

Iris was lying on her bed, her head propped on her arm, staring at me solemnly. "I never dreamed Lorraine was married to Chuck. He's just the sort of man with muscles and things that heiresses always seem to marry. But why on earth have they been keeping it secret?"

"It seems to have been Chuck's idea. He didn't want the world to know he'd married Lorraine without a cent to his name. Lorraine lent him the money to open the club. They were waiting for it to be a success. Then Chuck could appear in print as the wealthy Nevada businessman or what have you."

"But surely the Club must be successful enough by now. It's been coining money for a long time."

"That's it. They were all set to announce the marriage, anyway. That's why Lorraine asked the mythical Mr. Throckmorton to come. She was going to let him be the first to know and give his guardian's blessing. Incidentally, that's why she lugged us here and the Lagunos and the Flanders and the Wyckoffs. She wanted to reconcile them all and to have everybody happy to celebrate her own wedding."

Iris smiled wryly. "Poor Lorraine, things didn't pan out, did they?"

"Not exactly."

"But it's Mimi I don't understand, darling. Why on earth would Chuck fool around with a little fake like Mimi just now of all times when the marriage was going to be announced? I'm a woman. Maybe I don't know about these things. But is Mimi the sort of heady siren that makes men forget love, honor, and the Pleygel millions?"

"So far as I'm concerned, she wouldn't make me forget a five-cent candy bar."

"Then what was her strange power over Chuck?"

"Exactly," I said.

Iris' gaze started to rove aimlessly around the room. It concentrated on the dressing table. "Peter!" she exclaimed.

"What is it?"

My wife jumped off the bed and started running around the room, inspecting the dressing table and then the highboy. She came back to me.

"Peter, someone's searched this room."

"Searched it?"

"Yes. Things have been moved around on the dressing table. I always keep that perfume bottle on the left and—then the drawers in the highboy. I left them all shut, I know. Look, two of them are a little open. You haven't been in here since dinner, have you?"

"No."

"Then it has been searched."

I got up. "Anything missing?"

"I'll be able to find out in a minute."

Iris made a feverish search of our belongings. "No, darling. Nothing's gone. I've looked everywhere except the locked drawer."

"The locked drawer?"

"Where I keep my piggy bank. Where we put Janet's will. I've got Dorothy's bag in there, too."

Iris scrambled around in her pocketbook for a key and unlocked the drawer of the dressing table. I hurried to her side.

Everything was there. The blue piggy bank leered fatly up at us. Lying beside it was Dorothy's silver pocketbook and a folded piece of paper which I recognized as Janet's will.

Iris looked up excitedly. "Peter, it must have been the will or the pocketbook they were after. They must have been in too much of a hurry to risk breaking the lock. Lucky I locked it, isn't it?"

I was thinking. "No one knew we had Dorothy's pocketbook except possibly Wyckoff. I can't see any possible reason why he should try and steal it. It must be the will."

"Bill Flanders," said Iris. "Maybe Bill came up here hoping to be able to destroy the will himself. And then, when he couldn't get at it, he went to you."

"Or Laguno. If this will was out of the way, he'd inherit under the old one. I wouldn't put anything past that man." I bent and picked up the will and the pocketbook, putting them on the top of the highboy. "In any case, whoever tried once will probably try again. They're much too dangerous, both of them, to keep in a drawer with a ten-cent lock. As soon as the police come, we're going to turn both these little items over to them."

Iris looked meek. "I guess you're right."

She pressed the clasp of the pocketbook, springing its mouth open so we could see its interior. She pulled out Dorothy's gloves, and then stared at the little hoard of roulette chips. She smoothed out the right-hand glove, revealing the reddish smear on the middle finger. Suddenly she gave a disgruntled exclamation, picked up one of the chips, and fled into the bathroom.

"What on earth——"

I heard the sound of running water. Then my wife appeared again. She held the chip in one hand and a white face towel in the other. She brandished the towel at me miserably.

"Look, Peter."

I looked at the towel. Scrawled across the white linen was a reddish stain, very like the stain on the glove.

"Darling," she said, "and I was so sure that was curare on the glove!"

"But what——?" I began, fuddled.

"Look at the color of these roulette chips—reddish brown, the same color as the curare. They're made of cheap stuff. I just poured water on this chip in the bathroom and wiped the towel on it. Don't you see? One of the chips Dorothy played with at Chuck's must have been wet. That's how she got the stain on her glove. It isn't curare—it's dye."

She sank down on the edge of the bed. "Oh, Peter, there goes everything. We're back where we started from. The autopsy won't be able to prove Dorothy was killed with curare. The station wagon will probably be so burnt up they won't be able to prove the brake cable was filed through. There was never anything to show that Janet was murdered, anyway. The police will come. But what will we be able to prove? Just that three people had three accidents and that it's all very suspicious. That's all. No evidence of murder. Nothing. Darling, you may be a hero in the Pacific. I may be a movie star in Hollywood. But as detectives, we're—from hunger."

She was right as usual. The stain on the glove was about the only tangible thing we had to show the police. Unless something definite could be proved somehow, Inspector Craig would be just as stymied as we were.

I didn't care about it as much as Iris did. She had the detective bug worse than I. All I wanted right then was to be able to take her away from this plague-ridden spot and snatch a few days of peace with her before I had to return to my ship. That's the way it is with leaves. In the first days, I felt I had all the time in the world, time enough to dabble around in other people's mysteries. Now I was thinking in terms of having to be gone. Time was infinitely precious. I was grudging every second that wasn't a second with Iris.

I dropped down on the bed next to her. "Don't get churned up about it, honey. Let them all murder each other. Who cares?"

I started kissing her. It didn't take me long to forget that anybody had any problems. But at last Iris drew away from me.

"Darling, Inspector Craig will be here any minute." She got up and moved to the window. "We'll be able to hear his car coming if we stay here and listen."

I joined her, slipping my arm around her waist. Our window looked out rather unromantically on the garages, which were built in a neat white row beyond the front entrance of the mansion. The Nevada moon was shining brightly in a bare blue sky.

I stared down at the garages. The sliding door of one of them was half open, and a small pale object lying on the gravel outside caught my eye. As I glanced at it, a gust of wind lifted it and sent it skittering across the yard. It came to rest in a square of light from a downstairs window, and I saw that it was a woman's stocking.

Iris said, "A stocking. It came from the garage."

I looked back to the open garage door. Inside, dimly visible, was a low convertible coupé. I recognized its lines. "Iris, isn't that Chuck's car in the garage?"

"I think it is." Iris stared at me. "But Mimi said she was going to take it."

"She must have taken one of Lorraine's instead. But, come to think of it, I never heard a car backing out of the garages, did you?"

"No, I didn't. We would surely have heard it from here too. But, Peter, Mimi can't have been hanging around in the garage all this time. Maybe she decided not to go."

"It wasn't up to her to decide whether to stay or go. Lorraine threw her out. And the stocking! What's that stocking doing there?"

My wife and I stared at each other. I crossed to the highboy, picked up the will and Dorothy's pocketbook, and locked them back in the drawer of the dressing table with the piggy bank. I tossed the key to my wife.

"Come on," I said.

We left the room, locking the door behind us for good measure. As we started down the deserted passage, the door of Chuck's room opened. Chuck and Lover came out.

We went up to them. I said to Lover, "Did you talk Lorraine into letting Mimi stay?"

Lover looked distracted. "Why, no. I tried to talk to Mimi and then to Lorraine. They wouldn't listen to me, either of them. It's so unfortunate. I've been speaking to Chuck. He assures me there was nothing between him and Mimi, nothing at all. It's just that Mimi's such an affectionate child and——"

I broke into his maunderings. "Chuck, Mimi was driving your car into Reno, wasn't she?"

Lorraine's husband returned my stare defiantly. "Why not? She had to get there somehow."

Iris' hand pulled me urgently forward. "Come on, Peter."

While the two men watched us in perplexity, we hurried to the stairs and down into the empty hall. I swung open the big front door. We ran out into the drive and around under a high white arch back toward the garages.

The stocking was still lying, small and forlorn, near the house. Iris ran to pick it up. I hurried over to the half open garage door. Something was lying across the threshold of the garage. I almost stumbled over it, and as I veered sideways to avoid it, I saw that it was a suitcase. Its lid was open and its contents spilled out of it in a tumbled mess.

Iris' voice sounded. "It's a perfectly good stocking, darling. It must be Mimi's."

"It is," I said. "Her suitcase is here. It's been opened and searched."

My wife joined me. I stepped over the suitcase into the dark interior of the garage. I could just make out a light switch on the wall. I turned it on.

Behind me Iris gave a little broken cry.

I felt far from steady myself.

Mimi Burnett was sprawled beside Chuck's green coupé on the bare stone of the garage floor. The fur wrap splayed out from her shoulders like the wings of a dead bat. The medieval gown was crumpled and askew, and her head was lying in a pool of blood.

There was a rock with a jagged, bloodstained edge right there on the floor by her side. It was only too obvious for what purpose it had been used.

Shakily I dropped to my knees and bent over her. Her eyes stared blindly. Her lips, elfin no longer, were drawn back in a meaningless smirk.

I glanced up into my wife's haunted face.

"Peter," she whispered, "is—is she——"

"Yes," I said. "That's exactly what she is. Mimi's dead. It looks as if the era of accidents is over. This time it's murder, plain, honest-to-goodness murder with no question about it at all."

Part Five

LORRAINE

Sixteen

THAT THOUGHT nagged at me like an abscess as we stood in the starkly lighted garage. The rock which had crushed Mimi's skull was lying by her side for all the world to see. There had been no attempt to conceal the fact that her suitcase had been rifled. Dorothy . . . Janet . . . Fleur . . . Mimi. . . . Four of the six women in the Pleygel mansion had been murderously attacked in three days. The sequence of deaths was hurtling on with ever growing momentum. But that wasn't the worst part.

The worst part was that the murderer had come out into the open at last. He didn't care any more who knew that he had killed three women, tried to kill a fourth, and was probably planning to kill more. He was shouting it from the housetops.

That was what made the whole thing so terrible—and so mad.

Iris was standing close to me, not saying anything. I put my arm around her. There was something ominous about Mimi Burnett's dead, smirking face staring up from the oil-stained floor, something ominous about the dank smell of axle-grease and dust.

In a voice that sounded jarringly loud, my wife said, "Mimi dead! Peter, isn't it ever going to stop?"

That's what I was thinking, too. Even before Mimi's death, it had been impossible to find any reasonable motive to cover all the crimes. Now the whole picture had become as wild as a madman's dream. There would surely be no pattern to a holocaust that involved killing Dorothy, Janet, Fleur, and Mimi unless it was the pattern of a homicidal maniac intent upon snuffing out all the women in our party.

Lorraine and Iris were the only two as yet unscathed. From that moment on, I had but one modest ambition—to keep my wife alive.

"At least we won't have to call the police," Iris was saying. "Inspector Craig must be almost here."

As she spoke, I noticed for the first time that my toe was nudging against something on the floor. I bent to pick it up. It was a small, leather-bound book with arty gilt lettering. I read the gilt lettering which said, *Selected Poems of Edna St. Vincent Millay.* I had always thought of Mimi's poetry reading as just another aspect of her fake intellectual pose, but there was something pitiful about that book now. Poor Mimi, she no longer needed the spiritual uplift which Miss Millay could provide.

I slipped the book into my pocket.

My wife turned to the suitcase which lay by the open door. She was bending over it. I joined her.

"Don't touch anything. We've got to leave it for the police."

"I know." My wife threw a glance over her shoulder at Mimi. "We won't have any trouble now convincing Inspector Craig that there's a murderer on the loose."

"Exactly," I said.

Women are funny people. I who had lived and eaten and slept with death in the Pacific was still horribly conscious of Mimi Burnett's body lying there behind us. I wanted to get away from it. But my wife, now that the first shock was over, seemed to be taking the realistic point of view that what was done could not be undone, and the presence of a corpse did not feaze her. She was staring at the suitcase in a businesslike manner.

"It's maddening not being able to touch things. Whoever killed Mimi obviously wanted something she had in her suitcase. If only we could find out what it was, then maybe we could make some sense out of this. Maybe we could link it up with Fleur, Janet, and Dorothy."

I wished Inspector Craig would hurry up and come. "You can't link anything up with anything," I said morosely. "And you can't expect any sense from a maniac. Someone's crazy and someone's killing women. Let's leave it at that and hope to heaven he won't get the chummy idea of killing you."

"Nonsense." Even in the brash light from the bald ceiling bulb Iris looked lovely enough for a publicity still. "I don't believe in maniacs who manage to masquerade as normal people twenty-three hours out of the twenty-four. They only come in books. Be reasonable. Someone in the house must have done it. We know that. And we know them all. Frauds and phonies they may be, but which of them could possibly be a maniac?"

"I wouldn't put anything past any of them."

"I suppose you think that, come sunset, Lover transmogrifies himself into a plump werewolf, or little Fleur Wyckoff's teeth sharpen and start quivering for jugular veins. No, Peter, you can't shrug it off as easily as that. Some one person made four deliberate attacks for a very deliberate reason. It all seems idiot fringe to us simply because we haven't stumbled on that reason yet."

Iris was still beating the same old gong. Nothing seemed to discourage her. She turned to me. "Peter," she began.

"What?" I said.

"I was just thinking. Now Mimi's dead, the course of true love should run quite a lot smoother for Chuck and Lorraine." She broke off and I felt her hand on my arm.

"Listen," she breathed, "someone's out there in the yard."

We stood perfectly still. Trailing in from the darkness outside came the soft crunch of footsteps on gravel. At first I supposed it was Chuck or Lover coming from the house to see what had happened to us. Then I realized that the footsteps were not coming from the front door. They were approaching from the other direction.

Someone was slipping in from the garden.

I was in a condition then to sense danger in everything. Whispering to Iris not to move, I stepped out into the yard. The moonlight was strong enough for me to make out the stooped figure of David Wyckoff hurrying toward the arch which led to the front door.

I don't know what I had expected, but the sight of Wyckoff allayed my undefined fears. Of all Lorraine's heterogeneous guests he was the one I trusted most. Sooner or later he'd have to know about Mimi. He might as well know right now.

I called, "Hey, Wyckoff!"

He sprang round, peering through the darkness.

"Who is it? Is it you, Lieutenant?" He started toward me. "Fleur's asleep. I thought I'd take a little exercise while I had the chance. D'you want anything?"

"Yes," I said grimly. "I've got something to show you."

He came up to me. I could make out his eyes, faintly questioning. I turned into the garage. He followed, almost stumbling over Mimi's suitcase.

"Watch out," I said. "Don't disturb anything."

Wyckoff blinked at the light. He shot Iris a mechanical smile. Then the smile faded as he saw Mimi.

"My God!" he said.

It hadn't been fair, throwing him into it cold like that, but he took it on the chin. He did not say anything else. Very much the doctor, he dropped to his knees at Mimi's side. He didn't even touch her. I suppose he didn't have to. At length he looked up, his face bleak.

"She's dead," he said. "But I guess you know that already. This thing—isn't it ever going to stop?"

He had said exactly what Iris had said.

What else was there to say?

He got up. He glanced at the suitcase and then at me. I couldn't tell what he was thinking. He didn't have that kind of a face. In the methodical manner in which he might have extracted a patient's case history, he started to question us on the few facts we knew. I was still outlining the details when we heard the sound of a car coming up the drive toward the house.

Excitedly Iris cut in. "That'll be Inspector Craig at last."

I glanced quizzically at Wyckoff. "The whole thing's going to break now, you know. You're going to ask for an autopsy on Dorothy, aren't you?"

His mouth was grim. "Yes."

"And you've got your story straight? You think you'll be able to make your original diagnosis seem plausible enough to keep you out of trouble?"

"I hope so." I could tell that he was steeling himself for the difficult ordeal that lay ahead. "You two had better stay here. I'll go and bring Craig over. After all, Dorothy's old history." He glanced down at Mimi. "This is what's going to interest the police right now."

He hurried off to intercept the approaching car before it reached the front door.

Iris looked thoughtful. "You're not going to tell the police anything about Wyckoff's affair with Dorothy, or Fleur's stealing that letter?"

"I promised I wouldn't," I said. "Wyckoff obviously thought Fleur killed Dorothy and Fleur obviously thought Wyckoff did. I still think that cancels them both out.

They've had a tough enough time, both of them. We can at least spare them something."

"I guess you're right," said Iris noncommittally.

Soon Wyckoff reappeared with a short, brisk figure moving at his side. Apparently Inspector Craig had come alone. They joined us outside the garage. I could see something of Inspector Craig in the moonlight. He seemed youngish, with steady eyes.

"Dr. Wyckoff here tells me a woman has been murdered since Chuck Dawson called me," he said. "You two discovered the body?"

"Yes." I introduced myself and then Iris. Craig's eyes moved appraisingly over my wife.

"Iris Duluth," he said. "I've seen you in the movies. Good, too. Delicate thing for a movie actress getting mixed up in murder. We'll have to do our best to keep your name out of this as much as possible."

Iris said impetuously, "I don't care about my movie career. I'm bored with Hollywood, anyway. I'm only interested in getting this thing solved. My husband and I helped on some murder cases in the East and we've done a little investigation on this already. We've got quite a lot to tell you."

It seemed to me that a faintly sardonic smile passed over the Inspector's face as he watched my wife.

"Well, well." He turned to me and jerked his head toward the garage. "Wyckoff tells me nothing has been touched in there?"

"No," I said.

Craig started toward the garage door with Wyckoff behind him. He said over his shoulder, "Don't go, you two. I'll want to talk to you later."

The two men disappeared into the garage. They were gone quite a while. We could hear them speak to each other every now and then, but most of the time Craig seemed to prefer to work in silence. There was a telephone in the garage. There was a telephone in every room, nook, and cranny of Lorraine's mad house. At length I heard the Inspector using it. He was calling to have his regular homicide squad come up—and quickly.

After that, he and Wyckoff emerged again into the white Nevada moonlight.

The garage padlock was hanging on its metal catch. Craig pushed the door shut and snapped the lock, pocketing the key. He was obviously a man of few words and, equally obviously, he was not going to waste them. He said nothing about what he had or had not observed from his examination of Mimi's body. He turned to us, the steady eyes watching both our faces intently.

"I understand from the Reno police that a woman in Miss Pleygel's party died of a heart attack at the Del Monte two days ago. I also know from the Genoa City police that another woman was drowned here in the pool last night. I wasn't exactly surprised when Chuck Dawson called."

He just threw that out flatly, leaving the rest up to us.

Wyckoff blurted, "The woman at the Del Monte was a patient of mine in San Francisco. She had a—a serious heart condition. I was the one who diagnosed her death as heart failure. At the time it seemed logical enough, but I am no longer satisfied with my own diagnosis, particularly since Lieutenant Duluth here——" He was not doing a very good job with his apologia. "It's our belief now that Dorothy Flanders was poisoned. There's some reason to think curare was used. That's why Dawson called you."

Inspector Craig just stood there without offering any comment.

Iris, looking eager and enthusiastic, broke in. "We think Dorothy Flanders was murdered by some sort of poison trap fixed in her pocketbook. We have her pocketbook and some other things for you upstairs."

Once again I traced a distinctly sardonic expression on Craig's face. Very quietly he said, "If you had all these suspicions, it seems to me you might have come out with them before. Presumably you believe that Mrs. Laguno was murdered, too. There was an inquest on her this morning. No one from here seemed to quarrel with the verdict of accidental death."

"We didn't say anything because we weren't sure," I explained. "Both the deaths looked innocent enough. We had nothing to go on except our suspicions."

"That is," said Iris, "until this afternoon."

With a slight lift to his voice the Inspector said, "And what happened this afternoon?"

Wyckoff told Craig about the insane episode of Fleur and the station wagon.

The Inspector permitted himself the luxury of a comment. He gave a little grunt and murmured, "You certainly have been getting yourselves a time around here." His voice became blunt and impersonal again. "Well, we won't be able to take a look at that station wagon until morning. My men should be here pretty soon, but meanwhile—we'd better get in the house and see what we can find out about Miss Burnett." He glanced at Iris. "You say you have Mrs. Flanders' pocketbook and some other things? P'raps you'd be good enough to get them."

I said, "There's something else, too. Some Indian blow darts tipped with curare. Miss Pleygel has them in her trophy room. We think one of the darts has been tampered with. We'd like you to see them."

The Inspector looked at me with something akin to approval. "You seem to be keeping your eyes open, Lieutenant. Guess we'll take in those darts before we do anything else."

The four of us crossed the gravel yard, navigated the white stone arch, and headed toward the great front door.

No one in the house seemed to have heard the Inspector's arrival. The columned porch was deserted. So was the wide, unfriendly hall.

When we reached it, Iris started for the stairs to get the things from our room. As I watched her small figure being swallowed up by the vast staircase, I felt an absurd fear for her.

I said to Wyckoff, "Go with her, will you? I don't fancy the idea of her running around alone in this house."

Wyckoff gave me a brief, understanding smile.

"And while you're about it," I added, "the Inspector will want to see everyone, I guess. Lorraine's in her room—at least, I think she is. You might tell her that the police have come."

"Yes, Doctor." Craig was watching Wyckoff. "And I'd like to speak to your wife, too."

Some of the old wariness had slid into Wyckoff's eyes. Rather stiffly he said, "As my wife's physician I am afraid I must refuse to let anyone talk to her tonight. She's had a very bad shock."

The Inspector was still watching him. He gave a shrug. "Okay. Then that'll have to wait until tomorrow morning."

Wyckoff started up the stairs after Iris.

I led Inspector Craig to the trophy room. It, too, was empty. The house seemed to be as dead as those dead animals looking down at us from the walls. While elephants and alligators and zebras and the repellent portrait doll of Lorraine watched us glassily, I showed the Inspector the trophy cabinet that housed the three fan-groups of darts. I told him of the sixth dart which had been missing from the third group and had then reappeared. I pointed out the dart whose tip seemed to have been covered with some substance slightly different in color from the others. The glass top of the cabinet was locked. We would have to get the key from Lorraine before we could make a closer examination.

Craig was bending over the cabinet. It was the first time I had a chance to see him in a full light. He looked no more than thirty, with blunt, sensible features. I had been right about his eyes. They were the steadiest I had ever seen. Every now and then, as he stared at the darts, he blinked, but there was nothing indecisive about the blink. His lids flicked up and down as though with each flick some mental cash register recorded another observation.

"Doc Brown will be up with the boys," he said. "I'll have him take all the darts down for analysis. We'll know soon enough whether you've got anything here." He looked up at me. "You're certainly on the beam, Lieutenant. I'd appreciate it if you'd go along with me in this for a while. I think you'll be useful."

Preening myself somewhat, I said, "My wife and I will be glad to help all we can."

Inspector Craig smiled. It was a disturbing smile. "You," he said, "not your wife. I've no doubt she's a right smart girl. But she's a woman. I tell you frankly, Lieutenant, I don't go for women meddling around in men's jobs."

He said that amicably enough, but I could sense in him a stubbornness that rivaled that of my wife. I was glad that he was old-fashioned enough to think of Iris as an ornament rather than a detective asset. From now on, any kind of sleuthing was going to be dangerous. I welcomed the Inspector as an ally in my campaign for preserving my wife.

Craig was staring with slightly awed astonishment at the Lorraine doll when Iris and Wyckoff came in. My wife announced that Lorraine would be down and gave the Inspector Dorothy's pocketbook and Janet's last minute will.

It was not without satisfaction that I explained to Craig the unattractive role that Count Laguno had played in the activities to date. Iris, Wyckoff, and I let the Inspector know pretty much everything we knew about everything and everybody involved. We steered clear of Wyckoff's entanglement with Dorothy, however, and I made no mention of Chuck's marriage to Lorraine or of Lorraine's scene with Mimi on the front steps. I had promised Chuck to leave his marital explanations up to him. It would all be bound to come out soon enough anyway.

The Inspector listened quietly. It was a picture complex enough to make the soberest brain reel, but Craig took it in his stride—as if the seemingly motiveless murder of three women with an attack on a fourth was something that happened every day in Nevada.

All he said was, "This Mimi Burnett was engaged then to Miss Pleygel's half brother?"

"Yes," I said.

"Know where she came from or anything about her?"

"Nothing much. He met her in Las Vegas, I think."

The Inspector nodded. "Apart from Miss Pleygel and Mrs. Wyckoff and you three, there are four other guests in the house—Chuck Dawson, Miss Pleygel's half brother, Mr. Flanders, and this Count Laguno?"

"That's right."

"Where are they?"

"Around somewhere," said Wyckoff. "Must be. They're not upstairs."

"All right." Inspector Craig slipped Dorothy's purse under his arm and Janet's will into his pocket. "I'm ready to see them now. I guess they don't know about Miss Burnett's death—that is, I mean, none of you told them?"

I looked at Wyckoff. He shook his head. "No," he said. "We haven't told them."

"Well," said the Inspector, "there's one person in the house who didn't need any telling. It's up to us to find him —or her."

Saying it like that, he made it sound as simple as picking a needle up from the floor.

But, as far as I was concerned, the needle was still very deep in the haystack.

Seventeen

WE FOUND the four men in the library. They had put up a card table in the middle of the huge Aubusson carpet and were playing bridge. Under the circumstances it seemed an incongruous thing to be doing, and they made an incongruous foursome. The Count was leaning over his cards, sharp-eyed, like the kind of citizen one used to be warned against on transatlantic crossings. Bill Flanders, his crutch propped against his chair, showed sulky disinterest, while Chuck and Lover had the grim determination of people who were forcing themselves to keep from thinking about other and unpleasant things.

They were concentrating so intently upon having a bad time that our presence wasn't noticed until Inspector Craig gave a fromidable snort. Chuck, Lover, and Laguno sprang up, leaving Flanders at the table. With a poor imitation of a smile, Chuck strode over to us and pumped the Inspector's hand.

"Glad you got here, Craig."

The Inspector's bright gaze held Chuck under close scrutiny. "Quite startling news I hear about you in Reno, Chuck. So you've sold your club to Jack Fetter and his outfit."

That came out so smoothly that for a second I did not grasp it. An awkward flush deepened the tan of Chuck's handsome face. He looked like a boxer who had received a punch where he least expected it.

"News certainly travels fast," he said lamely.

"It's all over town. Fetter'd been trying to buy you out ever since you opened up, and now you suddenly decided to sell—quick like a bunny." The Inspector shrugged. "Cash sale, I understand, too. That's a lot of cash. But I guess you're right keeping any deal with Fetter on a cash basis."

"Yeah." Chuck was looking down at his feet. "I was cleaning up okay but—what the hell? A guy gets tired of being tied down. I sold the Club and I'm glad to be rid of it."

"Chuck, you've sold the Club!"

We all turned as Lorraine's voice sounded from the doorway, sharp and challenging. She had come in without our hearing her, and she went to Chuck, her eyebrows startled into arcs.

"Chuck, you can't have sold the Club. It's impossible. I mean you never told me anything. You——"

"I sold it this afternoon, honey. I had a good offer, so I just sold out like that. I was going to tell you, but——" His eyes, watching her, were pleading. "I did it on account of you, baby. This place isn't healthy for you any more. I don't want us to have any ties in it. I'm going to take you away."

There was something about the two of them as they stood there close together, something keyed up and jarring that kept us all interested in them to the exclusion of everything else. I was doing a little wondering about this remarkable news that Chuck had sold his club on a lightning cash deal with his local rival. His expressed motives for the sale were gallant enough. But, even for so gallant a motive, it seemed odd that he should have taken it upon himself, without Lorraine's knowledge or consent, to sell a club which had been financed entirely by her.

His wife was still gazing at him with enigmatic intensity. "But, Chuck, how could you have sold it? You know it was our idea from the beginning to tell Mr. Throckmorton that you owned the Club and were running it successfully, that he should see you there and——"

Chuck moistened his lips. "Listen, baby, this is something

for you and me to talk about later. There's plenty else to worry us right now." He indicated the silent Craig. "Inspector Craig."

Lorraine swirled around to the Inspector with an automatic hostess smile. "Oh, yes, Inspector Craig. How charming of you to come. How——" She seemed suddenly to recall that Craig's visit was not a social one. "Oh dear, yes, you've come about poor Fleur, of course. Or is it Dorothy—or Janet? I suppose it is all of them really." She gazed at the Inspector earnestly. "I only hope you'll be able to do something about it before anything else happens."

"I am afraid, Miss Pleygel," said the Inspector, "that something else has already happened."

There was an ominous quietness about him that impelled attention. They were all staring at him.

Lorraine said, "Something else? You mean—something we don't know about?"

Craig looked down at his nails and then up again quickly. "Yes. Lieutenant Duluth and Mrs. Duluth have just found Miss Burnett out in the garage, dead—murdered."

"Mimi!" Lorraine fluttered a small handkerchief to her lips and whirled round to Chuck. Her vivid face looked gaunt and spent. "Chuck, did you hear him? He said Mimi was dead."

"Dead! Mimi—dead!" Lover, his round cheeks as gray as uncooked biscuits, grabbed my arm. "You found her, Lieutenant?" he said hoarsely. "You found her dead and you didn't tell me?" He said that again and then again with the idiot reiteration of a victrola needle in a groove.

Chuck kept very still. Both Laguno and Flanders looked more relieved than anything else. I could guess what was going on in their minds. Mimi was none of their business. Her death, if anything, made things less, rather than more, uncomfortable for them.

Lorraine took a deep breath and said, "But why?"

"It's my job to ask questions not to answer them, Miss Pleygel." Craig's voice was unyielding. "In the first place I'd like you to tell me why Miss Burnett was leaving your house with a suitcase at this hour of the night."

Lorraine stammered. "Didn't Peter—Lieutenant Duluth tell you?"

"Lieutenant Duluth has told me nothing about Miss Burnett's movements."

"Then—then—"

Chuck broke in. "Mimi Burnett left because she decided to move to a hotel in Reno. She had become scared by the things that had been going on here. She didn't want to stay in the house any longer."

When I promised Chuck to keep quiet about the Mimi-Lorraine imbroglio, I hadn't dreamed that he was planning to lie to the police in so barefaced a manner. I didn't know exactly how to cope with this unexpected development.

"Miss Burnett was leaving the house because she was expecting to be attacked, too?" queried Craig.

Chuck was floundering. "I just mean that she—well, hell, three women had been attacked. She just didn't want to stick around any longer."

"I see," said Craig.

"So you do see, Inspector." Count Laguno stepped into the conversation. His voice was as trim and dapper as his suit. "It is most unfortunate that you do, because the thing you are seeing isn't true. Mimi Burnett wasn't leaving the house because she was girlishly afraid. She was leaving because Miss Pleygel had thrown her out."

Lorraine swung on him. "Stefano——"

"I don't relish discomforting you, Lorraine." Laguno showed his bad teeth in a bland smile. "But if we aren't prepared to tell the truth, what's the point of having the police here at all?"

Craig said sharply, "Is this true, Miss Pleygel? Did you ask Miss Burnett to leave the house?"

Lover blundered in then. In spite of his shaken condition he seemed to be trying to support his sister. "In a way Lorraine did ask Miss Burnett to leave. It was—ah—all a most trivial misunderstanding. It could have been cleared up immediately if they'd given each other a chance to explain, but——"

"I wouldn't call it a trivial misunderstanding." Laguno was still smiling. "There was quite a quarrel this evening, Inspector, between Miss Pleygel and Miss Burnett on the front steps. I happened to be passing through the hall and I could not help overhearing part of it. As I understand it, Miss Pleygel and Mr. French caught Miss Burnett in a most embarrassing embrace with Mr. Dawson. Miss Pleygel, in case you don't know, is secretly married to Mr. Dawson. She very naturally objected to what she saw. She ordered Miss Burnett out of the house immediately and in no uncertain terms. She——"

"One thing at a time," cut in the Inspector. "Miss Pleygel, are you married to Chuck Dawson?"

"I am." Lorraine was defiant. "Is there anything criminal about that?"

Laguno continued. "I lay no claims to being a detective, Inspector, and I certainly don t want to do your job for you. But since Miss Burnett apparently has been murdered, I assume you're interested in motives. I draw your attention to the fact that Miss Burnett was a definite thorn in the flesh of Miss Pleygel's secret married life; she was probably a serious embarrassment to Chuck; and she was certainly a disappointment to her fiancé, Mr. French. There, it seems to me, are three perfectly adequate murder motives."

Stefano Laguno played the role of rat with such zest that I could only suppose he enjoyed it. Lorraine's eyes were flashing as she glared at him. I had never seen her really angry before. It was an impressive sight.

"There must be a gutter outside somewhere," she said. "I wish I knew where one was so that I could ask Chuck to throw you into it where you belong."

She turned to Craig. "I'd like to remind you that poor Mimi isn't the only one who's been murdered. Dorothy Flanders was murdered and Janet Laguno was murdered. Now that the subject of motives had been brought up, it might interest you to know that the Count had been having an affair with Dorothy and had even threatened to kill his wife for her money. Everyone here can vouch for that." She added in vicious mimicry of Laguno's voice, "I lay no claims to being a detective. But there, it seems to me, is a perfectly adequate murder motive."

The Inspector seemed to be taking all this waspishness in his stride. "Lieutenant Duluth has given me Mrs. Laguno's new will." He turned to the Count. "I hope you'll be as willing to co-operate on the other deaths as you seem to be on Miss Burnett's, Count."

Laguno's bright insolence remained untarnished. Cocking his head at a jaunty angle, he said, "Naturally, Inspector. In fact, there is something I would like to point out to you right away. If you've read Janet's new will, you will have seen that she left all her property to Bill Flanders. No intelligent inspector is going to believe that I killed my wife merely to benefit someone else." He threw out his hands. "I make the humble suggestion that, in your search for suspects, you also give some consideration to Bill Flanders. He was far from fond of his wife and—well, Janet's death leaves him most comfortably off. I can't quite see how he fits with Mimi's death, but——"

"You swine." Bill Flanders gripped his crutch and swung himself to his feet. "You dirty swine. You think you can sling mud at everyone, don't you?"

Laguno smiled at him. "Give me a little more time, Flanders. I still haven't slung any mud at—Doctor Wyckoff, for example." His keen lizard eyes fixed on Wyckoff's face. "I don't want to confuse you, Inspector, by being too cooperative, but I think you should be interested in the fact that Doctor Wyckoff diagnosed Dorothy Flanders' death as heart failure when she was obviously poisoned. I think you might also be interested in the fact that Doctor Wyckoff's estranged wife was almost killed this afternoon when——"

"Cut that out, Laguno," flared Wyckoff.

Pandemonium broke out. Everyone started talking at once, hurling accusations at each other.

With difficulty Inspector Craig quieted them down. He gave up any further attempt at group interview, however, and announced his intention of questioning each member of the household individually. Lorraine was his first selection. He went off with her into the little yellow room that adjoined the library.

Left to their own devices, the rest of the party subsided into a stiff silence criss-crossed with animosities. For a long, tedious period while one person followed another into the Inspector's presence, we sat or strolled around the library doing nothing except pour an occasional drink. In the middle of it all, Craig's men arrived. There was a further delay while he went out with them to the garage. It was after two o'clock by the time the Inspector had finished his last interview and reappeared in the library.

He said, "I guess that's all for now, folks." He turned to Lorraine. "If it's okay with you, Miss Pleygel, I'll spend the night. Under the circumstances I think it's a good idea for me to be on the premises."

That sounded ominous, as if he, like myself, was prepared for anything to happen at any minute. Lorraine arranged for him to have a room and, at his request, found him the key to the cabinet in the trophy room. Craig gave the key to one of his men with instructions to get the poisoned darts for analysis right away.

I had no idea what conclusions, if any, the Inspector had reached, but he was obviously very much on the job.

Just before three, when we were all still assembled in the library, he returned and said, "You'd better get some sleep. There'll be quite a day for all of you tomorrow. Incidentally, I recommend you all keep your doors locked—particularly the women." The steady eyes settled on me. "Maybe you'd be willing to stay up a bit longer, Lieutenant. I'd like to speak to you."

I could tell that Iris was bursting with eagerness to hear what the Inspector had to say. Moving toward him with a ravishing smile, she said, "Why, yes, Inspector. Of course we'd be glad to stay up."

Craig's lips twisted wryly. With uncompromising politeness, he told my wife that it would be more than sufficient for his purposes to talk to me alone. Before Iris had time to realize what was happening, he was easing her out of the library in the wake of the others.

"But, Inspector," she protested, "my husband and I always——"

"Fine, fine." Craig gave a chuckle. "If you're interested in what we're going to say, I'm sure the Lieutenant will tell you all about it later on." He maneuvered Iris through the door. "Okay, Lieutenant, let's get our teeth into this thing and see whether we can't make some sense out of it."

Iris stared from him to me. "But, Peter——"

I grinned ruefully at the Inspector. "I'll just see my wife safely upstairs, Craig. Then I'll be right down."

As I guided Iris firmly through the hall, her indignation boiled over.

"Peter, what does he think I am? An infant with long golden pigtails? It's——"

"I'm sorry, honey. He's just the old-fashioned type. He

doesn't go for women detectives. Matter of fact, I'm glad. I've got a hunch the whole thing is still as dangerous as a volcano. I want you out of harm's way."

Iris sulked as we went up the great staircase. When we reached our room, she exclaimed vehemently, "Harm's way. I've been working on this thing from the very beginning. Now when it's getting really interesting, the little woman has to be kept out of—harm's way."

That stupid phrase echoed in my mind as I glanced around the zebra-striped walls. Only that evening someone had broken into this room, searching for something. Suddenly it occurred to me that by leaving my wife alone here I might well be putting her bang slap into harm's way rather than keeping her out of it. I had visions of someone breaking in again while I was downstairs with the Inspector, someone creeping to the bed, bending over Iris. . . . The evening had rasped my nerves to such an extent that the thought made me dizzy with anxiety.

I took Iris' arm. I tried to look very lord and masterish. I said, "Listen, baby, I want you to sleep somewhere else tonight."

"Somewhere else?"

"For all we know, whoever broke in here's going to try it again. Come on. Get your nightdress, your toothbrush."

Iris gave me a pained glance. "I may be a helpless female, but at least give me credit for being able to lock a door."

"I don't trust locks. I don't trust anything. I want you sound in wind and limb for the rest of my leave. I'm taking no chances."

My wife gave a little sigh. "All right, darling."

Reluctantly she rummaged around, collecting an exotic black nightgown, a housecoat, all the things she needed. Together we went out into the passage. Now that the mortality rate had been so high, there were plenty of empty rooms. I chose Janet Laguno's. Chambermaids had already obliterated all traces of its former occupant. Iris dumped her things on the bed and gave me a meek look.

"The little woman will wait up for her lord and master. Run along now to the Inspector and your masculine pursuits."

"Lock the door," I said, "and don't let anyone in. Anyone. When I come, I'll knock four times."

Iris grimaced. "Like a spy story. Okay."

"And no funny business. No dare-devil Iris Duluth, Hollywood's lone she-wolf crime-buster."

My wife shook her head. "Don't worry. I've no spirit left. I'm a broken blossom."

I kissed her, wishing that we were somewhere quite different and had never so much as heard the name Lorraine Pleygel. While my wife started fiddling with the black nightdress, I moved to the door. I wanted a cigarette. I felt in my pocket. Instead of the familiar package, I felt a hard, bulky object. I pulled it out. It was the *Selected Poems of Edna St. Vincent Millay* which I had absent-mindedly picked up from Mimi Burnett's side and completely forgotten.

"Here, honey." I threw it to my wife. "Something nice and feminine for you to read."

Iris caught the book. She read the title. "Edna St. Vincent Millay," she cooed. "How divine! There's nothing like poetry to nourish the soul."

"Exactly," I said.

Iris could bear it no longer then. She hurled the book down on the bed and flung the nightdress after it in frustrated fury.

"Damn Edna St. Vincent Millay," she said. "Damn Inspector Craig and his misogyny. Oh, damn the single standard!"

Eighteen

WHEN I JOINED the Inspector in the little yellow room, the fire was still crackling in the hearth. The atmosphere was incongruously peaceful. The police doctor was with Craig, and they were examining the reddish brown smear on Dorothy's glove.

"Doc Brown here's been comparing this stain with the curare, Lieutenant," Craig said. "He's inclined to think the stain was made by the stuff on the darts. Of course it'll have to be analyzed before we can be sure." He sighed. "They'll be analyzing the darts, too. And we'll have to get an exhumation order for Mrs. Flanders. There's a lot of things to be done before we can get really started."

He told me his men had removed Mimi's body and, having done all that could be done that night, had left. They would be back early in the morning to examine the wrecked station wagon. After a few moments the doctor departed, and Craig and I were alone.

The Inspector looked exhausted. He sat a few moments, staring into the fire. Then he filled his pipe and lit it. His lips drooped dispiritedly around the pipe stem.

"Well, Lieutenant, I don't rightly know why I asked you to stay up. I guess I've heard about everything I'm likely to hear from the others. They talked my head off, all of them. Not that it helped me straighten anything out." He stared at me rather wintrily. "We know Miss Burnett was murdered. I guess we've got to accept the fact that Mrs. Flanders and Mrs. Laguno were murdered, too, but that's as far as it goes. Frankly I've got no more idea of what's back of this business than I had before I even heard about it."

I wasn't surprised to learn that Inspector Craig was as confused as I. Most murder cases provide too little to go on. This one provided much too much—too many bodies, too many motives.

"It's crazy," mused Craig. "Almost all of 'em have a motive for one or other of the murders. Some have a motive for a couple of them. But there isn't any one person, so far as I can see, who could possibly have wanted to kill Mrs. Flanders, Mrs. Laguno, and Miss Burnett—let alone attack Mrs. Wyckoff into the bargain."

"Precisely," I said, which wasn't helpful.

"Now it might make sense," said Craig, "if Flanders had killed his wife and Laguno had killed his wife and Wyckoff had tried to kill his wife and either French or Dawson or Miss Pleygel had killed Miss Burnett. But—" he flung out his hands—"four murders and four different murderers! Who ever heard of four murderers under one roof. Don't they say that there's only one potential murderer in about three million people?"

Inspector Craig leaned forward and pushed the dying logs into place with a poker. That domestic gesture made him seem more human. He turned to me with a grimace.

"There's only one way to figure, Lieutenant. Somebody's killed three women and tried to kill a fourth. He can't have any real motive. I mean any real, sane motive." He puffed ferociously on the pipe. "There we are. This thing just can't be sane. There's someone in this house with a bug in his brain. All these women except Miss Burnett were wives planning to divorce their husbands. And Miss Burnett, so far as I can see, was double-crossing her fiancé, which kind of puts her in the same category. Someone's crazy, and that person's killing off women who don't stick by their men. I'm no psychologist or whatever you call them but I must admit I never heard of anyone nutty in just that way. However—"

he shrugged again—"what else is there to believe, Lieutenant? Just tell me. What else is there to believe?"

I stared back at him. "It's enough to give Freud high blood-pressure."

The Inspector's mouth moved in a fleeting smile. "You've been around, Lieutenant. I guess you never came across anything as crazy as this."

"Compared with the Pleygel mansion, the St. Valentine's massacre was a taffy pull."

Craig seemed lost in thought. "And yet, Lieutenant, what gets me is that the murderer has to be one of the people I talked to tonight. All the time I was talking to them, I was saying to myself, 'One of you people's got to be bats, insane, a maniac.' But—" he took the pipe out of his mouth and pointed it at me—"they all seemed sane enough to me. All of them, maybe, except Flanders. He's just been discharged from the marines, he told me. He seemed kind of jittery, embittered. I guess you can never be sure with a guy like that, poor devil. Shell-shocked, war neurosis——"

"I agree," I said. "When he got here, Flanders was one jump ahead of a breakdown. You could tell that. And yet my wife and I've decided Flanders is the one we could definitely eliminate. Before Janet Laguno was killed in the swimming pool, the lights were fused. It's much too much of a coincidence for the lights to have fused accidentally. Someone must deliberately have fused them. Anyone could have done that except Flanders. At the time, he was in the pool with my wife and myself."

"Maybe he had a confederate," said the Inspector.

"There you go tripping yourself up. That's just the point. If the murderer's a maniac, he couldn't have had a confederate. A murderer killing in cold blood can have confederates. But not a motiveless maniac."

"I guess so." Craig looked somber. "But the others, apart from Flanders—do any of them strike you as the kind of person who'd go berserk and kill women just for the fun of it?"

"They don't," I admitted.

"That's the point. In my day I've seen a couple of homicidal maniacs. By and large, homicidal maniacs don't look like ordinary citizens. That's my experience. I don't go for this Jekyll-and-Hyde storybook stuff. It's the bunk."

"Okay," I said. "You don't think there's any sane motive for the murders and you don't think any of the suspects is a maniac. So what do you believe?"

He grinned weakly. "There you've got me, Lieutenant. I just don't know." His dogged face went solemn again. "I can tell you one thing. I've met up with a lot of characters in my time, Lieutenant. I know a fraud when I see one and it strikes me there's plenty of frauds right in this house. That Count, he's phony as they come. And Wyckoff—he gave me a lot of glib talk about why he'd diagnosed Mrs. Flanders' death as heart failure. I didn't altogether go for it. I'm not saying he's not a good doctor, but I think he may well be pretty much of a fraud, too. And, from what I've picked up, this Miss Burnett and this Mrs. Flanders—they were both frauds from way back. For a wealthy, prominent woman, I don't think much of Miss Pleygel's taste in friends."

He paused. "And, on top of it all, she's married secretly to Chuck Dawson! Dawson's been around these parts some years. Everyone seems to know him. Most of 'em like him, too. But I doubt whether you could find one person in Nevada who knows exactly who he is or where he comes from. Maybe he's the biggest fraud of them all."

"So what?" I asked. "So they're all a bunch of frauds. What does that prove?"

"There you go again. So far as I can see, it proves just exactly nothing." The Inspector knocked out his pipe and slipped it into his pocket. "But there's one thing I'm sure about, Lieutenant. I wish I wasn't." His gaze moved somberly from the fire to my face. "Three murders—almost four murders—have been committed in three days. Since I can't figure out any reason why the whole thing started, I can't figure out any reason why it should stop." He gave a sardonic laugh. "I'll be in bad enough with the D.A. already for letting things get this far. If anything else happens, it'll be almost as tough for me as for the next victim."

That brought my own anxiety to the surface again. "Don't think I'm not worried, too, Inspector. You've only got a reputation to lose. I've got a wife." Impulsively I added, "I wonder if you'd give me a break."

"What is it?"

"I'm supposed to be on leave. I'm due to report back to my ship in ten days. Inspector, you don't suspect me or my wife, do you?"

Craig looked shocked. "Holy mackerel, no. You—or Iris Duluth? She's my favorite movie actress."

"Then let us clear out of this place tomorrow, will you? I want a chance to be alone with my wife somewhere where she isn't liable to end up with a knife in her back. Will you do that? Will you let us go? We'll keep you posted, of course. You'll always know where to find us."

Inspector Craig was watching me. Suddenly he grinned. "That's the least I can do for the Navy," he said.

I felt relief pouring through me. I grabbed his hand and shook it. "Thanks, Inspector. That's big of you."

He was still grinning. "Think you'll be able to get your wife to look at it your way? From what I've seen of her, she's a determined young lady and she seems to have her mind fixed on figuring out these murders."

"Don't worry," I said. "I can always carry her off over my shoulder if need be."

The Inspector glanced at his watch and rose. "Well, I guess we're not going to get anywhere tonight. I'm all in.

I'm hitting the hay." He paused. "By the way, before you walk out on me, Lieutenant, I wish you could give me a lead. You know these people much better than I do."

"From the start," I said, "my wife and I've figured out only one lead, and that's to concentrate on *how* Mrs. Flanders was killed. Anyone could have drowned Mrs. Laguno in the pool; anybody could have crept out and bashed Miss Burnett on the head in the garage; but Mrs. Flanders was killed in some fancy way. If only you could figure out how it was done, there's a good chance you might be able to pin it on some one person. Once you did that, half the battle would be won."

The Inspector didn't seem to think much of that lead. He grunted. "Well, I guess we'll know more about that after the autopsy and the analyses. Maybe you've got something, though." He yawned and started for the door. "Coming up?"

Now that I knew Iris and I would be able to pack up and go as soon as morning came, I felt like a man released. All sense of urgency left me. There was a whisky decanter on a side table. I was in the mood for a nightcap.

"No, Inspector," I said. "I think I'll stick around just for a while longer. Maybe I'll get an inspiration."

"Let's hope so." Inspector Craig reached the door, opened it, murmured, "Good night," and closed the door behind him.

I poured myself a drink and went back to the fire, relaxing in my chair, trying to think of a place where a man could take a movie-star wife without the local populace bringing out the brass band.

I slipped into a reverie thinking out all the nice things Iris and I could do to make up for the unappetizing days of murder and malice we had spent under Lorraine's roof. After a while, however, the unpleasant realities of the moment pushed the rosy dreams of the future out of my mind, and I found myself back struggling with the problem which, after only a few hours, seemed to have defeated Inspector Craig.

The Inspector's voice trailed through my thoughts. *It strikes me there's plenty of frauds in this house.* That statement was far more accurate than he knew. Lorraine's house party was a fraud's convention.

"I wouldn't wonder," I reflected gloomily, "if the murderer isn't the biggest fraud of them all."

That thought had been idle enough. But, as I mulled it over, I sat up straight in my chair. Taken all together, the murders did seem motiveless. But what if they were deliberately motiveless? What if that chain of random murders had been a colossal fraud? What if someone with a sound and solid reason for murdering one of those women had deliberately killed the others to create the illusion of a homicidal maniac and thereby camouflage his own motive?

The idea fascinated me. I was all set to rush upstairs and present it to the Inspector. But, as common sense took the place of enthusiasm, I found myself losing confidence. My theory was logical enough as a theory. But did it bear up in real life? Could anybody be as inhuman as that—inhuman enough to kill three innocent women purely as a smoke screen?

Lorraine's friends were frauds, but surely none of them could be as monstrous as that.

I subsided into my original state of frustration, but that flight of fancy had whetted my deductive appetite. For want of a better lead, I started to chew on the one I had given the Inspector—the problem of how Dorothy Flanders had been killed.

The police doctor thought that the stain on the finger of Dorothy's glove had been made by the arrow poison. If he was right, Iris' theory about its merely being dye from one of the henna roulette chips was wrong. As those two reflections merged in my mind, I had my second inspiration in so many minutes. Iris' experiment with the chip and the wet towel had brought to our attention something which should have been obvious from the start—that the color of the roulette chips was the same as the color of the curare.

In other words, if curare had been smeared on one of those five-dollar roulette chips, the person handling the chip would not have noticed that anything was wrong.

This elementary deduction seemed to lift a veil. With sudden clarity I saw exactly how Dorothy Flanders must have been killed. And, as I saw it, it seemed impossible that I shouldn't have realized it before.

Someone had made a crude poison trap out of a roulette chip. I could only guess at its exact construction, but it would have needed no particular expenditure of time or ingenuity. It would be simple, for example, to thrust a couple of broken off needle points, smeared with curare, into the side of a chip. The curare, merging with the color of the chip, would make the tiny points all but invisible. It would have been simple, too, for anyone in our party to have slipped a poisoned chip onto Dorothy's pile at the roulette table. A roulette player invariably handles and straightens his pile of chips before playing. Under normal circumstances, Dorothy would have pricked her finger and died right there in Chuck's Club. Under normal circumstances, there would probably have been no mystery whatsoever about the manner of her death.

But the circumstances had not been normal for one very good reason. Dorothy had been wearing her long leather gloves when she played. The smear on the finger showed where she had touched the curare but, as Iris had already deduced, the leather of the gloves had been too tough for a needle to penetrate. If it hadn't been for her greed, Dorothy would probably have been alive to this day and some wretched little croupier at Chuck's Club would have been the victim. But Dorothy had been greedy. She had bundled half her chips into her pocketbook without cashing them in. Among those chips had been the poisoned one.

The smallest details of that night came back to me with extraordinary vividness as I continued my excited reconstruction. When the sandwich had been brought to her in the Del Monte, Dorothy had peeled off her gloves. She had opened her pocketbook to put them away. She had noticed me glance into the pocketbook and, in her embarrassment at having me discover she had snitched the chips, she jammed the gloves in with unwonted violence. I even remembered how she had tugged her hand out of the bag as if she had been stung. I had never thought that gesture suspicious simply because I had attributed its nervous violence to the awkwardness of the situation.

But now its significance was only too clear. When she jammed her gloves into the pocketbook, her finger had jabbed against the poisoned chip which had been lying edgewise with the others in the bag. The remains of the curare, expedited by Dorothy's heart condition, had succeeded at the Del Monte where it had failed at Chuck's Club. Iris and I had been right in believing the pocketbook had been a poison trap. Our only error had been in supposing that the murderer had deliberately framed it as such.

The murderer had intended to kill Dorothy at Chuck's Club. It had been as simple as that. The confusion which surrounded the crime had been due, not to deviousness on the part of the murderer, but to the sheer accident of Dorothy's behavior. True, the murderer must have managed to sneak the poisoned chip out of Dorothy's pocketbook after the murder. But that had not been part of his original plan. He had merely adapted himself to a situation beyond his control.

The more I thought about it, the surer I became that I had stumbled on the truth. Rather dejectedly, however, I realized that my discovery did nothing to narrow the sphere of suspicion. Everyone had been milling around the roulette table during the few moments before Dorothy played. Any member of the party had had the chance to slip the poisoned chip onto Dorothy's pile.

A third thought came then which had so much punch to it that I found my brain reeling. A poisoned roulette chip would have been easy enough to put together, but it certainly could not have been manufactured on the spur of the moment. The needle points, or whatever had been used, had to be obtained. The dart with the curare had to be stolen from the trophy room. In other words, that lethal instrument must definitely have been made by the murderer *before* we left Lorraine's house for Reno, and he must have taken it to Chuck's Club with the deliberate intention of killing Dorothy at the roulette table. It seemed strange enough to me that anyone should have chosen so public and precarious a method of murder. But something was far stranger than that.

Although the murderer must have constructed the poison trap earlier in the evening, no one knew, before we left for Reno, that Dorothy was going to play roulette. She had said nothing about it; she hadn't even expressed the remotest interest in the game. In fact, it had been an accident that she had played the chips at all.

Dorothy Flanders had played roulette simply because Lorraine, who bought the chips, had decided at the last minute not to play. The pile of chips into which the poison trap had been slipped had not been Dorothy's pile of chips.

It had been Lorraine's.

If things had gone as scheduled, Lorraine would have played those chips instead of Dorothy.

That was the key. It opened a door to let in a blinding light.

Dorothy had died handling Lorraine's roulette chips.

Janet Laguno had been drowned wearing Lorraine's swimming suit—that dazzling silver suit which had gleamed in the darkness, making a perfect target for a murderer, that suit which Lorraine had discarded and given to Janet on the flimsiest of whims.

And that wasn't all. Fleur Wyckoff had almost died that afternoon in Lorraine's station wagon. Fleur's trip to Reno had been quite unpremeditated. No one, with the possible exception of Laguno, could have had the time to file through the brake cable after Fleur had decided to use the car.

But earlier in the day Lorraine had announced to all of us that she was going to take the station wagon down to the airport to pick up Mr. Throckmorton. Later she had received a wire informing her that Mr. Throckmorton had lost his reservation on the plane, but only Iris and I had heard about that.

If it hadn't been for that telegram, Lorraine and not Fleur would have driven off in the station wagon—to her doom.

There was sense now where there had been nonsense before—sense which had been hopelessly distorted by chance and the feather-pated irresponsibility of Lorraine's character. My hunch had been right. The murders were nothing but an immense fraud—a fraud brought about by a bungling murderer and a sardonic Fate.

Three traps had been set for Lorraine Pleygel. Each trap had caught the wrong woman.

The danger which had swooped through the house, seemingly attacking at random, had from the beginning been danger for only one person—Lorraine.

Mimi's death had still to be accounted for. That, surely, could not have been merely another unsuccessful attempt on Lorraine. But there was no time then for much coherent thought. I was plagued with anxiety for Lorraine.

A murderer who had persisted so doggedly would never stop until his purpose was fulfilled. Three women were dead but the real victim was still alive. Craig had been closer than he realized to the truth when he said the murderer might strike again.

Of course he would strike again. If he didn't, his whole bloody trail would end in a cul de sac. And he had nothing to lose. Thanks to the confusion he had created, Lorraine's death would appear to be just another wanton attack by the maniac.

I swallowed what was left of my drink and jumped up. My hand, as I put down the glass, was shaking. With the dreadful urgency of a dream, I ran through the dark, deserted library and out into the hall. The great staircase loomed dimly ahead of me. I started up it, hoping and praying that the truth had not come to me too late. For over an hour now, Lorraine had been alone. For over an hour the murderer had had his opportunity to steal through the darkness to her room and . . .

I reached the corridor which led away from the guest rooms to the wing which Lorraine kept for herself. My footsteps clattering against the bare boards sounded deafeningly loud but I didn't care whom I awakened. I came to the end of the corridor. I reached Lorraine's door. I knocked on it loudly. I knocked again. I called, "Lorraine—Lorraine——"

No sound came from inside the room. Beads of perspiration sprouted on my forehead. I knocked again. I tried the door. It should have been locked but it wasn't. It opened inward.

The room was impenetrably dark. I stepped in and closed the door behind me. I tried to find a light.

"Lorraine," I said sharply. "Lorraine, wake up. It's me—Peter."

I stopped then. For, trailing through the darkness, was a sickly sweet smell, a smell that no one could mistake.

The smell of ether.

Momentary paralysis gave place to wild activity. I started to stumble around blindly, searching for a lamp. At last I found one. I groped for the chain and tugged it. Blinking, I swung round so that I could see the huge, canopied bed.

The stench of ether invaded my nostrils. I stared at the figure which lay under the luxurious white satin coverlet. The bedclothes were drawn up to the neck, and I could trace the contours of the body through the thick material.

But I could not see the face.

That was what made it so horrible. Lorraine's face was invisible because a pillow had been thrown over it, completely smothering her sleeping head.

"Lorraine——"

I sprang to the bed. I picked up the pillow and tossed it away. What I saw under the pillow sent a cold shiver through me. I could see the outlines of her features, but I still could not see her face. Wrapped viciously tight around the head was a damp Turkish towel. And from the towel the smell of the ether came up to me in a blast, turning my knees to water.

"Lorraine——"

I touched the shoulder under the satin coverlet. Beneath my fingers the body lay stiff and rigid—with no life.

I felt a moment of complete despair. So it had happened. Snatching his last, desperate opportunity, the murderer had crept into Lorraine's room, wrapped the ether-soaked towel around her sleeping head, thrown the pillow on top as a double precaution, and had stolen away, leaving her to die.

The wheel of murder had come full circle. Lorraine had finally been trapped.

And I had been too late to save her.

Part Six

IRIS

Nineteen

I STARED DOWN. The stiff lifelessness of the body under the bedclothes had convinced me that Lorraine Pleygel was dead. The fumes of ether were making me lightheaded. Fighting against dizziness, I unwrapped the saturated towel from the face and flung it across the room.

Lorraine's face shimmered in and out of focus against the crumpled sheet. Something, however, was out of key. The eyes of a person who had been anesthetized and smothered would surely be shut. These eyes were open. And the cheeks would be pale or bluish. These cheeks were a rosy pink. Lorraine was lying there motionless as a corpse, but her red lips were fixed in the simpering smile of a store dummy.

As the effect of the ether began to wear off, the truth burst upon me. I grabbed the bedclothes and tore them off the prostrate form.

The figure which lay revealed was not wearing a nightdress. It was wearing a long, lime-green evening gown, and peeking out from beneath the wide skirts were the tips of lime-green evening slippers.

I stared at the dress and then at the vivid, pop-eyed face. I laughed from sheer relief. What I saw made no sort of sense, but this time the nonsense was on our side.

The murderer had crept into this room with his ether and his lethal intentions. He had come and gone, convinced that the day was his. But another colossal fraud had been perpetrated.

He had not smothered the sleeping Lorraine. He had merely murdered Lorraine's portrait doll.

My mind started clicking out questions. Who had set this booby trap? Lorraine herself? Had she guessed what danger she was in and thought out this fantastic trick of substituting the doll for herself in the bed? It was the sort of lunatic thing she would do. But where was she now?

I glanced around the room. There was nothing to give me a clue. I thought of Inspector Craig sleeping the sleep of the exhausted. I had enough information now to jolt him out of the deepest dreams. But I had not been listening when Lorraine allotted him a room. I did not know where to find him.

Iris had been there at the time, however. She probably knew. I felt guilty about my wife, anyway. She had insisted she would stay awake until I brought her the news of my interview with Craig. Nothing, I knew, would induce her to go to sleep until her curiosity had been satisfied. By this time she must have learned all of Miss Millay's Selected Poems by heart.

I hurried out of that room with its bizarre sham corpse and through the dark corridors to the room formerly occupied by Janet Laguno, which I had chosen as a fortress for Iris. Following my own melodramatic instructions, I signaled with four taps on the door. Footsteps pattered inside. A key scraped in the lock and the door opened.

The light from inside the room silhouetted a woman's figure at the door, wearing mad, candy-striped pajamas. I stared in astonishment because the woman standing there was not my wife.

She was Lorraine.

"Oh, Peter, angel," she said. "It's you. Come in."

She drew me inside, closing the door behind us. I kept staring at her stupidly.

"What on earth are you doing here, Lorraine?"

"Iris was scared of being alone. She lugged me out of bed and dragged me in here to keep her company."

I took a suspicious glance around the room. "And where is she?"

Lorraine shrugged the candy stripes. "Oh, wandering around somewhere."

"Wandering around!" Anxiety hit me like a blunt instrument. "But I made her promise—you mean, she's wandering around this no man's land alone?"

"It's all right, sugar-pie." Lorraine lit a cigarette. "She'd been gone quite a while and I was beginning to get anxious. But she was back just a few moments ago. She said not to worry. She was with the Inspector."

"The Inspector?"

"Yes, darling. I don't know what it's all about, but Iris said you weren't to worry or go searching for her."

"She said that?" I muttered weakly.

"Yes." Lorraine watched me through cigarette smoke. "Darling, whatever's the matter? You smell kind of medicinal and you look as if you'd just seen a corpse."

"I have," I said. "Your corpse."

"My corpse?"

"You were lying in bed in your own room, anesthetized and smothered."

I told her what I had just discovered. The absurd lashes batted over incredulous eyes.

"The doll? The doll from the trophy room? But, Peter, who put it in my bed?"

"I don't know," I said, although I was beginning to have very definite ideas of my own.

Lorraine's puckish face was deadly serious. "So it's become as mad as all that. Even trying to kill me!"

"It isn't a question of *even* trying to kill you, Lorraine.

You are the one the murderer's been after from the beginning."

I was worrying about Iris' mysterious escapade with the Inspector, but I felt the time had come to tell Lorraine the truth. The sooner she realized the immense danger she was still in, the safer she would be. I explained the whole crazy pattern as it had unrolled itself to me. Things had moved too quickly for me to carry my deductions to their logical conclusion. Now, however, as I watched the remnants of color fading from Lorraine's cheeks, the solution seemed almost ludicrously obvious.

Lorraine dropped onto the edge of one of the beds. When I finished, she was staring down at the carpet, her candy-striped shoulders sagging. In a thin voice she asked, "But—who, Peter? Who's been trying to do this to me?"

This was not going to be pleasant. I said, "You've never made a will, have you?"

"You know I haven't. I'd decided to make one when Mr. Throckmorton arrived. I——"

"That's what I thought." I put my hands on her shoulders to steady her. "When a married woman dies intestate, her entire estate goes to her husband."

She looked up, her face gaunt and white as linen.

"Peter, it can't be. No, no. You can't mean——"

She stopped as a knock sounded on the door. After a swift glance at me, she called, "Who is it?"

"It's me, baby." Chuck Dawson's voice sounded from the passage, gruff and urgent. "Can I come in?"

Lorraine sat watching the door as if it were a snake. Slowly she forced her gaze back to me. I nodded.

She called, "Come in."

Chuck strode in with a travesty of his normal swagger. His blond, cowboy face looked thin and bloodless. His eyes moved to me and then settled on his wife.

"They told me you were here," he said jerkily. "I came. That is—I wanted to make sure you were all right."

Lorraine was staring at him. "I'm all right. Only by a miracle though. Peter's just come to tell me that someone tried to murder me tonight."

Chuck stiffened. "Murder you! It's not possible!"

"Someone crept into my room to put me under ether and smother me while I was asleep. Luckily Iris had asked me to come in here with her, and somehow the portrait doll got into my bed as a booby trap." Her eyes still searched his face. "Chuck, don't you know anything about it?"

He dropped on the bed next to her. His hands went out to her. With a little shudder, she got up and moved to my side.

"Chuck, don't you know anything about it?" she repeated.

Chuck Dawson looked like a broken man with no fight left in him. He did not speak.

I was watching him all the time. Inspector Craig's words had risen again in my memory. *Maybe he's the biggest fraud of them all.* I thought of Chuck's anomalous relationship with Mimi. I thought of his startling sale of the Club that afternoon. It seemed pitifully clear. This was something that might as well be gotten over once and for all.

"Chuck," I said.

That was the first time I had spoken since his entrance. He started and said, "What?"

"You sold your club in Reno this afternoon, didn't you?"

He glared at me. "Why ask? You know I did."

"And you sold it for cash?"

"Yeah. It was a cash deal."

"Then where's the money?"

His eyes flickered. "I took it over to the bank, of course."

"That isn't possible," I said. "It was after three when

Dorothy's funeral was over. You sold the Club later than that. All the banks would have been closed."

A shiver ran through his big, athlete's body. "I—that is——"

I came in for the kill then. "Why don't you admit it?" I said. "You didn't sell the Club because you wanted to take Lorraine away. You sold the Club because you had to raise cash—a lot of cash—to pay someone who was blackmailing you." I paused. "But in the last analysis, you figured it would be easier and cheaper to murder Mimi rather than pay her off, didn't you?"

Chuck sprang up from the bed. He seemed to tower over us both. I found myself wishing I had my service revolver in my pocket. Lorraine grabbed my arm. Her nails dug into my flesh.

"No." Chuck's face was gray as cigar ash. "No. That isn't——"

Once again, at a dramatic moment, the door opened. This time Iris came in, shutting the door behind her. She was wearing a navy blue housecoat which flared out from her hips. She looked very beautiful. She also looked secretive and self-consciously innocent.

She gave me a smile and turned unconcernedly to Chuck. "I'm glad you got here," she said. "The time has come to talk of many—oh, let's skip the walrus."

"Where on earth have you been?" I said to her, still keeping a wary eye on Chuck.

"Oh, just around," said my wife meekly.

"You promised not to leave this room."

"I know, darling." Iris grimaced. "But the little woman got to thinking and the things I got to thinking about—well, I realized something had to be done, so I did it in spite of Inspector Craig's aversion to the sleuthing female."

Lorraine was staring at her. "Iris, you put that doll in the bed, didn't you? You saved my life. You knew there was danger for me so——"

Iris perched herself on the edge of the low vanity and lit a cigarette. "I felt awfully silly doing it, my dear, but it all turned out for the best."

My wife was deliberately playing for effect. She knew we were drooling at the mouth to hear what she had to say, but the actress in her was taking delight in prolonging the suspense. I could have wrung her neck.

She looked at me, puffing blue smoke. "It all started, Peter, because it suddenly occurred to me that the maniac wasn't a maniac at all. He was a perfectly ordinary murderer who was having lousy luck."

"I know," I said peevishly. "There's no need to be so Mrs. Raffles about it. I figured that out, too. I realized that each murder trap was intended for Lorraine and that the whole thing went sour through a series of accidents."

"Oh, no, dear, not through a series of accidents. I'd say there was an extremely good reason why each murder trap ganged agley." My wife glanced challengingly at Chuck. "Wouldn't you, Chuck?"

He swung away from her without speaking and moved to the window, where he stood staring out into the darkness.

At the risk of inflating my wife's ego even further, I had to ask, "Just how did you figure out Lorraine was the real victim? From Dorothy's death? I did. I realized Dorothy must have been killed by some sort of poisoned roulette chip."

Iris looked at me condescendingly. "Peter, how clever." She rose and crossed to a highboy from which she took a small cigarette box. She brought the box to me, removing the lid. "I would never have been smart enough to figure out the roulette chip by deduction. I just—found it. Here it is. Careful. Don't touch."

I stared into the interior of the cigarette box. Lying there was a henna five-dollar roulette chip. The trap which had killed Dorothy Flanders looked almost exactly the way I had imagined it would. A succession of six tiny needle points had been inserted into the cardboard side of the chip in a fan design. Their sharp points were just visible and smeared over them were still the vestiges of some sticky, reddish brown substance.

The curare.

I turned to gaze at my wife's placid face. "Where in the name of heaven did you find this?"

Iris put the lid back on the box and returned it to the top of the highboy. "Oh, it was around," she said maddeningly. She came back to me. "But it wasn't the chip that started me thinking, Peter. It was something you gave me. I'm surprised you didn't notice it yourself."

She leaned over the bed and picked up a book from the bedside table. I recognized it as Mimi's copy of Edna St. Vincent Millay.

"You told me to read it, Peter," she said. "I'm afraid I never got beyond the fly leaf."

She handed me the book.

"Chuck," she said softly, "turn round. You've got to listen."

Very slowly Chuck Dawson moved from the window. He stood sullenly, staring down at his blunt hands.

"I asked you to come here and talk to us, Chuck, because there's no point in your trying to hide things any more. You see, I guessed you sold the Club to get money to pay off a blackmailer. I guessed, too, that Mimi was the one who was blackmailing you. But I couldn't understand what your relationship with her was until I read the inscription in that book."

Feeling mildly crazy, I opened the book. An inscription had been written there in a round, clumsy hand. I read:

> To Mimi Dawson, my darling wife,
> from Chuck.

"Yes, Chuck," Iris was saying. "That's why she was blackmailing you, isn't it? And that's why she was murdered. Mimi Burnett never intended to marry Lover. She was just using him as an admission ticket to this house. She came here because she was your wife."

Twenty

I COULD HARDLY BELIEVE my ears. A dozen different explanations had occurred to me for Mimi's relationship to Chuck, but I had never dreamed of marriage. Neither, it seemed, had Lorraine. Her piquant face was crumbled with undiluted astonishment.

"You were married to Mimi, Chuck? But why—why didn't you ever tell me?"

Chuck avoided her gaze. Iris moved across to her side.

"Lorraine," she said, "I'm only telling you this because the whole tawdry thing has to come out into the open now. You've got to believe that. Chuck couldn't let you know about Mimi because—" she turned to Chuck, her lips tight— "because he's still married to her. They were never divorced."

"Never divorced!" Lorraine echoed the words like a child repeating a phrase it had never heard before. "You mean we're not really married?" Her voice dropped to a whisper. "It's bigamy?"

It was painful to see Chuck's face. He took a fumbling step toward her. "I couldn't tell you. I—oh, God, I swear it's true. When I married you, I never knew it."

Iris cut in crisply, "Surely, if you're planning to marry someone it's a good idea to find out first whether or not you're already married to someone else."

"What d'you know about it?" Chuck turned on her with a spurt of anger. "If only you'd listen to me instead of throwing accusations at me." His gaze moved back to Lorraine. "I'm going to tell you the truth, baby. Will you listen? Give me a chance?"

Lorraine gave a frigid nod. The Adam's apple was working convulsively in Chuck's throat.

"Yeah, I married Mimi," he said. "We were married seven years ago back in the East. We were both pretty young—and we just didn't make a go of it. A couple of years ago we split up. She had some sort of ambition to be an actress. She went off to Hollywood and I drifted out here to Nevada. We didn't get a divorce. We didn't bother. We just both of us agreed to give the other a divorce if either of us ever wanted to get married again."

He paused, wetted his lips. "I more or less settled in Reno, bought a small ranch, built up a kind of reputation for myself. Didn't make much money, but I had the right contacts. I was going along perfectly okay. Then—then sometime last year, Lorraine, I met you."

Lorraine stood stiff and silent.

"Oh, I know." Chuck's voice was bitter. "I know what you're going to say, that you're one of the richest girls in the world and that I just saw a good prospect. Say it if you like. Think it. I've given up caring any more what anybody thinks about me. But from the first day I saw you I was crazy about you. I couldn't believe it when you seemed to have fallen for me, too. Then that day—Lorraine, you remember. Out at Pyramid Lake. I asked you to marry me and you said you would."

Lorraine, Iris, and I were watching him in a strange, neutral silence.

"I almost told you then that I was married already, that I'd have to get a divorce first, but—" he shrugged—"I didn't. That's all. I just couldn't believe you'd really said yes. I was so scared that something, anything, might make you change your mind. So I kept quiet. I didn't say anything. But that night when I went home, I wrote to Mimi. I told her I'd fallen in love with you and asked her to give me the divorce as we'd agreed."

He hesitated. "She wrote back. It was a nice letter. She said sure, she'd give me a divorce but she wanted to be the one to get it. She'd go to Las Vegas right away, she said, and get it if I put up the money for the expenses. She hadn't been doing too well and didn't have the cash. Of course I was glad to give her the money. I'd saved a little, not much, but enough. I mailed it and she went off to Vegas."

He was watching Lorraine still. "You remember I insisted on our not getting married right away. I was waiting the six weeks for Mimi's divorce. And then, when the time was up, Mimi wrote me from Vegas that the divorce had gone through. I wrote back at once thanking her and telling her you and I were getting married the next day. And we did. We flew down to Mexico." His voice went husky. "Thank heaven, we decided to keep it secret.

"I might have guessed," he said, "that there was a snag in it. But I'd trusted Mimi. It never occurred to me that she'd do me dirt. When she called and said the divorce was okay, I took her word for it. I didn't bother to confirm it. Then, a week after you and I were married, Mimi showed up in Reno at my place. She didn't pull her punches. She came right out and told me that she'd never divorced me at all. She tricked me into committing bigamy. She'd gotten herself the neatest racket in the world. Now I was married to Lorraine Pleygel, she said, money meant nothing to me. She'd started the proceedings in Vegas, she'd established residence. She would be able to get the divorce any day she wanted it. She was willing to keep quiet and get the divorce as soon as I or Lorraine gave her one hundred thousand dollars in cash. If I didn't play ball, she was going to the press and have the whole story spread over the front pages by suing me for bigamy."

His hands went out in a helpless gesture. "She had me just where she wanted me. The bigamy suit wouldn't just have affected me; it would have thrown Lorraine's name into every scandal sheet in the country. What could I do? I knew when I was licked. I promised that somehow I'd raise the money for her."

Lorraine's pale lips half parted as if she were going to speak, but she didn't say anything.

Chuck went on. "Don't you understand, Lorraine? I couldn't possibly have gone to you and asked you to buy me off from Mimi for one hundred thousand dollars. You didn't even know of her existence, let alone that I was married to her. It—well, I was sure if ever you heard about it, you'd be through with me forever. Somehow I had to raise that money on my own hook. That's why I asked you to finance the Club. I've always had a flair for that kind of thing. I had the right contacts. I thought I had a chance to raise the hundred grand and still pay you back your original investment. I took crazy chances. Gambled everything on making a success of the Club. Nothing else mattered to me except to raise that dough for Mimi because until then I knew that neither of us had a chance for happiness."

I broke in. "But even with a big-time gambling club, clearing a hundred thousand dollar profit isn't child's play. As the months went by, I suppose Mimi got impatient. That's why she hitched herself on to poor Lover. She used him so she could get into this house and keep a constant threat over your head."

Chuck did not reply. He was still staring hollow-eyed at Lorraine.

Iris spoke then. Softly she said, "And things came to a crisis this week, didn't they, Chuck, because Mr. Throckmorton was coming. Lorraine was going to tell him about the secret marriage. You knew Mr. Throckmorton, as Lorraine's guardian and a hardheaded lawyer, would try to find out everything he could about you. There was a big risk of his finding out the marriage was bigamous. You realized you had to get Mimi back to Vegas to complete the divorce so you could marry Lorraine again before Mr. Throckmorton came. You were ready to promise Mimi anything, but she was through with promises then. She demanded hard cash, every cent you had. That's why you had to sell the Club. Mimi was planning to go to Vegas tonight and get the divorce tomorrow, wasn't she? And she was taking with her in that suitcase every cent in the world that you owned."

Chuck passed a hand across his forehead. "What's the use?" he muttered. "You seem to know everything, anyway."

"So you were going to pay Mimi off?" Lorraine's voice was small and bleak, the voice of a woman who has seen everything crumble to dust and ashes. "Then, at the last minute, you killed her instead. That doesn't seem so terrible to me. Any woman who could do a thing like that deserves to die. But—but that isn't all, is it? Two other women had been killed before that. They had been killed because they had fallen into traps set for me. You say you loved me. And yet, just because you were in a hole and needed money to save yourself, you were willing to try to kill me twice. Love!" A laugh was wrenched out of her. "That's the sort of love I got. A murderer's love."

Chuck seemed too dazed to take in what she was saying.

"Go on," said Lorraine. "Why don't you admit it and get it over with? Why don't you admit you killed Dorothy and Janet—as well as Mimi?"

Chuck took a step toward her. "Lorraine——"

Iris was watching Lorraine, too. There was an enigmatic smile on her lips.

"Oh, no, Lorraine dear," she said. "That isn't true. That isn't the way it happened at all."

Lorraine swung round to her. "Iris, what are you saying? What do you mean?"

"Peter said that it was sheer accident which saved you from those murder traps. He's not right. You're alive now simply because all the time somebody was doing everything humanly possible to keep you safe. Think, Lorraine. Who pulled you away from the roulette table just before you started to play those chips? Who kidded you out of wearing that silver swimming suit?"

She took Lorraine's arms and stared straight into her face. "You should be very proud to have Chuck. He did a lot of terrible things but he did them because he thought it was the only way to save your life, not to mention your reputation. If it wasn't for Chuck, you'd have been dead days ago."

Iris smiled at Chuck radiantly. "I'm sorry I was so rude. I didn't realize you'd been tricked into the bigamy. I see it all now and I, for one, believe you."

We were all watching her in expectant silence. A confused flush spread over Chuck's face.

"I know why you've been holding back," said my wife, "but don't you see? You've got to tell the truth now. You've got to tell them who the murderer really is."

Twenty-One

THINGS HAD BEEN RACING so quickly that I felt as if I had been left at the post. We were all watching Chuck. Lorraine, when she had accused him of the murders, had looked like a woman signing her own death warrant. Now there was a glimmer of hope in her eyes. Iris seemed completely self-assured, but I had a shrewd suspicion that she did not know as much as she wanted Chuck to think she did.

"Well, Chuck," she said firmly, "go on. Tell us. It's better coming from you."

"I guess it is." Chuck ran an uneasy hand around the collar of his cowboy shirt. It was almost as if he were trying to loosen an invisible lasso. "It's going to be hard to explain. Iris is right. I've done a lot of terrible things. I've protected a murderer whose guts I hate. I've lied. I've even put Lorraine into appalling danger although I never realized it at the time. If I hadn't been a coward, I guess I'd have gone to the police right away and faced the music. But I was a coward—a coward because I was scared of losing Lorraine."

His gaze moved starkly to Lorraine. "What I did, I did partly to save my own skin. That's true. If I'd acted any other way, I'd be under arrest now, probably as a murder accessory, certainly as a charlatan who'd exploited Lorraine Pleygel through a fake marriage. But that's only a small thing. Mostly, I was thinking of you, trying not to lose you, trying to save you from scandal because I love you."

He gave a shrug. "The laugh's on me in the end. When you've heard what I did, you'll be through with me, anyway—even if you aren't already."

Lorraine said quietly, "Tell us everything, Chuck. Don't hold anything back."

"I guess it's easiest to begin with Mimi. After I'd promised her the hundred grand, she stayed on in Vegas, got some sort of a job there in a night club. But she didn't like waiting. As the months went by and I didn't come across, she started getting suspicious. She'd have come to Reno on her own hook to make trouble, but something better turned up."

"The something better," put in Iris, "was Lover?"

"Yeah. She met him at the night club. She knew who he was, of course, and she realized it'd be a cinch if she could use him to get herself invited to Lorraine's where she could be right on the spot and really put the screws on me. She'd always been attractive to older men. She went into her fragile little poetry-lover act. He fell for it hook, line, and sinker. After a couple of days, he was so nuts about her he'd asked her to marry him."

He paused. "She hadn't figured on doing that good a job, but, as Lover's fiancée, she was in an ideal position. The very day she arrived here, she got me alone and told me that if I didn't give her the dough right away she'd have a showdown with Lorraine and blackmail it out of her. I was desperate. The Club was running very well and I was in sight of being able to raise the hundred grand without Lorraine's ever knowing. I pleaded with Mimi. I even handed her a couple of thousand to keep her happy. Finally, I managed to make her promise me a little more time."

He looked down at his big hands. They weren't very steady. "About a week later Lorraine dragged those women up from Reno and had her crazy idea of reconciling them to their husbands. What happened next I didn't know about at the time. Mimi told me later. But it seems that after dinner the first night the husbands were here, when we were all getting ready to go to Reno, Mimi went to Lover's room. She'd run out of cigarettes and she knew he always kept some in the top drawer of his bureau. He wasn't there. She went to the drawer and opened it. Inside, lying next to the cigarettes, was a woman's compact. She was always inquisitive. She thought it was queer his having a woman's compact. She picked it up and opened it."

Chuck Dawson nodded toward the cigarette box which stood on the top of the highboy. "Inside the compact, she found that roulette chip, fixed with the needles and the poison and everything."

Lorraine gave a gasp. "Then it was Lover!"

At last, after days of perplexity, I knew the name of the murderer. For some moments, while Chuck was talking, I had anticipated this and realized how wide of the mark my own half-digested accusation of Chuck had been. But, absurdly enough, instead of feeling embarrassment or shock, I merely found myself thinking how fantastic it was that we should all still refer to Walter French by Mimi's repulsive nickname.

"Lover!" Chuck gave a harsh laugh. "A hell of a name that turned out to be. Mimi couldn't make head or tail of the chip, of course. She was standing there with the compact open in her hand when Lover came in. He grabbed it away from her, shut it and slipped it in his pocket. He watched her in a funny way. Then he said, 'Well, I was planning to keep you out of this for a while. But now you've seen the chip, I think it's better for you to know.' She still didn't get it, and he started to explain. Until then she'd always thought of him as a sentimental, bumbling old fool, but the story he told was more cold-blooded and cynical than anything she'd ever heard."

He went on. "In the first place, he told Mimi quite calmly that he'd found out she was legally married to me. Mimi had always been careless about her things. She'd kept that book of poems I'd given her when we were first married, and Lover had found it and read the inscription the way Iris did tonight. On the sly, he'd put private detectives on her track in Vegas and they'd ferreted out the whole story. She thought her game was up. But, instead of threatening to expose her, he started to praise her. He loved her all the more, he said, for being an ambitious girl who knew how to take care of her own interests. All his life, he said, he'd been humiliated by being poor while his half sister was one of the richest girls in the world. He'd decided it was time for him to take care of his own interests, too. He'd thought out a plan which would make them both rich, which would make any scheme of hers look like chicken feed."

Chuck fumbled a cigarette out of his pocket. "He told her what the roulette chip was then, told her he was planning to murder Lorraine with it that night. She hadn't made a will. Her marriage to me was bigamous which could easily be proved. If she died before I could legalize the marriage, her whole fortune would go to Lover as her nearest living relative. When everything had blown over, he would marry Mimi, and they would be in clover for the rest of their lives."

His voice was grim now. "The set-up was ideal for murder. Lorraine had filled the house with husbands and wives who were at each other's throats. All of them would be crowded around the roulette table. No one, Lover said, could ever trace the chip back to him, and there was a big chance of the police's supposing that the chip had been intended for one of the wives by one of the husbands and that Lorraine had been killed by mistake. Whatever happened, there'd be so much confusion that his chance of going undetected was immense."

He went on. "When Lover'd finished, he gave a laugh and said, 'I'm glad I've told you. You're here to blackmail Chuck. Blackmail isn't very different from murder. I can count on your not going to the police. One has to take care of one's interests. I want you. Now that you know the plan, you'll have to stick by me once Lorraine is dead, because to all intents and purposes you'll be an accessory before the fact.' "

It was a story callous enough to make the blood freeze in your veins.

"By that time," said Chuck, "Mimi was really scared of him. She didn't want to marry him. She loathed him, and she didn't want to be mixed up in a murder. She was tough but not that tough. She promised she'd stick by him. She promised everything he made her promise, but she had another plan. The moment she got a chance, she got away from him and came sneaking over to my room."

I remembered how, on that first night, Iris and I had seen Mimi gliding furtively into Chuck's room.

"Yeah," he said, "Lover had her where he wanted her. But she was smart enough to realize she still had me where she wanted me. She was quick at thinking and she had her plan all set. She came to me just as I was ready to go downstairs and join the others. She told me that Lover had found out my marriage to Lorraine was bigamous and that he was planning to murder Lorraine before we could make the marriage legal. She said she was prepared to tell me what the plan was and help me save Lorraine's life on two conditions. First that I raised my ante to two hundred grand, and second that I promised, whatever happened, never to tell the truth to the police because, if I did, she'd be exposed as a blackmailer even if Lover didn't try to drag her down with him as his accomplice. She knew she was safe. She knew I loved Lorraine, that I'd do anything to save her life. She figured, too, that with a bigamy charge hanging over my head I'd never dare go to the police in any case. This way, she stood to get two hundred thousand dollars without getting mixed up in murder. She could thumb her nose at Lover into the bargain."

He was speaking jerkily now. "I was sweating blood

worrying about Lorraine. Since my only chance to save her rested with Mimi, I agreed. I'd have agreed to anything. She told me Lover's plan then. She said it would be simple to outwit him, but that we'd have to be very careful because if he guessed she'd double-crossed him, he'd turn on her. She knew he had the compact in his right-hand coat pocket. All she had to do was to snitch it. That way we'd not only save Lorraine, we'd always have the chip as evidence—something to threaten him with if ever he tried any other funny business."

Once again his eyes moved to Lorraine's white face. "I was too het-up to use my head. All I could think of was getting that chip before he killed you. We rushed downstairs only to find you'd all started without us. We jumped into my car. I drove like a fiend to get ahead of you, to get to the Club first, before anything could happen." He shrugged. "As you know, we got a flat. It was a nightmare changing that tire. First you all came by. We waved to Lorraine but she wouldn't stop. Then Lover shot by in the other car. Finally I got the thing fixed and we raced into Reno."

His eyes showed a memory of what he must have gone through that evening. "When we got to the Club, you were all already at the roulette table. We hadn't expected to be that late. Our plans were all shot. Then I saw that South American gigolo. I'd been talking to him the day before and he'd put on a big act of wanting to meet Lorraine. He seemed like a gift from God. I rushed over to the roulette table. I practically died of relief when I saw Lorraine hadn't started to play. My one thought was to get her away from danger. So I grabbed her. I grabbed Lover, too. I dragged them both back to Mimi and the South American. While I got Lorraine and the dancer together, I handed Lover over to Mimi. It was her job to get the compact. She started pawing him, pretending to be affectionate. After a few seconds, she nodded. I knew that meant she had the compact." He gave a wintry smile. "I thought everything was all right. I thought we'd saved the day."

From the beginning of that incredible story, Iris had been watching his face intently. Now she said, "You saved the day for Lorraine all right. But you didn't realize that Lover had already sneaked the poisoned chip into the pile and when you dragged him away from the table he had no chance to pick it up. He must have been on tenterhooks. He knew Dorothy would get killed if he didn't get back to the table and lift the chip. But you wouldn't let him get away. Then I hit the jackpot on the fifty-cent machine. Everyone rushed over to me. That gave Lover his opportunity. He ran back to the roulette table but, to his horror, the chip wasn't there. Dorothy had sneaked it into her pocketbook along with the others. From then on, the thing was out of his control. He didn't know where the chip was. He'd started the juggernaut and he couldn't stop it."

"I guess so." Chuck's fingers were twisting each other. "You see, Mimi didn't have a chance to look in the compact and find it was empty. Before either of us knew there was any danger for anyone, Dorothy was already dead."

He was staring at me. "When I helped you carry Dorothy off the dance floor, I knew that she'd been killed by Lover's poison trap. I realized what a terrible spot I was in. I had promised Mimi not to tell the truth to the police. Even if I broke that promise, the bigamy business would come out. Not only that. I had had foreknowledge of the murder plot and yet I hadn't done anything about it. I would be considered an accessory before the fact, too. I'd be in as deep as Mimi, almost as deep as Lover. I was suffering the torments of the damned. And then, out of the blue, Wyckoff diagnosed the death as heart failure. I hadn't any idea why he was doing it, but it was water in the desert to me. After all, Lorraine was safe. I didn't care much about Dorothy."

I said, "So that's why you kept quiet and used your influence with the police to have Wyckoff sign the death certificate?"

He nodded. "At least it gave me time. I had to talk to Mimi, but I got tied up with Wyckoff taking Dorothy to the funeral parlor and I got back here too late. I had to be terribly careful in contacting her, anyway, so as not to get Lover suspicious. It wasn't until the evening of the next day, after we'd come back from the trip on Tahoe, that the chance came. Mimi was waiting for me on the dock. Remember?"

"Of course," said Iris.

"The first thing she said was that Lover didn't suspect she'd double-crossed him. He thought my dragging him and Lorraine away from the roulette table had just been an accident. He didn't seem particularly worried that his plan had failed, either. Dorothy's death helped things rather than hindered them, he said. So many people had wanted to kill Dorothy that the police, even if they did suspect murder eventually, were bound to go haring off on the wrong scent. Then she dropped her bombshell. Lover was so sure of himself that he had planned another attempt on Lorraine."

He ran a hand across his cropped blond hair. "She said she'd tell me the plan and help me save Lorraine again provided I stick by my bargain. I was beginning to realize then how hopelessly entangled I had become. I couldn't have gone to the police by that time, anyway. I accepted Mimi's terms, and she told me Lover's plan. He was going to fuse the lights at the swimming party and drown Lorraine. He was banking everything on her silver swimming suit because, although he was shortsighted, he knew he'd be able to see it glimmering in the darkness. He had some ether, though he didn't want to use it unless it was absolutely necessary. As it happened, when the time came, he didn't need it."

He went on. "I saw immediately that I couldn't possibly

have Lorraine call the swimming party off without arousing her suspicion and Lover's. But I knew she'd always been sensitive about the things she wore. I figured out that idea of kidding her about the suit, making her think she looked silly so that she'd give up wearing it. We had to do it when Lover wasn't around, of course. We did. It worked. After dinner Mimi and I kept close to Lover. Later, when he fused the lights, I dove right into the pool, located Lorraine and stuck by her. I knew Lover'd never be able to see her in that black suit, but I was taking no chances."

He smiled a pale smile. "Once again we'd managed to save Lorraine, but we didn't stop a murder. What none of us knew was that Janet had brought no suit and Lorraine had given her the silver one. When Lover and Mimi and I reached the pool, both Lorraine and Janet were in the women's dressing-rooms. None of us knew Janet was wearing the suit, or Mimi and I would have done something about it. In the darkness Lover saw the suit gleaming. He murdered Janet—thinking he was murdering Lorraine."

He shrugged his shoulders wearily. "By then I was about at the end of my rope. It looked as if the thing would never stop. Lover would go on with his shortsighted slaughter until he finally got Lorraine. He didn't care that innocent women were being killed. In fact, each time there was another corpse, things would be better for him because his own motive would get buried deeper and deeper under a crazy surface that could only look like the work of a homicidal maniac."

Iris put in quietly, "Which, of course, is exactly what happened."

Chuck nodded. "I was ready to go to the police and confess everything then even though I knew it meant putting a noose around my own neck as surely as around Lover's. Then something occurred to me, something I'd never thought of before. There was a way of stopping the murders without going to the police. Lorraine's death was only profitable to Lover so long as her marriage to me wasn't legal. Mimi had gone through all the preliminaries of the divorce. She was a Nevada resident. If she went back to Vegas, she could get the divorce in a day. All I had to do was to marry Lorraine again legally, and Lover's motive for murdering was gone forever."

He paused. "I went to Mimi. I put it up to her. She was scared herself by then but not scared enough to forget her own interests. She said okay. She'd go to Vegas the next day if I'd sell the Club and give her every red cent I owned in the world. I didn't even try to bargain with her. Fetter had been after the Club for months. I knew it would be easy to make a quick sale. This afternoon I stayed in Reno after Dorothy's funeral. I made the sale. All the time I was in a blue funk that Lover would try to murder Lorraine again while I was not there to protect her."

"And that's just what happened," put in Iris. "Lover must have been on the desperate side himself then because Mr. Throckmorton was due to arrive and Lorraine had announced the evening before that she was going to ask him to draw up a will. A will would have stymied Lover as effectively as a legal marriage ceremony. When Lorraine said she was taking the station wagon to the airport, he realized he had to kill her before Mr. Throckmorton arrived. He didn't tell Mimi that time. He slipped into the garage and sabotaged the brake cable on the station wagon. We all know Fleur fell into that trap. Lover was coming up the drive at the time. When he saw Fleur instead of Lorraine in the car, he made that so-called gallant attempt to save her. It was a good opportunity to make himself seem heroic and he had nothing to lose."

Chuck nodded. "When I came back from Reno, I had the money for Mimi with me in cash. She met me on the steps. She told me about Fleur and the station wagon. That only made me more urgent. I handed the money over to her. She was going to leave right away for Vegas. But, unfortunately for us, she chose that moment of all moments to get sentimental with an almost ex-husband. I guess it was the money that did it. She said, 'I'm going to kiss you for old time's sake.'" He shrugged. "While she was giving me that last tender embrace, you all came out through the front door."

He continued. "Mimi and I had been careful to keep Lover from knowing we'd been meeting but we hadn't thought much about Lorraine. Through the days she'd begun to suspect we were having an affair and when she saw us kissing she was sure of it. She ordered Mimi out of the house. So far as Mimi was concerned that was fine. It gave her a reasonable excuse for leaving. But—" he grimaced—"that was one thing more for me to cope with. I'd been hoping to go to Lorraine tonight and make up some story about our Mexican marriage not being watertight. I was going to suggest we get married again secretly here before Mr. Throckmorton came. You see, I was still hoping crazily that I'd be able to keep her from knowing the truth. But Lorraine was so mad at me about Mimi that she locked herself in her room and wouldn't let me in." He paused. "I never seemed to get a break—not a single break in all those ghastly days."

His tired gaze moved from Iris to Lorraine. "I realized there was still terrible danger for Lorraine but at least she was safe in her room with the door locked. I thought things might still be all right. Tomorrow Mimi would call me from Vegas to say the divorce was okay. Maybe tomorrow I could calm Lorraine down and persuade her to marry me— legally this time. Lieutenant Duluth here had insisted on my calling the police. But that didn't worry me. I realized the murders were so hopelessly confused by then that there was practically no chance of anyone's stumbling on the truth. I went to my room and, after a little while, Lover came in."

A look of embittered hatred passed across Chuck's face. "He sat down and lit a cigarette. He was perfectly at ease. Quietly, as if he was telling me some trivial thing, he said that he'd just murdered Mimi. When he saw us kissing, he'd suspected she'd been double-crossing him and playing along with me to frustrate his plans. When Lorraine let it slip that Mimi and I had kidded her out of wearing the silver swimming suit, he had been sure. Just as calmly, he said that he had searched Mimi's suitcase, found the money I'd given her and pocketed it himself."

His gaze faltered. "It was awful to realize that I'd let myself get so horribly involved that I had to sit there and listen without even being able to sock him. As smug as you please, he said he'd come to make a deal with me. He pointed out a dozen good reasons, reasons I already knew only too well, why it was against my interest to turn him over to the police. He ended up by saying that if those arguments weren't sufficient and if I was still crazy enough to try and expose him, he was prepared to deny everything and throw the whole blame back onto me. If I stopped to think, he said, what with Mimi being my wife and everything, there was a much better case against me than against him. He was right, of course. I had absolutely no evidence against him now Mimi was dead. It would be my word against his. He was a respectable citizen. I was at best a charlatan who'd tricked Lorraine into a bigamous marriage. He told me his deal then.

"He'd got the money I had given to Mimi. He said he was perfectly satisfied with that. It was enough to keep him for the rest of his days. If I behaved sensibly, he would give me his word that he would make no other attempt on Lorraine's life. The police would come. They would try to solve the mystery. They were bound to fail. In time the whole business would become just a series of unsolved maniac crimes. He'd have Mimi's money. I'd have Lorraine. I could marry her again at my leisure. Everything would be swell for me."

His tongue came out again, wetting his dry lips. "He knew he had me just where he wanted me. I knew it, too. Under the circumstances I even thought he was giving me a break. I guess I didn't have much spirit left. Now Mimi was dead, there was nothing to stop me marrying Lorraine again, anyway. I said okay. I wouldn't go to the police."

He looked up, his face suddenly fierce. "Now I see he double-crossed me after all. All that about leaving Lorraine alone was just talk to lull me into a false sense of security. He knew he had me paralyzed. He also knew he'd built up the perfect smoke screen of a homicidal maniac. He did try to murder Lorraine again tonight." His gaze moved uncertainly to Iris. "I don't know anything about it, just what you've told me. I guess he finally decided to use the ether. But, thank heavens, somehow you managed to save Lorraine." He paused. "I guess that's about all except that—in a way I'm almost as bad as Lover and I'm ready to take the consequences."

He took a step toward Lorraine. "Honey, I just want to say one thing. You may not be able to believe it, but, through it all, I was always figuring how it would be best for you. I was a dope. Everything I did just made it worse. But—well——" His voice broke huskily. "Try not to hate me too much."

Lorraine was standing very still. She was staring straight at him. I was watching him, too. He looked completely spent, like a swimmer who had battled for hours against an undertow and had no more strength to battle on. As I reviewed that terrible story with its intricate pattern woven from conspiracy, counter-conspiracy, desperation, and fraud, I tried to think what I would have done if I had been in Chuck's shoes and Lorraine had been Iris.

Would I have shown up as a braver or more noble character?

Softly Lorraine said, "And you're ready to tell the police everything you've told us, Chuck?"

Chuck nodded.

"Whatever happens?"

He nodded again.

Lorraine's lips were quivering. Impulsively she went to him, putting her small hands on his big arms. "If they send you to prison, I'll wait for you."

He stared at her, his face incredulous. "Lorraine, you—you mean——"

"You fool." Lorraine's eyes were shining. "Haven't you any sense? Can't you see that I love you?"

For a moment Chuck just stood there holding her in his arms. He was transfigured, a man who didn't believe in miracles and was seeing one taking place. Then slowly his face clouded.

"It mayn't just be prison, honey," he said. "I don't have any evidence against him. He's much smarter than me, and it's my word against his. Maybe the police will believe him."

Iris got up from the bed then. My wife was looking glamorous and competent at the same time, a Hollywood conception of the executive woman.

"Oh, you don't have to worry about that, Chuck," she said. "You see, there's all the evidence in the world against Lover now. In fact, Inspector Craig has already arrested him."

Twenty-Two

THAT STARTLING STATEMENT brought the spotlight back to Iris. It made us conscious once again of the fact that it had been my wife who had precipitated the showdown. Uncannily she seemed to have spirited the complex solution out of thin air.

"Lover arrested!" Chuck stammered. "I can't believe it. I—I can't understand you, anyway, Iris. I thought the whole ghastly thing was so mixed up that no one would ever figure it out. And yet you seem to have——"

"Exactly," I broke in. I turned to my wife, trying unsuccessfully not to sound impressed. "In the first place, where in heaven's name did you find the poisoned chip?"

Iris was trying, also unsuccessfully, to look modest. "It was really just chance, Peter. You see, I was sitting here all by myself and I started thinking about the attempted robbery in our room. You and I had decided that the murderer must either have been after Dorothy's pocketbook or Janet's will. But it suddenly occurred to me that there was something else in that locked drawer—my piggy bank."

"Your piggy bank!" I exclaimed. "Why should the murderer want to steal your piggy bank?"

"I didn't know, but I did know I'd had it with me the night Dorothy was killed. So, when you'd gone downstairs to your misogynistic Inspector, I went back to our room and got the piggy bank out of the drawer. I decided that, if my hunch was right and the piggy bank was important, the murderer might come back for it a second time. I thought of that other piggy bank I'd bought for you and you'd never use. It was in one of the suitcases under the bed. I filled it with all the small change I could find and put it in the drawer as—as a decoy." She smiled meekly. "Then I brought my own piggy bank here. I broke it. Inside, with all those fifty-cent pieces from the jackpot, I found the chip."

"So, all the time, it was right there under our noses?"

"Yes, Peter. Once I saw the chip, I figured out that the murder trap must have been meant for Lorraine. And, as I looked back, I saw that Lover was the only one who could have put the chip in the piggy bank. Remember, Peter? When Dorothy died on the dance floor, Lover was back at the table alone with her pocketbook and my piggy bank. The moment Dorothy died, he knew she'd been poisoned by the chip and that it couldn't be anywhere else but in her bag. He didn't know that the murder was going to be hushed up by Wyckoff. He'd naturally have expected that the police would search everyone. He couldn't risk keeping the chip in his pocket. My piggy bank was the ideal cache—something in no way connected with him, something he could always get at later on when it would be safe to retrieve the chip and destroy it. As things turned out, when he did try and get it back, we'd locked the piggy bank in the drawer and he was in too much of a hurry to do any lock picking." She shrugged. "I'm glad to say that, by and large, Lover had the lousiest luck of any ambitious murderer in history."

We were all watching her then.

"The rest is simple. I realized there was still great danger for Lorraine. Without making her suspicious, I persuaded her to get out of bed and come in here where she'd be safe. I saw that Lover's bad luck had a way worked out to his advantage and that, with everyone believing in a maniac, he still had a wonderful opportunity to kill Lorraine and get away with it. Any man who had tried and failed three times wasn't going to stop there. So I thought out something. I snuck downstairs and lugged up that loathsome doll and planted it in Lorraine's bed. It looked extremely lifelike and I knew Lover was shortsighted, anyway."

My wife grimaced. "Feeling awfully silly, I hid in the clothes' closet with the door ajar and waited. Sure enough, Lover showed up, and sure enough he murdered that doll with all the stealth of the King pouring the poison in Hamlet's father's ear. I'd witnessed an actual murder attempt. That was all I needed. When he slipped out of the room, I went after him. I saw him tiptoe down the corridor to our room. He was after the chip in the piggy bank, of course. I'd left the door open as a lure. I'd also put the key on the outside of the lock to make things easier for me. Once he was in our room I just closed the door on him, locked it, and went to wake up the Inspector."

She smiled at me. "He was rather suspicious at first. But when I told him I'd caught Lover red-handed, trying to kill Lorraine, he leaped out of bed. I left him just now coping with Lover. I wanted to come here and have Chuck tell us the whole story because everything still wasn't quite clear in my mind."

I stared at her. I gulped. I had been laughing at her when I called her, "Dare-devil Iris Duluth, Hollywood's lone she-wolf crime-buster." Now the laugh was on me. With Iris as an eye-witness of his attempt on Lorraine, Lover was as good as in the death cell already.

Iris slipped her hand into mine. "It was a miserably tangled up case, Peter, partly because Chuck and Mimi were complicating things all the time, but mostly because Lover was such a darn elaborate murderer. Chuck thinks he's smart. I don't. He was ruthless enough, heaven knows, and ingenious. Too ingenious. If I wanted to kill one person, I'd kill that one person not three other people. In my humble opinion, Lover, as a master mind, was a fraud."

She turned to Chuck. "You mustn't worry, Chuck. I told the Inspector a couple of the things you'd done and I pointed out the ghastly spot you were in. He likes you. Everybody does. I don't think you'll get into much trouble. And—well, he's really a most sympathetic man. He's promised to soft-pedal everything that involves Lorraine and your marriage."

Chuck and Lorraine were both watching her as if she were one of those things in miracle plays that come down from the sky at the last minute and organize happy endings. With a quick movement Lorraine stepped forward and kissed her.

"Darling," she said, "you're wonderful. You're perfectly wonderful."

Iris grinned sheepishly. "Nonsense," she said. "Just luck and Edna St. Vincent Millay."

At that moment the door opened on Inspector Craig. He looked slightly mad in a shabby raincoat and, so far as I could see, nothing else. He had eyes for no one except Iris.

He said, "Mrs. Duluth, I've got one of my men up from town. He's watching French downstairs. French isn't talking yet, but with your evidence we've got him where we want him. There's one thing that stops me though. That money Chuck got from selling the Club, the money he gave to Miss Burnett—you told me French would have it. I've torn his room down but it isn't there."

"I know." Iris looked apologetic. "It was awfully stupid of me. I should have had enough sense to realize where it would be. Come on. I'll get it."

Inspector Craig gawped. So did the rest of us. But we followed Iris humbly out into the corridor. She hurried to Chuck's room and turned on the light. While we crowded behind her, she went around opening drawers and prodding things. At length she came to the bed and yanked up the mattress.

There, splayed over the top of the box spring, were thick packages of treasury notes.

Iris glanced at Chuck. "I thought so. You were right. He was planning to throw the blame on you. I guess he'd have planted the poison chip here, too, if he'd been able to get at it."

Inspector Craig gave a long, low whistle. The woman-hater stared down at the money and then with dogged adoration at my wife.

"If I ever make another crack against women," he said, "shoot me."

My wife smiled delightedly. "I'll treasure that for my memory book."

The Inspector was scooping up the packages of money and stuffing them into his pocket. "You'll get this back, Chuck, but right now I'd better keep it. Since you're all awake, no point in wasting time. Maybe you'll come downstairs and start making your official statements."

As we trooped out of the room, Iris slipped her hand through my arm. "Darling," she said, "let's sneak away from here tomorrow. Now it's over, we can have ten lovely, glorious days. I'm bored with being a movie star. I'm bored with being a detective. I want to be a——"

"A what?"

"A little woman."

The world which had been so dark a few hours before was very bright again. "Where'll we go?" I asked.

"Anywhere so long as we're alone. If need be, we'll rent a prison cell from Inspector Craig."

As we passed Fleur Wyckoff's room, the door opened and Fleur and Wyckoff appeared, she in a revealing pink negligee, he only in pajama pants. They stared anxiously. Wyckoff said, "We heard voices. Is everything all right?"

"Sure," said Chuck showing white teeth in a spontaneous grin. "Everything's all right. Come on and join the procession."

They unembarrassedly came as they were. We made a

motley group trailing down the giant stairway. Craig headed the party, his bare legs sticking out beneath the raincoat. The Wyckoffs, in their various states of undress, followed hand in hand. Lorraine and Chuck came next, with Iris and me bringing up the rear.

As we reached the hall, I saw Lorraine look up at Chuck, her little pug face ecstatic. "Thank heavens, darling, that Mr. Throckmorton was thrown off the plane. He's frightfully Bostonian about morals and things. He'll explode when he finds out we weren't properly married. But now at least we'll be able to become respectable before he arrives."

We were moving through the hall toward the open door of the living-room when the front doorbell jangled. Everyone stopped and stared.

"Who on earth——"

The Inspector went forward and threw the door open.

A man was standing on the threshold, a large, square, elderly man, in a black suit with a fat black brief case under his arm. He had a formidable, old-fashioned mustache. He looked like a visitor from the Watch and Ward Society.

"Lorraine!" Pushing past the Inspector, the newcomer moved ponderously into the hall. "I took a train and then a bus and then I managed to find a taxi. It has been a most exhausting trip but since you seemed so eager for me to——"

He looked around the group then. His eyes widened in outraged disapproval as they played on Lorraine's pajamas, Fleur's negligee, and Wyckoff's torso. Finally his glance settled upon the Inspector's legs thrusting out from beneath the inadequate raincoat.

"Who are these people?" he boomed with immense umbrage. "Who are these naked men? These indelicately clad young women? Have I come all this way to take part in an orgy?"

He stood there glaring in terrible wrath. Lorraine was

speechless. Even the Inspector quailed. It was Iris who stepped into the breach.

With a smile that would have disarmed the Recording Angel, my wife moved forward and held out her hand.

"Mr. Throckmorton, I presume."

Mr. Throckmorton ignored her. His gaze was fixed now on the open door of the living-room. Just inside it, Lover was visible, with Inspector Craig's burliest plain-clothes man standing very close at his side.

"Ah, Walter, my boy!" Mr. Throckmorton brushed past Iris toward Lover, smiling benevolently. "Thank goodness you're here. Thank goodness there's at least one solid, respectable citizen to protect Lorraine from this riff-raff."

I looked at Iris. Iris looked at me.

"That," said Iris, "is one of the great curtain lines of all time. Come on, Peter, let's get a drink."

THE LIBRARY OF CRIME CLASSICS

CHARLOTTE ARMSTRONG
The Balloon Man
A Dram of Poison
Lemon in the Basket
A Little Less Than Kind
Mischief
The Unsuspected

JACQUELINE BABBIN
Bloody Soaps
Bloody Special

GEORGE BAXT
The Affair at Royalties
The Alfred Hitchcock Murder Case
The Dorothy Parker Murder Case
"I!" Said the Demon
The Neon Graveyard
A Parade of Cockeyed Creatures
A Queer Kind of Death
Satan Is a Woman
Swing Low Sweet Harriet
The Talullah Bankhead Murder Case
Topsy and Evil
Who's Next?

ANTHONY BOUCHER
Nine Times Nine
Rocket to the Morgue

CARYL BRAHMS & S.J. SIMON
A Bullet in the Ballet
Murder a la Stroganoff
Six Curtains for Stroganova

CHRISTIANNA BRAND
Cat and Mouse

MAX BRAND
The Night Flower

HERBERT BREAN
The Traces of Brillhart
Wilders Walk Away

JOHN DICKSON CARR
Below Suspicion
The Burning Court
Death Turns the Tables
Hag's Nook
He Who Whispers
The House at Satan's Elbow
The Murder of Sir Edmund Godfrey
The Problem of the Green Capsule
The Sleeping Sphinx
The Three Coffins
Till Death Do Us Part
WRITING AS CARTER DICKSON
The Gilded Man
He Wouldn't Kill Patience
The Judas Window
Nine - and Death Makes Ten
The Peacock Feather Murders
The Plague Court Murders
The Punch and Judy Murders
The Reader Is Warned
The Red Widow Murders
The Unicorn Murders

LESLIE CHARTERIS
Angels Of Doom
The First Saint Omnibus
Knight Templar
The Last Hero
The Saint in New York

CARROLL JOHN DALY
Murder from the East

LILLIAN DE LA TORRE
Dr. Sam: Johnson, Detector
The Detections of Dr. Sam: Johnson
The Return of Dr. Sam: Johnson, Detector
The Exploits of Dr. Sam: Johnson, Detector

PETER DICKINSON
Perfect Gallows

PAUL GALLICO
The Abandoned
Love of Seven Dolls
Mrs. 'Arris Goes To Paris
Farewell To Sport
Too Many Ghosts
Thomasina

JAMES GOLLIN
Eliza's Galliardo
The Philomel Foundation

DOUGLAS GREENE & ROBERT ADEY
Death Locked In

DASHIELL HAMMETT & ALEX RAYMOND
Secret Agent X-9

REGINALD HILL
A Killing Kindness

RICHARD HULL
The Murder of My Aunt

E. RICHARD JOHNSON
Cage 5 Is Going To Break
Dead Flowers
The God Keepers
The Inside Man
Mongo's Back in Town
Silver Street

JONATHAN LATIMER
Headed for a Hearse
The Lady in the Morgue
Murder In the Madhouse
The Search for My Great Uncle's Head
Solomon's Vineyard

VICTORIA LINCOLN
A Private Disgrace
Lizzie Borden by Daylight

MARGARET MILLAR
An Air That Kills
Ask for Me Tomorrow
Banshee
Beast in View
Beyond This Point Are Monsters
The Cannibal Heart
The Fiend
Fire Will Freeze
How Like An Angel
The Iron Gates
The Listening Walls
The Murder of Miranda
Rose's Last Summer
Spider Webs
A Stranger in My Grave
Vanish In An Instant
Wall of Eyes

BARRY MALZBERG
Underlay

WILLIAM F. NOLAN
Look Out for Space
Space for Hire

WILLIAM O'FARRELL
Repeat Performance

ELLERY QUEEN
Cat of Many Tails
Drury Lane's Last Case
The Ellery Queen Omnibus
The Tragedy of X
The Tragedy of Y
The Tragedy of Z

PATRICK QUENTIN
Puzzle for Players
Puzzle for Puppets
Puzzle for Wantons

S.S. RAFFERTY
Cork of the Colonies
Die Laughing

CLAYTON RAWSON
Death from a Top Hat
Footprints on the Ceiling
The Headless Lady
No Coffin for the Corpse

CRAIG RICE
The Corpse Steps Out
8 Faces at 3
The Wrong Murder

GEORGE SANDERS
Crime On My Hands

HAKE TALBOT
Rim of the Pit

DARWIN L. TEILHET
The Talking Sparrow Murders

P.G. WODEHOUSE
Full Moon
If I Were You
Service with a Smile
Who's Who In Wodehouse

Write For Our Free Catalog:
International Polygonics, Ltd.
Madison Square, P.O. Box 1563
New York, NY 10159